Someone wa[s] in the house...

Sarah waited in the dark for an endless minute before creeping forward and soundlessly turning the doorknob. She slipped into the hall like a wraith, marveling that the thunder of her pulse could be contained within her body instead of echoing throughout the darkened house.

He could be right beside me, she thought in sudden panic. *He could be right here and I wouldn't even know it until he touched me.* For a few moments she simply stood in the hall, steadying her breathing, absorbing the night sounds. Suddenly a flutter of movement, a whisper of sound chilled her, freezing her in place.

The den. He was in the den! On the periphery of her vision, a shadow, fractionally darker than the nighttime gloom, floated across the floor. Slowly she turned her head and the specter took shape. A man, moving away from her to the far side of the room, so stealthy and silent that she was tempted to doubt his existence.

"Don't move," she said, amazed that she could sound so controlled, "not even an inch. This thing has a hair trigger."

ABOUT THE AUTHOR

Leigh Daniels is a Texas writer who has been in love with romantic suspense for as long as she can remember. "I grew up on Mary Stewart and Daphne du Maurier," she says, "and I desperately wanted to be like those heroines, living a life of adventure and happy endings. Through my writing, I can have as much of those things as I like, and I never even have to leave home!"

On the Run
Leigh Daniels

Harlequin Books

TORONTO • NEW YORK • LONDON
AMSTERDAM • PARIS • SYDNEY • HAMBURG
STOCKHOLM • ATHENS • TOKYO • MILAN

For Aimee, and for the Condors

Harlequin Intrigue edition published January 1989

ISBN 0-373-22106-1

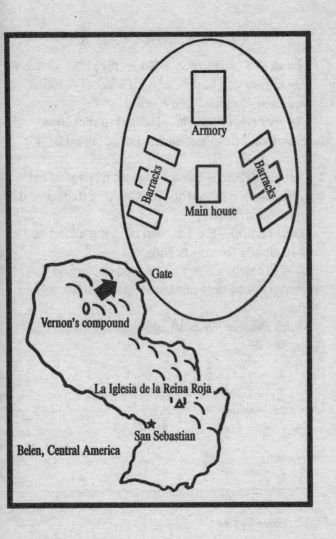

Armory

Barracks

Barracks

Main house

Gate

Vernon's compound

La Iglesia de la Reina Roja

San Sebastian

Belen, Central America

CAST OF CHARACTERS

Sarah O'Shaughnessy—She thought her greatest adventure was in the pages of a novel—until a *real* hero dropped into her life.

Aubrey Glen Macklin—He had to race to save his niece, but others seemed determined to stop him.

Patrick O'Shaughnessy—Could he protect his sister from a man who was courting danger and possible death?

Paul Vernon—He dreamed of being a king and had finally found his kingdom.

Kay Macklin—She was trapped in Vernon's fantasy, and only her Uncle Mack could save her.

John Bridges—Would he salute the flag . . . or betray it?

Prologue

A pale light spilled through the lacy lamp shade, casting dark, elongated shadows across the bedroom, creating shapes oddly at variance with the soft femininity of the furniture. In the predawn stillness, the hurried scratching of pen on paper, though faint, sounded much too loud, and every few seconds the young woman who sat on the edge of the bed glanced up from her work and paused to listen.

As she wrote, her hand trembled, distorting some of the words into nothing more than meaningless squiggles, but there wasn't time to rewrite the note. She would just have to trust that Mack—if he ever received it—would be able to decipher her scrawl. She closed her eyes against the sudden chill of despair that quivered through her. Mack was her only hope, her only chance for rescue. Why hadn't she listened to him?

Outside, the wind off the Pacific rose suddenly. The whistle of its passage around the corner of the house raised the fine hair along her forearms. She shivered, then angrily dashed away the tears that clung to her lashes, blurring her vision. She wouldn't cry; she wouldn't. She *mustn't*. If *he* were to walk in and find her in tears, he would be furious. And anger made him cruel.

Hurry, hurry, the wind urged. *Hurry, before it's too late....*

Abruptly—magically—the wind died, and she caught the sound of a soft footfall outside her door. The narrow drawer of the nightstand was still open, and with desperate haste she thrust the sheet of paper, along with the pen, against the back panel, then quickly slid the drawer closed.

The bedroom door opened, and he entered the room noiselessly, on cat's feet. His strangely pale eyes, alert and penetrating, darted around the room, finally coming to rest on her. She squirmed, feeling like a bug about to be pinned to a board.

"What's wrong, darling?" Like the man himself, the voice was deceptively tender. "Couldn't sleep?" He crossed the room to kneel beside her. "I understand. I feel it, too. The excitement, as well as the frustration. But I have some good news." He paused and looked at her, his eyes narrowed in what she had come to recognize as anticipation. "The problems have been worked out more quickly than I expected. By this time tomorrow, we'll be there, in a new country, a new life. It will be wonderful, *mi reina roja*, just as I promised."

Tomorrow? She felt sick. There would be no time to mail the letter, no time for Mack to come for her. She'd just disappear, and no one would ever know where she was.

He gathered her into his arms, pressed her down against the mattress, covered her mouth with his. She wondered how he could fail to notice how his touch chilled her—she felt frozen, brittle, as though her very flesh would soon shatter. But the man merely ran his hands over her slender arms, while a faint smile tugged at his thin lips. He watched her, in much the same way he might study his favorite piece of porcelain.

Presently his breathing changed, becoming rapid and shallow with arousal, and he kissed her again.

When he reached out to click off the lamp, she rejoiced in the covering darkness. If he couldn't see her face, maybe he wouldn't discover the depth of her fear and revulsion. Maybe she would be safe for another day....

Chapter One

A woman sprawled invitingly across his bed wasn't precisely what Bothwell had been expecting when he unlocked the door to his apartment. She was blond, voluptuous—and an absolute stranger. Bothwell had the gut feeling she was also a nicely packaged bundle of trouble.

"I thought you'd never get here," she purred, letting her icy blue eyes trace the lean length of him, from wavy black hair to expensive black shoes. She must have liked what she saw, for she daintily licked her upper lip before she continued, "What kept you?"

"I had to drop by the morgue to say goodbye to a friend."

Sarah O'Shaughnessy grimaced. "'I had to drop by the morgue to say goodbye to a friend,'" she read aloud, testing the last sentence.

She shook her head in disgust, her red curls bouncing almost violently in the skirmish between the sudden movement and the Pacific breeze. The words sounded no better spoken than they looked in the center of page one hundred sixty-one. With a deep sigh, she flung the typewritten pages down beside her. They fluttered for a moment against the brightly striped, oversize towel on which she sat, then wafted gently to the sand while she stared out at the waves of Carmel Bay breaking against the rocks.

She had to face it. Chapter Eight of *Kill Me with Love* just wasn't working, and she didn't have a clue about how to fix it.

At this rate, David T. Bothwell, intrepid private eye and all-American hero, would never grace the pages of anything except discarded typing paper. She'd never had this kind of problem with Bothwell before. In fact, the compulsion to write had been so strong she'd even set aside an entire month away from her own research business to complete the manuscript and get it submitted.

So what the devil was wrong? She had all the right ingredients. *Kill Me with Love* was a fast-paced, contemporary mystery with a setting that was neither too commonplace nor too exotic, and Bothwell had emerged as a straight-talking, hard-hitting personality—the epitome of dark, smoldering, cleft-chinned perfection. Add to all that an entire file of meticulous research on illegal arms trading, an interested editor and ideal working conditions, and the sum total should have been No Problem. But the dreadful reality was that in the past week she'd managed to grind out only fourteen measly pages. She'd done better than that in her own apartment after working ten hours a day.

She flopped over on the beach towel to lie on her stomach, wondering what she could do to start the juices flowing again. This wasn't like her, not at all, and she was beginning to worry. Common sense told her she could write this book. But what if her common sense was wrong? What if all she had was the idea, the fantasy, instead of a real manuscript?

"Oh, stuff it," she said aloud, disgusted with herself. "You've probably just been out in the sun too long." She sat up again and brushed the sand off her legs, then picked up the errant manuscript pages littering the sand, and glared at them, thinking furiously. This entire trip would be a waste if she didn't pull herself out of this funk.

"The Authoress." That was what Raylene called her, singing Sarah's praises to anyone who'd sit still long enough to listen. "Mah friend and former roommate, The Authoress." Until now, Sarah had believed it of herself, so full of hope and confidence that failure had never occurred to her. Well, it was occurring to her now, and the prospect was unpleasant in the extreme.

Bothwell had been a part of her for years. He represented every romantic, adventurous fantasy she'd ever had, and the more she thought about him, the more real he had become, until she knew him inside out. Bothwell, the perfect hero. Now it all seemed to be ending, not only Bothwell, but her dream of an exciting career as a novelist.

What would she say to her friends? Dolly and Raylene had been so proud of her, so supportive and helpful. Through her locator business, Dolly had found this house-sitting assignment for her, teasing her about the need for "writer's solitude." And Raylene, bless her practical, Georgian heart, had added Sarah to an already overcrowded list of answering service clients, only too happy to field the numerous calls from Sarah's own clients. Not to mention the O'Shaugnessy brothers, who drove their sister to distraction on a regular basis. Each of them phoned Sarah at least twice a week—Frank, to ask if she needed anything; Robby, to pass along fabricated messages from their father; and Patrick, to ask when she was coming home. Thank God, she reflected, she'd had enough sense not to tell them about the book. At least she wouldn't have to listen to their I-told-you-sos.

The late September wind, steady and brisk, whipped her hair into her eyes, and she brushed the strands away with an irritated gesture. She certainly couldn't fault her present living arrangements for this…*block*, or whatever it was, she thought, looking around. Whoever owned this place had exquisite taste, and enough money to indulge it. The panoramic view was breathtaking. The seas of Carmel rose and fell in ever-shifting shades of blue. The waves were capped by frothy white peaks where they beat against the craggy rocks crowned by the delicate shapes of cypress trees that stood majestically atop the distant cliffs that defined Point Lobos. Closer at hand, at the top of a steep, sandy slope, the sleek house gleamed in the sun like a new penny, and the breeze carried the tinkle of wind chimes, which were strung along the flagstone patio.

Another sound, faint but recognizable, drew her attention. A car, moving very slowly, was driving past the house. She frowned. Hardly anyone used the narrow road, which wasn't unusual, since it ended in a cul-de-sac almost at the front door. But there'd been a sharp increase in engine noises the past couple of days, sometimes quite late at night. After a moment, she heard the car make the tight circle and pass again in the opposite direction, back toward Highway One. Probably vacationers hoping to catch a glimpse of one of the best views on the peninsula, she thought absently.

And who could blame them? Her own apartment in San Francisco was nice, covering the entire top floor of a turreted, turn-of-the-century house. But this place was more than nice—it was Paradise.

For a few minutes, she glanced aimlessly through the pages of the manuscript, letting her mind wander. Her writing wasn't really bad, but it seemed to lack the punch, the crispness that characterized the first six chapters. The tone had changed from taut excitement to…complaisance? Outright boredom?

She considered her choice of adjectives. At home, she had used her writing as an escape from a routine existence. But here on the coast, next door to picturesque Carmel-by-the-Sea and lively Monterey, she had nothing to escape from. Each morning she slept later, each day her time at the typewriter became shorter and each night she lay awake longer, bemoaning yet another unproductive twenty-four hours.

With a sigh she drank in the picture-postcard view of the bay and gradually brought her thoughts into focus. What should have been the adventure of a lifetime had turned into a dull chore, something closely resembling an obligation. She's said it herself; paradise was not conducive to creativity. She needed to bring back the spark, the sense of adventure. And since adventure rarely came knocking on the door, she'd just have to go out and actively hunt it down. The thought stirred her, and she felt a touch of excitement returning. There were probably dozens of new and thrilling scenarios lurking in this beautiful locale, just waiting to be discovered.

A self-satisfied smile curved her generous mouth, and she sprang to her feet, grabbing the beach towel. She would start right away, tonight in fact. Both Carmel and Monterey were only ten miles away to the north, and the bars along Cannery Row were exactly the kind of places Bothwell would frequent. She could probably get some wonderful character ideas from talking to the bartenders and patrons.

Immensely pleased with her newfound resolve, she hurried up the slope toward the house. From here on, she promised herself, nothing, absolutely nothing, would interfere with her writing.

THE MAN ON THE RIDGE surveyed the beach from the cover of low, dense evergreens that marked the boundary of the beach house property. As he watched the young woman hurry across the sand and up to the house, he wore an expression of grim confusion and his thoughts spun furiously.

What the devil was going on? He'd spent days finding this house, and he was certain he'd made no mistakes. This had to be Paul Vernon's place, the hideaway where Paul and Kay always spent their weekends and vacations. The house from which Kay had made that last telephone call, now nearly three weeks ago. The house from which she had disappeared. . . .

Locating it hadn't been easy, but he had stuck with it doggedly because it was his last hope. He'd thought that he had everything pulled together, with nothing to do but wait until dark to enter the house, find what he was looking for and be out in an hour. But that wouldn't work now, not with the house occupied.

At least he'd had the good sense to curb his impatience and not go charging in until he'd looked things over carefully. During his first run past the house, day before yesterday, something had triggered a faint alarm, a tingle along his nape that told him the house wasn't empty as he'd expected. It simply hadn't had that *deserted* feel to it. So he'd settled in to wait and watch.

His caution had paid off. First, he'd scouted around on foot, staying a safe distance from the house but close enough to see the occupant through the windows and, later, walking back and forth to the beachfront. She was a young woman, with flaming red hair that whipped like a banner in the wind. When he'd first seen her, he'd been paralyzed for an instant by a flare of hope. Kay's hair was that exact shade of red; she held her head the same way, too, up and slightly tilted to catch the sun. Then reason had reasserted itself as he took in the details. This woman's hair was short and curly, not long and straight, and her face was more round than angular. Still, her abrupt appearance had been startling.

He'd spent the first night in his car, trying to put the puzzle together. Who was she? A friend of Vernon's, a partner in crime? Or a federal plant, in residence as bait for any of Vernon's cronies who hadn't yet been rounded up? Neither possibility really satisfied him. Quite simply, the lady was an enigma.

Then, to further muddy the issue, a brown Pontiac had taken to driving past the house, making the circle without stopping as he himself had done several times, then cruising back to the main road. The first time it happened, he'd assumed the two men inside were simply tourists. But it had soon become clear that they, too, were scouting, and he was grateful they hadn't spotted him or his vehicle, which was parked on an overgrown track forking off the private road.

Something was very wrong here, something that threatened to upset all his plans. Soon, his source had told him, the Treasury boys would make their move. Once they hit Vernon's property everything would be wrapped up, confiscated. He wouldn't have a prayer of getting through their security.

"Damn!" he now swore, watching the woman disappear into the house. Too many complications had popped up too suddenly, and he simply didn't have time to sort them out. If he didn't find Kay and bring her home, *soon*, she would go down with Vernon . . . or worse.

He forced the negative thoughts away. He would find Kay, but he had to have a starting point. That point was the beach house. Which brought him back to the unknown woman.

The next time she left, he decided, he would follow her. He needed only to determine if she would be away long enough for him to make a thorough search. As for her newly acquired shadows, she was on her own unless they interfered with his plans.

But he couldn't help wondering about her, especially about why she was under surveillance from this new source. He had a strong feeling that someone else was looking for

Paul Vernon, too, or anyone who knew where he was. The little lady, whoever she was, most likely had trouble nipping at her heels.

But that wasn't his concern. His first and only objective was to get inside Vernon's house, where, overlooked or forgotten or unnoticed, there would be a clue, an indicator pointing him toward Paul Vernon and, ultimately, toward Kay. And he would find that indicator, no matter what it took, no matter who he had to go through.

SARAH HURRIED through her shower, eager to put her plan into action. She towel-dried her hair and fluffed out the curls with her fingers, then rummaged through the clothes hanging in the bedroom closet. There were few enough of them, for she'd never seen any point in spending her limited income on fancy dresses and suits she'd probably never wear. Her work consisted mainly of long hours spent either in the library or at her computer, and her social life, such as it was, ran more to Becker's Bowling Alley than to dinner at the Ritz. Accordingly, jeans and loose, comfortable shirts made up the bulk of her wardrobe. After several minutes of frustrated searching, she finally settled on a pair of reasonably blue Levi's, a thin knit white shell and an old navy blazer left over from her college days.

Making up her face was a much easier matter. She had long ago decided that trying to cover up her freckles was an exercise in futility, so she never did more than darken her lashes and gloss her lips.

She stood in front of the mirror when she was finished and grimaced at the depressing reflection. No wonder Dad and the boys still treated her like a child, she thought; to look at her, no one would guess that her twenty-eighth birthday loomed alarmingly near. The pointed chin and wide blue eyes, the hideous freckles, the bright mop of curls, all combined to create an image of youthful innocence she would gladly do without. She looked like a taller version of Little Orphan Annie, except with more curves, and even those hadn't come out right. Her breasts were too small, her hips too wide, and she didn't have a snowball's chance in hell of ever being taken for the classic femme fatale.

She dug through the box that held her few pieces of jewelry and came up with a pair of gold hoops. Slipping them into her earlobes, she surveyed her reflection once again. A definite improvement, she thought; at least she now looked postpubescent.

Relieved to have the dressing ritual behind her, she went back into the den and busied herself with making last-minute notes—details to incorporate into the remaining chapters of the book; items to take with her; things to do, places to see....

Her pencil flying across the paper, Sarah was so engrossed in her plans that she almost missed the sound. Another car, moving just as slowly as the first, and it was directly in front of the house. Why had her little road suddenly become so popular, she wondered, going into the front room to peek out between the drapes.

The vehicle had already made the turn and was heading away, so she caught only a glimpse of GM taillights set into a dark brown body before the car disappeared from sight. Maybe the absentee owner had arranged for someone to drive by periodically just to check things out. But if that were the case, why had he arranged for a house-sitter?

She shrugged and turned away. Certainly there was nothing sinister about a couple of cars using the road, she told herself, sinking into her usual chair. But she couldn't help regretting that the phone service had been disconnected. What if someone broke in? For that matter, what if she fell and broke her leg?

That daunting thought had never before occurred to her. Sarah wasn't by nature a timid person, but neither was she foolhardy. First thing tomorrow, she decided, she would see about having the phone reconnected. Not only would it be a comfort, but she wouldn't have to drive into town to check in with Raylene and get her messages.

Which brought her to another matter she should have attended to several days ago. She hadn't talked to Raylene since the beginning of the week, so that should be the first item on her agenda for the evening. *Call Raylene,* she scribbled on the steno pad and, on the next page, *call phone company.*

She flipped back through the pages to make sure she hadn't omitted anything vital, smiling as she remembered Dolly's incessant teasing. "You and your notes, O'Shaughnessy. I'll bet you don't get up in the middle of the night for a drink of water unless it's written down."

Well, she wasn't quite that extreme, and the habit of planning her days in writing had always been more help than hindrance. First, it had kept the O'Shaughnessy household on schedule after her mother's death, ensuring that everyone got his chores done without skipping his homework or being late for class. And later, it had helped her balance her college classes with several part-time jobs, eventually providing the basis for her own business. Once she recognized her natural talent for observation and organization, she had become an independent researcher, finding and cataloging data for an impressive list of clients.

One more thing to do, she realized as she looked through her notes. *Tape recorder, replace batteries.*

She hurried into the bedroom, pulled out the skinny top drawer of the nightstand. The minirecorder was one of Sarah's standard items. She never embarked on any research project without making sure it was neatly tucked away in the bottom of the canvas bag. She now found it buried under a ream of typing paper; if she could only locate the new batteries . . .

Her groping fingers finally brushed against the edge of the package, but as she pulled she realized one corner of the cardboard backing was wedged in a crack of the drawer. She yanked and the package came out, along with something else—a piece of paper, crumpled and torn. Smoothing out the wrinkles, she examined the fragment, though in truth there wasn't much to see. It was merely a skinny, jagged strip of what appeared to be stationery, devoid of writing. Now that she thought about it, she'd recently run across an entire box of stationery that matched this piece, with the initials "KM" embossed in gold in the upper right-hand corner. She fleetingly wondered why it had been left behind. But perhaps "KM" had a box of the stuff printed up for each residence, in coordinating decorator colors, of course.

Shrugging, Sarah wadded the scrap of paper into a tight ball and tossed it into the wastebasket on the other side of the nightstand. She had more important things to occupy her mind, such as finishing *Kill Me with Love*. When Bothwell became a bestseller, she'd have her own stationery, as many boxes as she wanted, with "SKO" in huge, ostentatious letters across the top.

The whimsy amused her, and once again she felt a surge of excitement for her research expedition. Swinging her bag over her shoulder, she headed for the garage. She patted the yellow Volkswagen's dented fender affectionately as she passed it to raise the garage door. Poor old Lucille hadn't been out in days; a change of scene would do them both worlds of good. As she checked to make sure the vinyl convertible top was securely snapped down behind the rear seat, she found herself humming a tune. It was an old song, one she'd often heard on her mother's lips. She couldn't remember the name of it, but the melody was cheerful, and she sang it over and over as the little convertible raced down the road to her first stop.

SARAH LEANED AGAINST the outside wall of the convenience store, cradling the receiver of the pay phone and listening as Raylene's honeysuckle-and-mint-julep voice flowed clearly through the wire from San Francisco. In the past five minutes, Sarah had learned that one client was unhappy with the last research report he'd received; another was threatening to bring his young life to a particularly gruesome end if Sarah didn't help out with his thesis; Mrs. Lambert, Sarah's former landlady, and Greg Roberts, her former boyfriend, were leaving cryptic messages; and Patrick, her much-loved and thoroughly infuriating brother, was on his way for an impromptu visit.

"Well, the clients can wait," she said, raising her voice to compete with the noisy pickup that had chosen that precise moment to chug its way past the store on Highway One. "If they call back, tell them I'll be in touch sometime next week. And I'll try to get by to see Mrs. Lambert when I get back to the city. She's probably just lonely."

Now that the clatter of bad valves had faded, Raylene's sigh was clearly audible, even long distance. Just as clearly, it held a note of exasperated confusion. "I don't know, Sarah. She seemed to think you were in some kind of trouble. And Greg Roberts said almost the same thing."

Sarah sighed. "What exactly did he say, Raylene?"

"Well, first he said, 'Is Sarah all right?' So I told him that of course you were fine, and he said, 'Tell her I'm here for her if she needs anything.' Doesn't that sound strange to you?"

Sarah felt the hair on her forearms ripple and rise, as though blown by a soft, chilly breeze. "Are you sure that's what he said?" There were days, she thought, when absolutely nothing made any sense.

"Of course I'm sure," Raylene said, bristling. "Sarah, I take messages for a livin'. I know what the man said."

Again Sarah found herself straining to hear. A good bit of the traffic routed itself to and from the little store, creating a mild cacophony of engine noise. At the moment, a brown Pontiac with a badly dented rear fender had chosen to idle in the parking lot just a few yards away, and it could have used some serious muffler repair.

"Okay," she told her friend, "I'm sorry. What about Patrick? Did he say how long he was going to stay?"

"No, just that he'd be here in a few days. Of course, that was a few days ago."

Sarah closed her eyes and prayed for patience. Why now, of all times? "Well, I'll just have to drive back to the city for a couple of days. Whatever you do, don't tell him where I am or what I'm doing."

"I know how to keep a secret, Sarah." Raylene sounded huffy. "I told him you'd gone into Oakland to do some research. And he'll be spittin' nails if he finds out I lied to him. Why don't you just tell him about the book? I mean, he's not a monster."

In spite of her aggravation, Sarah didn't miss the slight softening of Raylene's tone when she talked about Patrick. The nonromance between her brother and her ex-roommate had been going on for years, ever since the first time Patrick had visited Sarah in San Francisco. But neither of them could work up the courage to make a commitment, so they both pretended to be coolly indifferent.

"Not where you're concerned," Sarah teased, knowing how Raylene would react. "He's probably just using me as an excuse to see you, anyway. Why don't you give the guy a break? You know he's crazy about you."

Sure enough, Raylene wasn't in the mood for what she termed Sarah's "mawkish adolescent streak." "That is *not* funny, Sarah Kathleen. If you're not goin' to write down your messages, I'm goin' to hang up. You called collect, remember?"

Sarah laughed. "Okay, don't get yourself in a tizzy. I'll see you sometime tomorrow. Give Dolly my love, okay? And if Patrick calls back, give him *your* love."

Raylene made a rude noise and hung up.

Chuckling, Sarah replaced the receiver. Raylene and Patrick were both obtuse, insecure and bullheaded. But they were also ideal for each other. It might take a little time, but Sarah suspected that someday Raylene would find herself firmly entrenched in the bosom of the O'Shaughnessy family, riding herd on several miniature Irish hooligans.

She stepped away from the pay phone onto the parking lot pavement, carrying the pleasant domestic picture with her. But as she headed for her car, Raylene and Patrick faded from her mind and she found herself pondering those cryptic messages.

Mrs. Lambert's call couldn't be taken seriously, but Greg Roberts was another matter. Sarah had dated him only a few times, though they'd remained good friends. But she hadn't seen him for months. Where on earth could he have gotten the idea she needed help?

As she backed the VW out of its space, she glanced in the rearview mirror. The brown Pontiac she'd noticed earlier was still idling in front of the phone. For some reason, it reminded Sarah of a vulture, dark, brooding and patient, waiting for something to die.

Amazed at the morbid turn her imagination had taken, she pushed the unpleasant thought aside and shifted into first gear. By the time she found a break in the traffic and joined the stream of commuters heading for Carmel, the endless adventures of David T. Bothwell, Private Investigator, had once more assumed priority. Mrs. Lambert, Greg Roberts and the brown Pontiac faded from her mind.

BY THE TIME SHE REACHED Monterey, Sarah's spirits were soaring, and she approached Fisherman's Wharf eagerly.

Along the boardwalk, everything seemed to vibrate with
energy. The shops were colorful and varied—shoes and
clothing, souvenirs, arts and crafts, jewelry—and for a while
she forgot that Bothwell would hardly be browsing through
gift shops while chasing the bad guys. She didn't remember, in fact, until she had paid for not one, but two pairs of
sandals and an alarmingly expensive straw sun hat. Only
then did she notice the disappearing daylight and recall
herself to the task at hand.

Across the wharf was a seafood restaurant that would
make a perfect setting for a scene in Chapter Five, she
thought. But as she headed in that direction, her oversize
tote bag collided with her new purchases, and she decided
to tuck the nonessentials in the VW. The parking lot wasn't
far, and she preferred the extra walk to the prospect of
trying to juggle an armful of shopping bags.

She was just locking her car door when she noticed the
brown sedan. If its rear end hadn't been sticking out,
prominently displaying the dented fender, she wouldn't have
given it a second look. Yet there it sat, glaringly familiar,
and Sarah's curiosity was instantly aroused. She approached it carefully, trying to appear casual just in case
anyone was watching, then looked more closely at the
crumpled fender. It was definitely the same car she'd seen
earlier, a dark brown Bonneville, five or six years old,
bearing Nevada license plates.

She frowned. Not an hour before, as she'd left the tiny
city park in downtown Carmel to walk back to the VW,
she'd noticed the same car. It had cruised the street slowly,
leaving her with the impression that the driver
was . . . stalking her. At the time she'd thought the notion
ridiculous, but now she wasn't so sure. Either there were
several identical cars scooting around the Monterey Peninsula, or else she and the unknown owner of this one had

chosen to travel the exact same route. Yet the odds against either eventuality had to be astronomical.

It was a puzzle, and she couldn't decide whether or not to worry about it. Just take it easy, she told herself. If the car was still here when she finished in the restaurant, she'd call the police and tell them she was being harassed by a perverted Pontiac.

After another quick scan of the parking area—which revealed no sinister lurkers or suspicious-looking kidnapper types—she hurried back along the wharf to the restaurant. When she pushed open the heavy glass door and surveyed the interior, she felt a keen surge of pleasure. Class, she thought. Pure and simple class. Exactly the kind of place Bothwell would like.

As Sarah gazed, enraptured, at the huge, square fireplace that dominated the spacious dining area, the hostess claimed her attention with a discreet little cough, then escorted her to a table near the back of the room. From there she had an unimpeded view of both the room and, through the floor-to-ceiling windows, Monterey Bay. Several charter fishing boats rocked hypnotically at their moorings, while farther out a number of sailboats skimmed the water for one last fling before darkness set in.

Sarah exhaled a breath of pure delight. Then, almost so real she could touch him, Bothwell materialized at the table next to her. Sitting beside him, their arms touching, was his faithful girl Friday and only true love, Traci Stevens. Sarah felt the stirrings of a creative flash, and within seconds it had flashed into a brilliant idea.

She suddenly became aware of the waiter interposing himself between her and her characters—from his expression, Sarah deduced he'd been waiting for some time—so she hurriedly ordered a drink and a seafood salad. As soon as the waiter disappeared, she jerked the steno pad from her bag and began a furious scribbling:

From across the table, her face delicately shadowed by the candlelight, Traci smiled. Bothwell smiled back.

"Oh, David T.," she breathed—Bothwell loved the way she breathed—"you're too good to me."

Sometime later, Sarah laid her pencil aside and read the last two paragraphs with profound satisfaction:

Traci looked as though she'd just been fed worms. "Why, you lying, good-for-nothing snake! This is the third time you've canceled our trip, and it's always the same reason. An important case or a client who's in trouble. Well, I've had enough."

Bothwell glanced around nervously, hoping nobody was staring at the scene Traci was making. No such luck. At the bar, a man looked their way, his eyes steady and penetrating.

Sarah smiled. This was fantastic! An entire scene had just played itself out in her head, and it worked beautifully. The trip into town was just what she'd needed to clear out the cobwebs and get things rolling again.

She leaned back in her chair and arched her feet under the table, gratefully stretching her legs. Now that the burst or creativity had faded, she felt a bit tired. And a bit something else, which she couldn't quite identify. Unease? Maybe it was nothing more than the inevitable letdown after—she checked her watch—after twenty minutes of an adrenaline high.

On the table sat her drink and the seafood salad, apparently placed there by the unobtrusive waiter while she wrote. She reached for the glass, wrapped her hand around it and sipped. If the rest of her foraging trip went this well, she'd have the book finished in record time.

The drink was good, cold and fizzy, and she raised the glass again. Then she stopped before the rim touched her lips. The unease had deepened into actual discomfort, except that now it was more localized and she quickly pinpointed it. The spot between her shoulder blades was burning, had been burning for some time, but she only just realized it.

Someone was watching her....

Chapter Two

Imagining the unknown eyes boring into her back with an almost physical force, Sarah stiffened.

"Not again," she whispered, appalled by the uncharacteristic flights of fancy that were assailing her. Stalked by cars, watched by strangers in restaurants. She was certainly immersing herself in Bothwell's world today, and the sensation was as disturbing as it was unexpected. This had never happened to her before.

She pulled the salad toward her, arranged the napkin in her lap, picked up the fork. The feeling persisted.

She raised a tiny pink shrimp to her mouth, then turned suddenly in her chair.

He sat at the bar, not the only one there, but the only one who'd quickly turned away. She could only see the back of his head and his blue windbreaker. His sandy-brown hair, cut rather short, was neat and well groomed, and his broad shoulders strained the thin material of the jacket as he placed his elbows on the bar. His height was difficult to judge, but he wasn't a small man. She retained a fleeting impression of hard, blunt features set beneath heavy eyebrows, of sun-browned skin and of a mouth tightened into a grim slash above an aggressive chin.

All in all, she thought, he didn't present the classic picture of a man on the make. Instead, he looked more like a man with a score to settle. She fervently hoped he hadn't picked her as the girl most likely to settle it with.

Determined not to encourage him with even a brief show of attention, Sarah turned back to her dinner and thoughts of the book. She'd been hoping to find a way to spice up Bothwell's love life, and this new scene fit the bill perfectly. Maybe she could use the Traci-Bothwell conflict as a subplot, even bring Traci into the final confrontation.

The plot of *Kill Me with Love* managed to distract Sarah for only a few minutes. Soon the prickling heat between her shoulder blades reminded her of her unwanted . . . admirer? Surely not. She'd seen his face only briefly, but she was certain his expression hadn't held anything as flattering as admiration. Curiosity and speculation, maybe, but she just couldn't reconcile any kind of sexual appraisal with those hard, impersonal eyes.

She forced herself to finish eating, and by the time the last crouton had disappeared, she was amazed to find she had become so attuned to the stranger's regard that she could tell not only when he looked at her, but exactly when his gaze turned away. Right now, for instance, she'd bet that he had turned back to the bar or was looking at something else.

Turning slowly in her chair, she discovered that she was right. Perched on the bar stool, his profile to her, he was examining a watch on his left wrist. His eyebrows were drawn together in a scowl, and something in his posture suggested impatience.

Of course, she thought with relief, *he's waiting for someone who's late, and all those negative vibes are hitting me by mistake.*

The man at the bar chose that moment to glance up. Their eyes met, and Sarah could have sworn that his flickered in surprise, but why? Because this time she'd been the surreptitious peeper? Feeling benign and a bit superior, Sarah smiled at him. Not a full-fledged flirtatious smile, just a slight, lip-tilting, caught-you-in-the-act smile.

Apparently he wasn't used to being one-upped, for he frowned again and, with an abrupt motion, turned away. Sarah also turned, pleased with herself. And, she admitted, more than a little relieved to find that her growing apprehension had been unfounded.

Putting the stranger out of her thoughts, she finished her drink and made a few more notes before leaving the table. But she couldn't resist one final glance at the bar as she left the restaurant.

The man was gone.

HE WATCHED HER as she hurried along the boardwalk toward the parking lot, a compact little figure illuminated by the overhead lights that had flickered on at dusk. After a few seconds, he slipped into the thinning stream of pedestrians and followed her.

Before she got into her car, he saw her pause beside the brown Bonneville. In spite of the fact that the two men were pitifully inept in trailing procedures, he was a bit surprised that she'd noticed the car. But, as he'd learned in the restaurant, she was observant—too observant for his purposes. Or maybe he'd simply allowed himself to become too eager, too tense, and therefore careless. At any rate, she'd gotten a good look at him and he couldn't afford to let it happen again. He'd have to be more careful than ever, or he'd never get into the beach house.

Slipping into his own car as she backed the VW out of its parking space, he watched in the rearview mirror to see which way she turned. If she headed back to Carmel, he'd be stymied for another day, and each day he lost would take Kay that much farther from rescue.

He didn't even realize he'd been holding his breath until he released it in a sigh of relief. She'd turned right, toward

Pacific Avenue and the Cannery Row area, so she wasn't going home just yet. But he was puzzled. It was too dark for sight-seeing, and most everything along Cannery Row was closed by now. He'd have to follow her again. Maybe, if luck was with him, she'd settle in at a bar or a friend's house and he could go about his business.

Just as he gained the parking lot exit, another car pulled in front of him, cutting him off. The Pontiac.

"Damn," he breathed. He hated working blind, with no knowledge of the other players, but at this point he had no choice. He found himself hoping the redhead, whoever she was, would be able to handle the trouble that had so obviously dropped into her lap. He sure as hell wouldn't be able to help her.

The thought nagged at him as he drove, once again taking last place in the ridiculous convoy. He just wouldn't let it bother him. Whatever happened, he didn't have time to get involved. If she was mixed up with Paul Vernon—and it looked as though she must be—she probably deserved the worst that could happen to her.

But what if she's not? a perverse inner voice prodded. *What if she's an innocent who just happened to be in the wrong place at the wrong time—like Kay?*

"Damn!" he said again, more loudly. He didn't have an answer. And he didn't want to have to come up with one.

The taillights of the Pontiac mocked him as he drove along the winding street, wondering when—and how—this cat-and-mouse game would end.

PERFECT, SARAH THOUGHT gleefully, stuffing the recorder back into her bag. The place was perfect. She relaxed against the cane-backed bar stool and took another look around at the small, dimly lit lounge. As with the restaurant, she had no trouble at all visualizing Bothwell in this setting.

The bar was intimate without being seedy, and the clientele was exclusively male, with the exception of the woman she'd just interviewed. Louise Harper—"Just plain Lou to my friends," she'd said—owned fifty percent of a fishing boat, and she'd given Sarah some priceless anecdotes and insight into the tightly knit fishing community.

Even the decor seemed designed for a hard-hitting detective novel. Dark wood paneling; compasses and sextants and barometers; a rusty anchor; no dance floor, but an old jukebox with hits from the forties and fifties. This was definitely an old-timers' hangout, no kids, yuppies or tourists allowed.

She broke off her survey and turned back to the bartender, who had just set a fresh drink in front of her.

"What's this?" she said in surprise.

"Compliments of Lou," he explained, nodding toward the stout, gray-haired woman who'd rejoined her friends at a corner table. "Says to tell you that if you ever want another interview, you know where to come."

Sarah smiled and waved her thanks across the room, though she really didn't want the drink. She'd had a couple already, one at the restaurant and another during the interview, but she supposed she should at least have a sip or two, just out of courtesy.

But as she raised the glass to her lips, she became aware that, once again, she was under scrutiny. This time she had no trouble identifying the source. Two men, seated against the opposite wall, were eyeing her with what she could only describe as hostility.

Her breath caught in her throat. What on earth...? If she hadn't known better, she would have sworn there was something personal in the way they stared, but she'd never seen either of them before.

The smaller man, dark and intense, had the thin, pinched face of a fanatic. His eyes were narrowed, either against the curling smoke from his cigarette or in concentration, and his mouth was drawn into such a tense line he seemed to be nearly lipless. Sarah thought he looked like a weasel or a ferret.

Ferret-face's companion was larger, his face florid and covered with a sheen of perspiration. He twitched his right hand rhythmically and occasionally tugged at his shirt collar, which appeared to be too tight for his pudgy neck. While not as overtly menacing as his friend, he appeared too desperate to be considered harmless. Sort of a feral version of Porky Pig.

Sarah tried not to squirm, but it was difficult. On the bar stool, with no one else sitting near, she felt exposed and vulnerable—and very puzzled. Why was she attracting so much negative attention? First the man in the restaurant, now these two.

Keeping her face impassive, she stared back, hoping her coolness would intimidate them into looking away, but the tactic had no immediate effect. Ferret-face and Porky kept their eyes trained on her for another eternal, nerve-racking minute, until finally Porky turned his head and said something to his pal.

Soon the two men were involved in deep conversation, and Sarah spun around on her stool, grateful that she'd managed to give as good as she'd gotten. She had no idea what point they'd been trying to make, but whatever it was, she felt she'd successfully made an important point of her own. Sarah O'Shaughnessy was not a pushover.

Now she would take another swallow of her drink, then quietly leave—being careful, of course, to make sure she wasn't followed. Maybe she should check out the rear entrance....

As her gaze slid across the obligatory mirror behind the bar, she stiffened in alarm, immediately forgetting about the two men and their apparent interest in her. Now she had a much bigger problem. There, right in front of her, was the reflection of an uncomfortably familiar breadth of shoulder, clad in a blue windbreaker and partially hidden by the jukebox and a potted palm.

Hardly daring to breathe, she sat stiffly, waiting in an agony of suspense. Then the shoulders moved and she had her answer. There was no doubt—it was the man from the restaurant. Quickly she lowered her eyes, afraid that the mirror would work against her.

Her heart began to race. He *had* been following her! But why? She forced herself to stay put and not go running for the nearest exit. With a trembling hand she toyed with her glass, swallowed the drink without tasting it, finally grasped the straps of her bag and slid off the bar stool. Then, carefully picking her way through the tables, eyes fixed straight ahead, she headed for the back of the bar. Tucked away at the end of a short, dark hall she found two doors, appropriately labeled Buoys and Gulls. She also found what she was really looking for—a third door marked Exit.

She turned the knob and pushed it open only a few inches at first, peering through the crack. Satisfied that no one waited in the darkness to pounce on her, she slipped outside and quietly closed the door behind her.

On the narrow street with its line of parked cars, she soon saw the brown Pontiac. Carefully, and with frequent nervous looks over her shoulder, she circled around the car. Her fingers found the rusted dent in the fender, final proof that she wasn't just imagining things.

A sudden flash of anger, intense and somehow frightening, swept over her. How dared he track her down, invade her privacy, threaten her well-being? She didn't even have recourse to the police at this point, because he hadn't actually *done* anything to her, except scare her witless. Well, she might not have any hard evidence against him, but she knew what she knew. She'd be an idiot to just passively accept whatever he was planning.

With a savagery she didn't know she possessed, Sarah brought her heel down on the stem that protruded from the right rear tire, then repeated the blow. The quick hiss of escaping air satisfied her need for revenge and she smiled. She enjoyed the sensation so much, in fact, she decided to perform the same surgery on the front tire.

But by the time she reached the VW, her satisfaction had drained away, leaving her tense and anxious, and she drove out of Monterey with at least half her attention on the rearview mirror. Whenever a car followed too closely or for too long a time, she slowed to let it pass. Somehow she couldn't shake the notion that, in spite of two flat tires, the brown Pontiac was somewhere behind her, driven by a madman bent on revenge.

At one point, the feeling grew so strong she pulled off the road where she would have a clear view of each car that sped by. After forty minutes, she conceded that she wasn't being trailed and finished the drive home.

At twelve-nineteen, according to the radio announcer, Sarah pulled into the dark garage, but she didn't immediately switch off the engine. She was, quiet simply, scared to death. Even within the relative security of the garage, she hated the thought of walking the few steps through the darkness to the kitchen door. Now, reminded of the isolation of the house, she shivered as her childhood fears of the bogeyman came rushing back, and she remained in the car for interminable minutes, hugging the security of the headlights to her like an old, warm, familiar blanket.

Idiot, she told herself. *You can't sit in the car all night.* But neither could she face the darkness. Logic simply wasn't enough to combat her primitive fear of the unseen and the unknown.

After what seemed hours, she decided on a reasonable compromise. She left the engine running and the headlights on, dashed from the car to the wall and fumbled the light switch on. Instantly the interior of the garage was flooded with the welcome, blessed glow of a hundred of G.E.'s finest watts. Then she hurriedly closed and locked the garage door before killing the headlights and the engine.

She trembled as she unlocked the exterior kitchen door, then relocked it; she trembled all the way down the hall. She still trembled as she reached the sanctuary of her bedroom, flipped on the light switch and firmly closed the door behind her. From across the room, she caught sight of her reflection in the mirror. She could see the pale oval of her face, lent color only by her too-wide eyes and the slash of her mouth, while her head was surrounded by a shock of frizzy hair that seemed to be literally standing on end.

"Okay, that's it." She spoke aloud for comfort, but her voice held a tremor. "Get a grip on it." With an angry twist of her forearm, she flung the tote bag to the floor beside the bed and plopped down on the mattress. What had really happened, anyway? She had seen the same car and the same man a couple of times, assumed the two belonged to each other and, with malice aforethought, had attacked two defenseless tires. Maybe the man *had* been following her, but if so, it was over now. He had no way of knowing where she lived, so she was safe. Her car was hidden in the garage; the house was locked up tight. And there was no such thing as the bogeyman.

But later, as she finally drifted off to sleep in the comforting glow of the low-watt shell lamp, she wondered what she would have done if the man *had* followed her home. Like it or not, her days of being the reclusive artist had come to an end. Tomorrow she would call the phone company.

IN HER DREAM, she was arguing with a faceless editor about the manuscript that lay on his desk. "This is *garbage!*" he shouted. With a sudden movement, he swept the pages off the desk onto the floor, and with them a heavy ashtray. It shattered when it hit the floor, and Sarah found that awfully strange, because his office was carpeted. . . .

Her eyes flew open. She blinked repeatedly, trying to readjust her perspective from the dream to reality. The digital clock on the nightstand winked its red numbers at her— 2:31. Her first thought was that she'd been in bed only a couple of hours. Her second was that the breaking noise had come from inside the house.

Groping for the short robe laid across the foot of the bed, she thrust her arms into the sleeves and fumbled with the sash, but the satin ends slipped from her nerveless fingers. She didn't know which prospect frightened her more, staying shut in the bedroom like a rat in a cage or venturing out into the dark, inimical house with nothing to protect her.

She forced herself to walk toward the door, all the while frantically searching her memory for something, *anything*, that could be used as a weapon. But there were no convenient knives or hammers or ice picks strewed about the neat bedroom. She took two tentative steps, then two more. The door was nearly within reach. . . .

When she crept past the dresser, her eyes locked on the heavy hairbrush nestled innocently between the spray cologne and her makeup bag. Quietly, carefully, she closed her fingers around the wooden handle. One part of her mind, the tiny portion that remained remote and uninvolved, recognized the absurdity of trying to confront an intruder with such an insignificant weapon. But another part of her didn't care how silly she looked—the hairbrush was solid and reassuring, positive evidence that she still retained some semblance of control.

With her free hand she reached for the doorknob, then quickly stepped back. The lamp. She'd forgotten about the lamp. Dim as the light was, the glow might spill into the hall when she opened the door. Her only advantage was the element of surprise, and she couldn't afford to give it away. With short, jerky steps, she sidled her way back to the nightstand, keeping her eyes on the door, and clicked the lamp off. The noise seemed as loud as a cannon shot in the otherwise silent room.

She waited in the dark for an endless, nerve-racking minute before she crept forward again and soundlessly turned the doorknob. Then she slipped into the hall like a wraith, marveling that the thunder of her pulse could be contained within her body instead of echoing throughout the darkened house.

At first the blackness seemed to stifle her with its thickness and weight. *He could be right beside me,* she thought in sudden panic. *He could be right here and I wouldn't even know it until he touched me.*

If she gave in to fear, let it defeat her, she would be doing the intruder's job for him.

For a few moments she simply stood in the hall, steadying her breathing, absorbing the night sounds. When her eyes had adjusted to the darkness, she made her way toward the kitchen, forcing one foot in front of the other. At least she didn't have to decide which way to go. Only the kitchen and the den were tiled. If the intruder had knocked something to the floor in any other room, the carpeting would have absorbed the noise.

With that much reasoned out, Sarah decided to play a hunch. *If* the intruder had gained entrance to the house from the patio, he had probably bumped into the avocado plant on the bar. And *if* his blunder had startled him into immobility, at least for a minute or two, she thought she knew where to find him—crouched beside the bar, about six feet from the patio doors.

Heartened by her cool logic, she advanced a few more paces, feeling with her bare foot for the spot where the carpet met the tile. Cautiously she peered around the wall into the kitchen. There was the bar, its bulk unmistakable. Moonlight filtered through the window above the sink, illuminating a small patch of floor; just at the edge of the dim light, a shard of earthenware told its tale. She'd been right. He must be there, only a few yards away, backed into the dark corner formed by the bar and the kitchen counter.

Suddenly a flutter of movement, a whisper of sound, chilled her, freezing her in place. The den. He was in the den! Just on the periphery of her vision, a shadow, fractionally darker than the nighttime gloom, floated across the floor. Slowly she turned her head, and the specter took shape. A man, moving away from her to the far side of the room, so stealthy and silent that she was tempted to doubt his existence.

She drew in a huge breath and, with a supreme effort, propelled her body across the distance between them. The hairbrush jabbed into the small of his back, and she heard him gasp.

"Don't move," she said, amazed that she could sound so controlled. "Not even an inch. This thing has a hair trigger."

He slowly extended his arms away from his sides, his hands palms up. "You're the boss," he answered, but she detected no fear, no uncertainty in his voice.

She jabbed him again. "Over there, in that chair."

He obeyed, walking cautiously. Just as cautiously, he turned and lowered himself into the armchair beside the sofa. In the velvet darkness, with nothing more than vague moonlight for illumination, he was merely a shadowy bulk. But the memory of how he had looked in the restaurant, his

broad shoulders outlined by the thin windbreaker, brought
to her mind an impression of controlled strength that could
suddenly erupt into violence. He seemed to be looking up at
her, and she wished she could see his face, his eyes. Instinctively she reached for the light switch, then jerked her hand
back. If he saw that she didn't have a gun...

"I guess you'll be wanting to call the police," he said in
a low, conversational tone as she moved behind him, out of
his line of vision.

She stiffened. He certainly didn't *sound* like a man who
was worried. "I guess I will."

"Too bad your phone doesn't work."

She gritted her teeth. "How do you know?"

She thought she saw his broad shoulders move slightly in
a shrug. "I checked."

"Well, the phone may be dead," she bluffed, "but this
gun works just fine. Why the hell did you break into my
house?"

He didn't say anything for a moment. Then, reluctantly
it seemed, he told her, "Actually, I was trying to break out."

The words didn't register. "I beg your pardon?"

"Out," he repeated. "I was trying to get out."

She felt dizzy with confusion. "Then when did you get
in?"

"While you were out bar hopping. By the way, you forgot to lock that window."

"Oh, shut up!" She tried to pace, but gave it up when she
discovered she couldn't do it without turning her back to
him. "This is crazy! I flattened two of your tires, and the car
was still parked at the lounge when I left. There's no way
you could have gotten here ahead of me. And how did you
know where I lived, anyway?"

That shrug again. "I don't know whose car you vandal-
ized, lady, but it wasn't mine. And as for the house—let's

just say I have an interest in it. Now why don't we cut this short? I'll go my way and you can go back to bed."

He started to rise, then dropped back into the chair when she jabbed the brush roughly against his shoulder blade.

"Don't you move again," she ordered. "Why have you been following me?"

He sighed. "Look, lady, you're just wasting time. You can't call the cops." He rose slowly and turned to face her. "And I'm betting you won't pull that trigger. I'm going to leave."

Abruptly, without warning, he lunged. Caught too off guard to turn and run, Sarah dived to the side, but his arms locked around her waist and they both fell against the sofa. Squirming, bucking, kicking, she desperately tried to free herself, but he held her firmly in place. Her struggles accomplished nothing except to work her robe off her shoulders and down around her arms, making her uncomfortably aware that the brief teddy she slept in left her nearly naked.

Then, lithe as a panther, the intruder sprang to his feet and yanked her upright. "Give me the gun," he demanded. His fingers, brutally strong, forced her wrist upward. Until then she'd forgotten about the brush, which was still clenched in her frozen fist. Now she felt one of her fingernails rip as he tore the puny weapon from her fingers and shoved her aside.

He cursed. She backed away, stumbled, moved again until the back of her leg bumped the chair.

"A hairbrush?" His voice was harsh with incredulity. "You backed me down with a goddamn *hairbrush*?"

Swearing steadily, he grabbed her again and pushed her toward the sofa. "Now you're going to sit down, lady, and you're going to stay put. You're also going to answer a few questions." He swore again. "A *hairbrush* . . ."

She gasped when she fell against the sofa cushions, more with indignation than fear. "*Me* answer questions? You're out of your mind!"

In her mind's eye, he suddenly swelled with menace and loomed hugely above her.

"Shut up," he said, his voice rough with anger and impatience. "Where's Vernon?"

The question startled her. "Vernon?"

"I don't have time to be nice, lady. Where's Vernon?"

"I don't know anybody named Vernon." She drew the open edges of the robe together, as though the flimsy fabric could somehow protect her.

"You're living in his house, so cut out the act. I told you, I don't have time."

Suddenly he stopped talking. Even in the dark, she could tell that his body had tensed. The way he held himself, rigid, with head half turned as if he were listening to something, made her uneasy. Very uneasy.

"What's wrong?" she asked, wishing she could escape from this living nightmare.

"Quiet," he whispered.

"But what ... ?"

Instantly his hand covered her mouth.

"Quiet," he repeated. "Are you expecting company?"

She shook her head. Then in the silence she heard it. A metallic scraping, faint but definite. Someone was trying to jimmy the lock on the patio doors.

He let his hand fall away from her mouth and she drew in a greedy breath; in the very next instant, she gasped when his hand painfully gripped her upper arm. He yanked her to her feet, pushed her ahead of him toward the hall.

"Listen to me," he said, still whispering. "I want you to go into the bedroom, close and lock the door, and stay there. Understand?"

She nodded, realized he couldn't see her, and finally found her voice. "Yes."

He pushed her forward again, the touch of his fingers at the small of her back burning through the robe.

She tripped on the ridge of carpet where it met the tile, but his hand steadied her. She was so confused. What was happening? This man had trailed her like a bloodhound, broken into her house, wrestled her to the floor. But he hadn't hurt her. Not even after she had pushed him around and smashed his ego with a hairbrush. And now he was apparently trying to protect her from someone else. But who? Who was Vernon? Why had the beach house suddenly turned into Mystery Mansion?

At the bedroom door she stopped. "In here," she said quietly. Now she was eager for the haven of the cool, smooth sheets. Maybe if she burrowed beneath the covers, hid her head like an ostrich, all this madness would go away. She'd wake up in the morning to find that it had all been a dream.

Suddenly he flattened himself against her, pressing her hard against the wall. Instinctively she struggled. "What . . . ?"

"Shh." His voice was scarcely more than a stirring of air. "Listen."

In the dark she could see the faint gleam of his teeth; he seemed to be grimacing, and she wondered why. *She* didn't hear anything.

Then she did. The scuffle of footsteps, a few words spoken in a soft murmur. She felt faint. *More* strangers, intruders, and this time there were at least two of them. She found her hands gripping the front of his jacket with quiet desperation.

Gently, it seemed, he loosened her grip. Then he silently urged her into the bedroom. He grasped her upper arms, pulled her very close, so close that his breath feathered across her ear. "Lock the door. Stay inside."

When he drew away, she wanted to reach for him, bring him back. Somehow, sometime, he had become her friend and ally—her only security. But he backed out of the room, closing the door soundlessly behind him. He was gone, and she was alone again.

She had no idea how long she stood there after he left, but eventually she found herself pressed against the door. She could hear nothing. No voices, no footsteps, no thumps and bumps in the night. Only the sound of her breathing, ragged and uneven.

A multitude of thoughts assailed her. A brown Pontiac had been following her. *He* had been following her. She'd disabled the Pontiac, but it didn't belong to him. Ergo, she had been twice-shadowed, double-trailed, twin-tracked. Two sets of thugs. What did they want with her? Did they know each other? If so, why work separately? And who was Vernon? He—her friendly enemy—said that she was living in Vernon's house. He obviously wanted to find Vernon, but why? Were the others also searching for Vernon, or were they your common, garden-variety thieves?

Something strange and dangerous was going on, and she had managed to land smack in the middle of it. Suddenly the conversation with Raylene came back to her. The cryptic messages from Mrs. Lambert and Greg Roberts now took on an alarming significance—mere coincidence or specific warnings? How had those two people, who played only marginal roles in her life, become embroiled in the intrigue that now surrounded her?

Sarah felt overwhelmed by a flood of disconnected data that had no form or definition. While potentially violent strangers stalked each other—and her—through her house, she could do nothing but cower and hide. She had become a pawn in a game where she didn't know the players, the rules, or the goal. The only thing she knew for certain was that she was in danger, and if she didn't help herself, no one else would.

Coming to a swift decision, she found the lock in the center of the doorknob and twisted it. Then she felt for her bag on the floor where she had tossed it earlier and scrabbled through its contents until she found the car keys. The house was still silent—she heard no sounds of struggle, no shouts or curses. *Maybe they've all gone away.* She felt a momentary surge of optimism before reality claimed her again. *Or maybe the second intruder was only a ruse. The first guy gains my trust, then lets his buddies in for the dirty work.*

"Damn!" The sound of her own voice, unnaturally loud in the dark bedroom, spurred her to action. She ran to the window, pulled the drapes and fumbled for the latch. The window slid open noiselessly, and she ran her fingers around the inside edges of the screen, searching for the tiny release mechanisms. There. She had it loose.

Carefully she lowered the screen to the hedge that bordered the front of the house; with a hop-twist, she climbed onto the sill, extended her legs outside and boosted herself over the shrubbery. Luckily the hedge wasn't very wide. Unluckily it was very rough. As her feet hit the ground, she felt every scrape and rip of the tough stems as they tore along the backs of her bare legs. But the pain didn't matter. She had gained a measure of freedom.

While she debated her next move, she realized that freedom was indeed relative and, in her case, fleeting. She couldn't get to the Volkswagen. The garage was locked from the inside, and the only way into it was through the kitchen. *Think, Sarah.*

It came to her then, a simple solution. She'd use one of *their* cars. If their cars weren't being guarded, and if they had been gracious enough to leave the keys in the ignition....

Outside, the moonlight favored her with its faint but steady glow. She could see clearly, and within seconds she had crossed the front lawn to the road. Swiftly she scanned one way, then the other. The road was empty. No cars, at

least not nearby. They must be beyond the curve, out of
sight out of the house.

She started down the road at a dead run, trying to ignore
the surrounding trees that now seemed much larger than she
remembered. She had gone only a few yards, when the sharp
report of a gunshot sent her sprawling, belly down, in the
hard-packed dirt.

An instant later she was on her feet, hugging herself
tightly. The shot had come from inside the house, not outside. Her collusion theory vanished. Partners in crime
wouldn't be shooting at each other, and they weren't shooting at her. She wanted to keep running, but each passing
second hammered an unwelcome truth into her head. The
man she'd caught had tried to protect her, and she was, quite
literally, running out on him. He could be wounded, maybe
dying, while still trying to protect her. Illogical as it seemed,
she owed him something. But what could she do?

Before the implications of the gunshot had time to para-
lyze her with indecision, she darted toward the house,
around the garage, to the back. The patio was directly ahead
of her. The wind chimes swung gently in the ocean breeze,
glinting silver in the moon's glow. Beneath the chimes sat a
round wrought-iron table and matching chairs. Several large
blooming plants in ceramic pots stood grouped in a semicircle behind the furniture, framing the rock garden. A
charming scene, but regrettably devoid of weapons.

From inside the house came a sudden crash, then the unmistakable splat of knuckles striking unprotected flesh.
Someone yelled out the beginning of an obscenity, but the
words ended abruptly.

Sarah took two running steps across the rock garden, and
stopped in midstride. Quickly she knelt and touched the
small, white stones underfoot, Individually they were
worthless, but together...

With a shrug, she wiggled out of her robe, then grasped
a sleeve and shoulder on either side of the seam and yanked.

The sleeve separated with a satisfying tear. Working so swiftly her fingers felt disconnected from the rest of her, she knotted the torn end of the sleeve, knelt again to scoop the stones into the slender bag thus created, and knotted the other end. She hefted the makeshift blackjack, comforted by its weight, and ran for the open patio doors.

The den and kitchen were still unlit, but her eyes were now accustomed to the darkness and she had no difficulty distinguishing two men locked in brutal combat. A few feet away from the battle lay a third man, alive but obviously injured. As she watched, he struggled to his knees, then fell sideways and was still.

Sarah sidestepped the two men grappling on the floor, keeping the wall to her back. If only she could tell who was who... But their sudden shifts and turns, their total absorption in destroying each other, made their faces nothing more than shadowy blurs.

Another movement claimed her attention. The injured man had again pulled himself upright. He now stood, swaying on his feet, one arm extended before him as as if he were pointing at something. Or *aiming* at something....

Sarah launched herself at the man, wielding her bag of rocks to good effect. The homemade bludgeon struck his face, and as she bounced into the wall, he fell to his knees with a screech of pain and outrage. The cry seemed to herald a rapid descent into sheer bedlam.

Either in pain or in desperation, maybe both, the man clutched at the brass-and-glass étagère that served as a divider between the kitchen and the den. It teetered for a moment, then crashed forward. The two combatants, who had been startled into separating, jumped in opposite directions, but one of them was too slow. He stumbled and went down under the weight of the shelves, while his opponent darted to one side and clutched at Sarah.

"What the hell...?"

"Get me outta this...!"

"Run! Get out of here!"

The voices melded in a brief, harsh chorus of excitement and confusion. Then, like a stage play gone haywire, the scene erupted into hurtling bodies, flying furniture and some very imaginative curses.

Sarah reeled from the impact of someone's beefy shoulder and fought to keep both her balance and her grip on the satin blackjack. In the next instant she was lifted from her feet. Flailing and kicking, she managed to twist free from the muscular arms. She whirled in a blind panic, and the heavy cudgel followed the momentum of her arm, flying in a deadly arc. It connected hard with something, and the sickening thud sent a jolt all the way up to her shoulder. She heard an abbreviated grunt, and then she felt herself falling, carried to the floor by the heavy weight of a body.

She landed on her back. Her lungs, painfully crushed between the floor and the man on top of her, felt ready to explode. Her head cracked against the hard tiles. She saw a brilliant explosion of white behind her eyelids before she surrendered to the velvet fog that swept her away....

An irritating brightness penetrated the mist and she turned her head to escape it. But she couldn't escape the voice, loud and filled with disbelief.

"Sarah Kathleen! By all that's holy, girl, you should be ashamed of yourself!"

She couldn't see the man behind the flashlight, but all the same, she knew who he was. Her brother, Patrick. And he had just walked in on his worst nightmare.

His baby sister, all but naked, lay brazenly entangled in the arms of a man he'd never seen.

Chapter Three

Held immobile by shock, not to mention the deadweight sprawled atop her body, Sarah had trouble framing an appropriate response, but she did the best she could.

"Paddy... What are you doing here?"

"Never mind what I'm doing here," her brother's voice growled from what seemed an absurd height. "The question is, what are *you* doing *there*?"

Pushing futilely at the inert form that pinned her to the floor—and fervently hoping that in this case the word *deadweight* would prove to be merely a figure of speech—Sarah groaned. Her head ached; her chest hurt; the scratches on her leg burned. She had been attacked, the house had been ransacked and she quite possibly had killed someone. She wasn't in the mood for Twenty Questions.

"Patrick," she said through gritted teeth, "do you suppose you could postpone your righteous indignation long enough to get that flashlight out of my eyes and help me up from here?"

"Help, is it?" Paddy's voice rose to a dangerous level. "And whose help did you have gettin' yerself onto the floor?"

She groaned again. For reasons unknown, Paddy invariably fell into their father's Irish cadences whenever he was winding up for a serious lecture. "Oh, Lord, not The Brogue, Paddy. Anything but The Brogue."

But, warming to his theme, Paddy continued. "Ah, Sarah Kathleen, if Mother were to see you now, she'd be turnin' over in her grave. 'Tis shameful, shameful."

"Argh!" Sarah drummed her heels against the floor. "You're right, Paddy, I admit it! I'm a shameless hussy! I've disgraced every generation of O'Shaughnessys all the way back to the year zero. Now will you please get this man off me!"

At that moment, a low moan, pitiful in its implied agony, sounded from somewhere near her head, and the man lying on top of her stirred.

Paddy immediately dropped to his knees, waving the flashlight up and down. "Sarah, are you hurt? I didn't know you were hurt!"

Sarah pushed at the man again, and this time she felt him shift his position slightly. "Not me. *Him.* I knocked him out. See if you can roll him off me."

"Out? He's unconscious?"

"Did you think he was just too overcome with passion to lift his head? Really, Paddy, I worry about you sometimes." She had to pause to draw in a breath, painfully conscious of the throbbing at the base of her skull. "Now hurry, I can't breathe."

With Patrick's weight behind the task, Sarah was soon free and on her feet, though her legs felt none too steady and she had to fight against a wave of dizziness. She groped through the dark room, gingerly stepping over obstacles, until she reached the light switch and flicked it on. After a quick glance around, she wished she were still in the dark. The room was a shambles.

The beautiful brass-and-glass étagère lay on its side, three of its five shelves shattered. Several pieces of Waterford crystal were likewise smashed, and a delicate shell lamp, mate to the one in her bedroom, was now unrecognizable. Half a dozen books, along with their marble bookends, were strewed across the floor, intact but battered. An intricately carved ivory pipe that had once graced a small oak rack would never again be smoked; its stem had been snapped, its age-yellowed bowl cracked.

And in the midst of all this debris, the largest piece of flotsam began to move. First an arm, then a leg, finally the head. The movement was accompanied by an occasional oath, weak in tone but quite provocative in originality. Sarah reflected that anyone who could swear like that couldn't be too badly hurt. She hoped so, anyway, because she had recognized his voice. This was the *first* man, the one who had tried to protect her. Her aim had been good, but she'd hit the wrong target.

She heard Paddy's quick intake of breath. "Sarah, what happened here? Who is that guy?"

"Paddy, see if you can help him," she interrupted. "I'm going to get a towel and some water."

"And some clothes while you're at it," her brother said. Then, seeing her questioning glance at the man on the floor, he added, "For yourself, Sarah. You're half-naked."

Looking down at herself, Sarah realized he was right. The teddy was skimpy by design and obviously not made for the sort of exertion she'd just been through. One shoulder strap hung loose, leaving her right breast barely covered, and the thin nylon was torn in several places. A side seam, ripped from hem to waist, flapped open, exposing an indecent amount of white skin, as well as a rapidly darkening bruise on her hip.

She looked at Patrick, at the face that was a masculine version of her own, and was both amused and exasperated to see that he had blushed a shade of red that outshone his hair. "My brother, the prude. Never mind," she said over his sputtered protest, "I'll get dressed. Just see what you can do for him, get him a pillow or something."

"Typical," Paddy groused. "First you knock him senseless, then you want to mother him."

Sarah left both brother and victim, one muttering, one cursing, and hurried to her bedroom, where she quickly shed the offending teddy. She wiggled into a pair of jeans, trying to ignore the way the denim aggravated the scratches and abrasions on her thighs, and pulled on a lightweight, sleeveless sweater. Then she darted to the bathroom to grab a washcloth, a towel and a tube of first-aid ointment.

When she got back to the den, she found the patient sprawled on the sofa, while Paddy leaned sullenly against the wall, his arms akimbo like a disgruntled schoolmaster. "Sarah, I want an explanation."

"You're not the only one," she retorted on her way to the kitchen. She took some ice cubes from the freezer and wrapped them in the towel, then carried the ice pack to the man on the sofa. "This should help the lump on your head," she said. "Does it hurt much?"

"Hell, yes, it hurts!" He snatched the towel from her hand and cursed again when he pressed it to the side of his head. "What did you hit me with?"

She glanced away from him. "A sack of rocks."

"That figures." He regarded her quizzically, his head cocked to accommodate the ice pack. "You're resourceful, I'll give you that much. Hairbrushes and rocks—got any more surprises up your sleeve?"

"Not at the moment," she said coldly. His attitude was beginning to grate on her sense of justice. After all, technically speaking, *she* was the injured party. "If you intend to make a career of breaking and entering, pushing people around, you sort of have to expect that someone might push back."

Surprisingly, his face softened. When she'd first noticed him in the restaurant, his features had seemed harsh and forbidding. Now, she admitted, they were actually rather nice. His mouth wasn't really grim, especially when it relaxed in a semismile, as it was doing now. And his eyes, nearly the same color as his sandy brown hair, were framed by the most incredible lashes.

"I'll have to remember that," he said, and Sarah thought she heard a hidden laugh in his voice. "I suppose the other two got away."

"If you mean the two bozos I passed on the road, they're probably halfway outta the county by now," Patrick said loudly, apparently fed up with being a bystander. "Seemed to be in a hurry to get into a car that was pulled off in the bushes."

"What?" Sarah shrieked, whirling to face her brother. "You didn't even try to stop them?"

"Stop them from what?" Paddy shouted back. "Getting into a car? As far as I know, Sarah Kathleen, that's not a crime. And you still haven't told me what this is all about." He shifted his angry glare from Sarah to the stranger, evidently keeping his temper only by dint of a mighty effort.

Sarah sat down suddenly, sinking into the armchair nearest the sofa. "Paddy, please don't shout," she said, rubbing her arms. Her stomach had started to churn and she felt cold. Terribly cold.

Patrick hurried to her side, tilted her chin up to look at her face. "You're white as a sheet. I thought you said you weren't hurt."

Though his voice was rough, his fingers were gentle. Sarah knew he was troubled and confused; he only barked to hide his concern. She wanted to reassure him, but she couldn't. Everything had just that moment begun to sink in, and she couldn't even reassure herself.

"I'm not hurt," she began shakily. "At least I don't think so . . . I mean . . . I don't know what I mean . . ."

"You're scared." The stranger spoke quietly as he rose from the sofa, carelessly tossed aside the ice pack. "You have a right to be scared. I'm just surprised it's taken this long to hit you."

He held up one hand in a gesture of subtle command when Patrick stepped forward and opened his mouth to speak. Sarah watched in amazement as her burly, tough brother intercepted and obeyed the unspoken order by retreating a step and remaining silent.

"If I had any sense at all," the man continued, "I'd get out of here right now. But after what's happened, I think you deserve an explanation. And you just might be able to help with something that's important to me. Very important."

He paused, and Sarah caught the expression of fatigue that showed only in his eyes. She also sensed that he was seething with frustration.

"An explanation would be nice," she said sarcastically. "I don't even know you, yet you've been following me all over the peninsula, and tonight you broke into this house. And while you're at it, explain those other two creeps. What did *they* want, and why were you shooting at one another?"

"Shooting?" Patrick exclaimed, throwing his hands up. "Sarah, what are you involved with?"

"I'm not involved with anything," she answered, her voice rising. "I don't even know these people. I don't know what they want. In fact, I don't know *anything*!"

The stranger started to shake his head, then winced and rubbed at his temples. "If you're not involved, why are you living in Paul Vernon's house?"

Was there really a hint of accusation in his voice, Sarah wondered, or had she only imagined it? No, she decided, it was real. In spite of the fact that he'd tried to protect her, he obviously suspected her of something. But what?

"You seem to be confused, mister," she said coldly. "You're the one who should be answering the questions, not me. Let's start with your name."

Again his eyes expressed what he was feeling—extreme irritation. "I don't owe you anything."

"Aubrey Glen Macklin," Patrick said.

Both Sarah and the stranger faced him with surprise.

Patrick smiled smugly and showed them the wallet he held carelessly in his right hand. "Security consultant, lives in Los Angeles. Six feet, one hundred seventy-five pounds, about...let's see...thirty-eight years old." Abruptly he tossed the wallet across the room to its owner. "I'm Patrick O'Shaughnessy, and this is my sister, Sarah. Now that we're all acquainted," he continued in a deceptively mild tone, "why don't you tell us just exactly what the hell's going on."

TWENTY MINUTES LATER, as the three of them sat around the dining table, Sarah stirred another spoon of sugar into her coffee and frowned. "Okay, so your niece is romantically involved with this Paul Vernon, who's the classic bad guy. Fraud, income tax evasion, smuggling. Now she's disappeared, along with Vernon, and you think he's kidnapped her. So why are you watching this house if you already know they're not here? And why you in the first place, instead of the police?"

Mack—who strenuously objected to being called "Aubrey"—shrugged. "Just a hunch. About three weeks ago, she called me, said she wanted to visit me for the weekend. I got the impression that she was having second thoughts about her relationship with Vernon and wanted out. Anyway, she never showed up and I couldn't reach her by phone. So I figure Vernon skipped out in a hurry and took Kay with him. If he was nervous, pressed for time, there's a chance he left something behind that could tell me where they've gone."

"All right, that's why you're here," Sarah conceded. "But it still seems like a police case to me."

Mack smiled grimly. "Not a police case. A federal case. The government's issued warrants for Vernon—and for Kay. She's listed on all Vernon's corporate papers as an officer, and her signature appears on several questionable documents. In short, she's considered a coconspirator, and she'll be prosecuted right along with Vernon." He sighed heavily. "When I told them I thought Vernon had kidnapped her, they practically laughed in my face."

"Maybe that's the best thing that could happen," Patrick said. "The feds bring them in, Kay testifies against him and she's off the hook. Unless you're afraid she's just as guilty as her boyfriend," he added nastily, eliciting a strong desire in Sarah to slap the smirk off her brother's face.

Mack glared at Patrick. "You don't know Kay. I do. Yeah, she was a fool to get mixed up with Vernon, but she's not a criminal. Besides, I'm afraid she won't live to be arrested. I think her life's in danger."

He turned away from them abruptly, but not before Sarah had seen the desolation that blanketed his face like a mask.

"Why?" she asked gently. "You said she was in love with him, that they'd been together for several years. And since he's taken her with him, you have to assume that he cares for her. Surely he'll protect her."

Mack stared at her as though she were an alien life form. "Do you ever have trouble seeing through those stars in your eyes? Okay, okay," he said quickly to forestall Sarah's outraged exclamation, "I'm sorry. But you don't know the situation and I do. Vernon's not sane. His dossier reads like another *Snake Pit*. 'Egomaniacal' and 'paranoid' are two of the nicer labels. The bottom line is that if he's cornered or feels threatened, he's capable of murder."

"All right," Patrick said. "I grant you that your niece is in a bad position. But what the devil do you think you can do about it? She's gone, man, and if the federal government can't find her, nobody can."

A shutter seemed to close on Mack's face, robbing him of everything except ruthless determination. "Maybe they're not looking as hard as I am."

Sarah felt a chill come over her, as if a silent, cold wind had blown into the room. Aubrey Glen Macklin, she sensed, was not one man, but two. Sensitive and warm, protective of those he loved; yet, because of that protectiveness, dangerous and brutal. And she suspected that he wasn't even aware of the paradox.

"What about the rest of your family, Mack?" she asked, hoping to banish the unease that had settled around the table. "Kay's parents?"

For a moment she thought he was so lost in his dark thoughts that he hadn't heard her. Then he pushed his coffee mug toward her, and she refilled it, content to wait until he was ready to speak.

He sipped at the hot coffee, grimaced and cradled the mug between hands that were tanned and weather roughened. "There's just the two of us," he began. "She's my brother's child. He died in 'Nam when she was five. Not long after, I enlisted, and when I came back home two years later, I found out my sister-in-law had dumped Kay on a baby-sitter and left town. Kay was in foster care. Her mother's family didn't want her, and my parents were dead, so I took her." He took a huge gulp of coffee, set the mug down softly and stared at the wall. "She was a tiny thing, with these big blue eyes that sort of cut right through you. Seven years old, and already she knew that nobody wanted her. No child should ever feel that way."

"How old is she?" Sarah asked. What she really wanted to do was put her arms around him, try to ease his sadness.

"Twenty-four," Mack said. "And she's really a good kid. Worked all during college and still managed to stay on the dean's list. But she's too gullible. I tried to warn her about Vernon, but that just made her more determined to have him."

Patrick cleared his throat self-consciously. "When you love somebody, it's hard to watch them make mistakes and not want to step in and take over." He glanced at his sister, and once again a blush of embarrassment rushed up his neck and covered his face.

Sarah laughed. Mack had inadvertently hit upon the one topic closest to Paddy's heart—taking care of family.

Patrick's response even elicited a grin from Mack. "I get the feeling that playing big brother hasn't been easy. She ever hit you with a bag of rocks?"

"Not yet," Sarah interjected, "but not because it hasn't occurred to me. Don't waste your sympathy on Paddy. There are two more at home just like him, and they run me ragged."

"With good reason," Patrick insisted. "You should be at home, Sarah, where you belong. I told you California was too wild for you, and now look what's happened. You could've been killed tonight!"

"Well, I wasn't, and I'm not going to be. And this isn't the time to rehash the family fight, okay?" She looked at him pointedly, then continued. "Mack's got a problem, and I think we should help him."

"Hey, wait a minute. This isn't any of our business, Sarah."

"Your brother's right," Mack said. "Besides, there's nothing you can do."

"Sure there is," Sarah told him emphatically. "You said you wanted to look for clues, right? So we can help you look, especially me. I know this house, Mack. Just tell me what you're looking for, and I'll know if it's here."

"Look, I appreciate what you're trying to do, but you're missing the point. I don't *know* what I'm looking for. I'm just going on instinct. Kay knows I'd come looking for her, and that I'd eventually find this place. I believe she'd try to leave *something*. But I don't know what."

Patrick shook his head. "How could she leave something that Vernon wouldn't find?"

"First of all," Sarah said, "if he had to leave in a hurry, like Mack said, he wouldn't have time to be careful. Besides, it might not have occurred to him that Kay wanted to get away from him." She gestured with impatience when the two men looked at her blankly. "Well, think about it! Kay implied that she wanted to leave Vernon, so it stands to reason that something about him was making her uneasy or frightened. If I were in her place, I wouldn't broadcast my intentions. I'd play along until I had a chance to get away."

"I think you're right," Mack said thoughtfully. "When she made that last call to me, she seemed to be choosing her words, like Vernon was in the room with her. I could tell she was nervous, but maybe he couldn't."

Sarah bit her lower lip, trying to visualize what had happened from Kay's point of view. "So she told you she wanted to spend the weekend with you. Would Vernon let her do that?"

Mack nodded. "She usually came every three months or so. Vernon and I didn't exactly get along, so I never visited them."

"Then obviously she didn't know he was planning to leave. Which means that either he was deliberately keeping her in the dark, or else he felt like somebody was getting too close and he decided to run for it."

"Could be," Mack conceded. "About six weeks ago, he lost his business in L.A. to the bankruptcy courts, and right after that, he was indicted. I didn't know any of this until later, but now it makes a lot of sense. He brought Kay here, where they'd be out of sight until he could find a way out of the country."

"And he must have figured it would take a while." Sarah began to feel excited as her theory took shape. "I mean, why move to Carmel for just a few days when it would've been easier to use phony names and stay at a hotel in L.A.? No, I think he planned to be here a while, but something panicked him, forced him to move up the timetable. He left here in a hurry."

"And Kay didn't have time to let me know."

"But she might have left a message where Vernon wouldn't see it," Sarah finished, looking from Paddy to Mack in triumph. "At least it's worth a try."

Mack smiled at her then, a *real* smile, free of irony and weariness, and Sarah wondered how she could ever have thought of him as cold and forbidding. Even his voice had lightened, and if he didn't sound really hopeful, she reflected, at least he no longer sounded *hopeless*.

"So where do we start, Pollyanna?"

THEY STARTED in the kitchen, taking everything out of the drawers and cabinets, examining each scrap of paper, looking under cans and boxes and cartons. Next they finished tearing apart the dining room and the den, moved on to the formal living room and finally dissected the closets, the two bedrooms and two bathrooms.

Two hours later they stood in the kitchen again and surveyed the dubious fruits of their labors. Their net find amounted to an empty suitcase, a stack of magazines, the box of embossed stationery that Sarah had noticed before and a cigar box that held several check registers, a stack of clipped coupons, an invitation to a baby shower and a scrawled shopping list. The items offered no obvious clues, yet Mack handled them almost reverently.

"Kay and her coupons," he said softly, turning the small bundle over in his hands. "They're like a game with her. She's always trying to top her last refund."

"What about the check registers?" Patrick said, nodding toward the small books Sarah held.

Sarah shrugged. "The writing's so bad I can barely read them. Anyway, the last entry was nearly a year ago."

She tossed one of the books to Mack, and he thumbed through the pages. "It's Kay's," he confirmed. "I can read most of it, but it doesn't look important. Supermarkets, department stores, utility payments. No checks to individuals, nothing to travel agencies or airlines. Here's one to UCLA for two-hundred-fifty dollars, noted 'final payment/student loan.'" He flipped back page by page until he reached the front of the register; then, with a sound of disgust, he threw it on the table. "She made the same payment on the fifteenth of every month. Some criminal, huh?"

Sarah reached into the cigar box for the last two items. "'Sandra Jamison,'" she read from the shower invitation. "Do you know her?"

"Yeah," Mack answered, running his hands through his hair. "She was Kay's roommate at school. I checked with her a couple of weeks ago. She hasn't seen Kay since the shower."

"Seven—no, eight months ago." Sara frowned. "That's a long time to stay away from a close friend."

Mack was reading the shopping list and didn't look up when he answered. "Apparently Vernon didn't encourage her to do much socializing. I checked with all her old friends, and they all said the same thing. When they telephoned, Kay would talk to them, but she never asked them to visit, and she always turned down their invitations. So they finally stopped trying."

Patrick had started leafing through the magazines, shaking them and riffling the pages to loosen any stray sheets of paper. Now he tossed the last one on the floor with the others. "Nothing here. What's left?"

"Just the suitcase and the stationery," Sarah said, "but I've already been through both of them. Nothing."

"And this is just what it looks like," Mack said, crumpling the shopping list and throwing it across the room. "Milk, eggs, paper towels, mushrooms. Damn!" He kicked one of the chrome chairs and it slid across the floor, then toppled with a thud.

Sarah felt a sudden rush of sympathy. He looked so tired, so dejected, and she wanted, more than anything, to help him.

Tentatively, wondering if he would accept the gesture, she reached out and touched his arm. "Mack, I'm so sorry."

"Yeah." Surprisingly, he cupped his hand around her neck and lightly squeezed it. "Thanks for helping. You could've thrown me out after what I did to you. I apologize for all the trouble—and for scaring you to death."

Patrick stepped to his sister's side and grinned. "Well, she got you back for that," he said, pointing to the lump on the side of Mack's head. "I'd say the score's even."

Sarah flushed to the roots of her hair and neatly elbowed her brother in the ribs. "Patrick has a warped sense of humor," she said. "Listen, why don't you rest for a while? I'll fix us some breakfast, another pot of coffee."

But Mack was already heading for the door. He paused to pluck his windbreaker off the sofa. "Thanks, but I've got a room in Carmel. I'll crash for a few hours, then get back to L.A."

"But where can I reach you—just in case I run across something?" It was a lame excuse, she knew, but suddenly she couldn't bear the thought of watching him walk out of her life.

"'Run across something'?" Patrick exclaimed. "Sarah, we've searched this place from top to bottom. There's nothing here!"

Sarah ignored her brother, for Mack's eyes had just met hers. She read the unspoken message: if things were different, if they'd met another time, in another place, then maybe...

Quickly, before he had time to change his mind, she hurried to the kitchen counter and sorted through the mess until she found a pencil and a notepad. She thrust them at him and stepped back to wait.

Again their gazes met and held. Then he scribbled several lines and handed the notepad back to her. "Just in case."

Clutching the slip of paper close to her breast, Sarah watched him walk out the door. Then she sighed and turned, to find Patrick glowering at her, his hands angrily jammed into his pockets.

She took one look at his face and knew the storm was about to break.

"Don't start with me, Paddy," she warned, hoping to cut off the budding lecture before it bloomed. "I've had a rough night, and I'm not in the mood to listen to your moralizing."

His chest swelled with indignation. "Moralizing, is it? I call it just plain common sense. This wouldn't have happened at home. You've got no business out here, Sarah. If Dolly hadn't told me where you were, there's no telling what would've happened."

"Dolly told you? Well, I might've known," she said, hands on hips. "What'd you do, browbeat the poor girl until she came up with a map?"

"As a matter of fact," he replied, his voice rising, "she asked me to come. She was worried about you, for all the good it did." He shook his head. "You know what your problem is, Sarah? You've got no gratitude, that's what."

Sarah ignored his last remark, concentrating instead on what he'd just said about Dolly. "Worried about me? Why?"

"Why not?" he said with heavy sarcasm. "Every time you have fifteen free minutes, you're hatching up another daredevil scheme."

"Which *you* always manage to blow all out of proportion! How many times do I have to tell you, I can take care of myself."

"Like you were taking care of yourself tonight? People breakin' in, shootin' at each other, and you right in the thick of it, brawlin' like an Orangeman!" He took a deep breath, and Sarah could hear The Brogue rising in his throat, like a song he was compelled to sing. "What would I be tellin' the family, Sarah Kathleen, if I have to take your poor, broken body home in a pine box?"

She suppressed a sudden desire to giggle. Really, one had to admire his voice, his delivery. Patrick O'Shaughnessy would have made a fine thespian if he hadn't decided to become a truck driver.

She listened for a few moments longer, from her lack of "proper behavior," through her penchant for "dangerous shenanigans," right up to her blasphemous refusal to "settle down and raise a family like a good Catholic girl."

When he finally began to run out of steam, she interrupted. "Give it a rest, Paddy. I've had my say, you've had yours, and as usual, it's not getting us anywhere."

His jaw was tight with exasperation. "If you'd listen to reason, it'd get you back home, away from all these California lunatics, where you'd be safe."

"Don't be ridiculous," she said sharply. "What happened last night was *not* my fault, and it had nothing to do with my life-style. I just happened to be in the wrong place at the wrong time. The same thing could have happened in Iowa."

"In Iowa you wouldn't have been holed up in some strange house that doesn't even have a telephone." His eyebrows drew together in a frown. "What are you doing out here, anyway? Raylene and Dolly wouldn't give me a straight answer."

Sarah didn't want to give him a straight answer, either, but she couldn't think of a convincing lie. "Well, the thing is—I'm writing a book, Paddy. There were too many distractions in the city, so I took some time off and came down here to finish the manuscript."

"A *book*?" To have called his expression incredulous would have seriously understated the matter. He was thunderstruck. "A book? Why in heaven do you want to write a book? You've got a good business that seems to pay your bills on time. Don't tell me you're going to throw it away for something as silly as writing."

She felt her hackles rise again. "I'm not throwing anything away, and it's not silly. If you're going to start yelling again, you can just leave."

"Okay, okay." He ran his hand through his hair, making the red curls stand out in comic disarray. "Just tell me why, okay? Because I don't understand you, Sarah. I really don't."

And that, she thought sadly, was the unvarnished truth. Patrick had never understood her and probably never would. "It's just something I want to do, Paddy. It's important to me. If you don't approve, then let's not talk about it."

"Seems to me there's a lot that's not being talked about. Look, Sarah, if you want to take some time off for this book thing, why not come back home to do it? Not to stay, just to visit . . . and write."

If they gave out medals for persistence, Sarah thought wryly, Patrick would have too many to count. "No," she said as firmly as she knew how. "I am *not* going back to Iowa. I *am* going back to San Francisco, though, and I could use some help with the packing."

"Thank the Lord for small favors," he grumbled. "But I still don't see why..."

He never finished what he'd started to say, because Sarah was already walking away.

"You can start in the bathroom," she said over her shoulder. "Everything should fit in my overnight bag."

He followed her down the hall to her bedroom. "C'mon, Sarah, it's five o'clock in the morning, and I've got to pick up a load later today. Can't we sleep first?"

"Not on your life." She rummaged in the closet and came up with a scuffed but serviceable blue case. "I'm not staying here a minute longer than it takes to pack and clean up this mess," she said, tossing the case to him. "Those goons may decide to come back, Paddy, and I don't intend to be here if they do."

As though he'd almost forgotten the reason for his arguments, he blinked, then nodded. "Right. The bathroom it is. But we've still got some talking to do, Sarah."

She sighed, wishing with all her heart that Patrick had waited a while before paying her this particular visit—say a year or two.

AT THE PENINSULA MOTEL, Mack unlocked the door to his room, fumbling with the key in the predawn darkness. It had been over twenty-four hours since he'd slept, and then only for a few restless hours in the front seat of his car. The room didn't offer much in the way of luxury, but it had a bed—a king-size, firm-mattressed, clean-sheeted bed that, at the moment, was the only luxury he needed.

He switched on the light and shut the door, thumped his heels against the carpeted floor to dislodge his shoes before he started to undress. Then he set the alarm on the small travel clock that rested on the dresser top.

Three hours wouldn't begin to make up for all the sleep he'd missed, but he couldn't afford more than that. With this last setback, and no new leads to follow, he had to get back to L.A., make some more phone calls, call in some more favors. But if he didn't get some rest first, even if only for a few hours, he wouldn't recognize a lead if it walked up and spit at him.

He slipped the chain lock into place and turned off the light, then got into bed with a grateful sigh. Damn, he was tired. Too little rest, too few leads, too many dead ends. And time was running out. Every turn he took seemed destined to end in failure, and each hour he lost carried Kay farther away. For the past few weeks, his life had been a waking nightmare. He could only imagine the hell Kay must be going through.

His eyelids, heavy with the weight of worry, gradually closed. Behind them, he allowed his mind to replay the events of the past twenty-four hours. He'd built up so many hopes around the Carmel beach house. But right from the start, nothing had worked out the way he'd imagined it. How could such a simple operation have gotten so fouled up?

Restlessly he tossed, seeking a more comfortable position. His body ached in a hundred places, most noticeably his ribs, where several solid blows had landed. And his head, of course. Mack had taken his share of hard knocks over the years, but this was the first time he'd been coldcocked by a sleeveful of rocks.

An unwilling smile tugged at his lips. That little redhead certainly had spunk. She didn't panic, she was resourceful, and he envied her natural ability to absorb and process details into a meaningful pattern. And she wasn't afraid to get involved. She'd put as much effort into searching the house as he had, and when they'd come up empty, he'd felt an absurd desire to comfort her.

Too bad he couldn't get that kind of cooperation from other people. Except for one of Vernon's shipping clerks who'd dated Kay right after she started work, not even her co-workers would talk to Mack, and the young man hadn't known anything, of course. Another dead end.

He shifted again, heard himself groan. If he didn't shut down his thoughts, the alarm would go off before he ever fell asleep. He willed his tense muscles to relax, imagined his mind was a slate that had just been wiped clean. Within seconds, he felt the soft, feathery edges of sleep curling around him.

His last conscious image was of a perky, stubborn woman with soft, red-gold curls, who had briefly lessened his despair by sharing it....

SARAH HAD SAVED her bedroom for last, after straightening out the shambles in the kitchen and den. Now, as she neatly stacked her folded clothes on the bed, she marveled at the multitude of changes that had overtaken her life in a mere twenty-four hours. Yesterday her major problem had been finishing a manuscript, her only danger a figment of her imagination.

Now she was up to her eyeballs in *real* intrigue—criminals, kidnap victims, armed thugs. Paradise had changed its face, had become an arena of violence and mystery. She could have been injured last night, maybe even killed, and so could her brother.

And what about Mack? What would happen to him now? He wasn't the type simply to abandon a mission. He'd keep searching, prying, taking risks. Facing danger and fighting time, no matter what the odds were.

She dragged the suitcases out of the closet and put them on the bed. She'd needed only two, just enough space for a few clothes, some toiletries, several books and her writing supplies. The idea had been to simplify her life, clear away the clutter to make room for Bothwell and company.

But somehow the simplicity had faded, leaving her exposed to the harsh realities of a world she'd once found so exciting in theory. When Bothwell faced the bad guys, it was a glamorous adventure. Knuckles didn't connect with real skin; bullets didn't inflict real damage. And the hero always lived happily ever after.

She paused in her packing and closed her eyes. Mack was the hero of this scene, and she knew how it would end if she were writing it. But in this case, "happily ever after" was only a much-desired goal, not a foregone conclusion. She hoped with all her heart that he would find Kay and bring her home.

And she hoped she would see him again....

She shook away the troubling thought with a toss of red curls. Aubrey Glen Macklin was gone, and if he'd stirred up a longing she didn't want to acknowledge, she'd just have to learn to deal with it. The best therapy would be to write *The End* to this brief episode and get on with her life. She had a book to finish, a career to launch.

Her clothes were packed. After double-checking the closet and the dresser, she turned to the nightstand. Besides the novel and the clock radio, there were two more books on the bottom shelf and typing paper and sundries in the single drawer.

She retrieved her possessions, but as she bent to place them in a suitcase, one of the extra batteries slipped from the open pack, bounced on the floor and rolled under the bed.

"Cripes," she muttered, dropping to her knees and groping under the bed. Her fingers met with nothing except carpet, so she lay on her stomach and peered beneath the box springs. The battery had rolled to the wall. She wiggled and stretched until her hand closed around it, then braced herself on her free palm and started to rise.

The nightstand was directly beside her head, with the open shelf yawning at eye level. As she turned her head, a patch of light color against the darkness of the wood caught her attention. Something protruded from the rear of the drawer, down into the unenclosed area of the shelf, lying flat against the back panel of the stand. She reached for it and tugged. It was only a piece of paper, but it was jammed.

She worked it back and forth, pulling it loose by degrees. When at last she held it, she recognized the embossed "KM." But this sheet wasn't blank. Half of it was covered with writing, in a hand she remembered from Kay Macklin's check register.

The unfinished letter was so badly scrawled Sarah could make out only a few words. But the salutation was fairly clear: *Uncle Mack*. As Sarah read the two words, she felt a surge of excitement.

Getting to her feet, she quickly scanned the lines.

"Please come...don't know...going away..." There was a word that looked like "guns," though it could have been "guess" or "guru" with a little squiggle on the end. But one phrase was crystal clear: "I don't want to go."

This was no run-of-the-mill duty letter. This was a plea for help. Sarah read it over and over, amazed that she'd actually found the clue Mack had so desperately searched for. When she thought how close she'd come to missing it, she shivered.

Mack had to see it at once. But first she had to find him.

Chapter Four

After spending nine quarters and fifteen minutes at a pay phone, Sarah had finally located Mack, and now she pulled into the parking lot of the Peninsula Motel, driving slowly to look at the room numbers. There it was—number sixteen, the corner unit. She parked in an empty space and got out of the car, patting the pocket of her jeans reassuringly. This letter could be the breakthrough Mack needed; hopefully he'd be able to make more sense of it than she had.

As she approached the door, she hesitated. He'd still be asleep, she knew; it was only a little after eight, and remembering the utter weariness on his face, the dark circles under his eyes, she hated to wake him. But she also knew that he'd be furious if he found out she'd waited one second longer than necessary to give him Kay's letter.

She raised her hand and rapped twice on the door, then dropped it to her side when she saw how badly it was shaking. Surprised at her reaction, she smiled wryly. There was no way she could fool herself that she was simply nervous about having to wake a sleeping man. She had wanted badly to see him again, and now that the moment was here, she was skittery as a colt. *Get hold of yourself,* she chided.

She raised her hand again just as Mack jerked the door open, and she nearly knocked on his nose.

"Hi," she said inadequately, taking in the fact that aside from a white towel riding low on his hips, he wasn't wearing a stitch. His hair was wet and rumpled, and droplets of water glistened along his shoulders and in the hollow of his throat.

For a moment he stared at her.

"Hi, yourself," he answered at last. "What are you doing here?"

She wrenched her eyes away from his damp chest and dug into the pocket of her jeans. "I found something," she said in a rush. She offered him the much-folded sheet of stationery. "I found it in my bedroom. It's from Kay...."

He grabbed her elbow and dragged her inside, then snatched the paper from her fingers. "From Kay?" he said, sitting down heavily on the unmade bed.

Sarah noticed how his voice shook. His hands were none too steady, either, as he unfolded the paper and smoothed it. She stood silently, watching as he read. Finally he lifted his head and looked at her. "I was right," he said hoarsely. "He's taken her somewhere, probably out of the country." He rubbed his hands over his face. Sarah heard the scrape of coarse whiskers against his palm. "And she's afraid of him."

"But at least it's something."

"It's a piece of paper that doesn't tell me a damned thing!" He sounded hollow, as if all the vitality had been wrung out of him. "Rambling, hysterical words without a single concrete fact."

Instantly Sarah sat beside him and laid her hand on his arm. "Maybe not," she insisted, almost fiercely. "You've hardly looked at it. Go over it again, Mack. Maybe you missed something, a name, a clue." She paused, then boldly added, "We'll do it together."

She let her hand drop. The seconds ticked by slowly, and while she waited for his response, she studied him closely.

His face was expressionless, and she couldn't read his hooded eyes. What was he thinking? Probably the same thing she was—that she was too pushy for someone he'd met only a few hours earlier.

But then the tense line of his mouth relaxed and he looked at her quizzically. "You really came through for me, Sarah. Thank you." Under the light from the ceiling fixture, his eyes seemed flecked with gold, and his scrutiny brought another blush to her cheeks.

He stood then, pulling her up with him. "Okay, Pollyanna, let's get busy and put this puzzle together." He squeezed her shoulder briefly, then made a grab for the towel, which had slipped dangerously low.

"Maybe you should get dressed first," she said with a teasing smile.

"Maybe you're right." Grinning, he turned and walked to the bathroom, leaving Sarah with a fleeting glimpse of tanned, muscular legs and a funny little quiver in her stomach.

SOMETIME LATER—she didn't know how long because she'd lost all sense of time—Sarah looked at the steno pad that lay open on the table before her. Silently she reread, for the umpteenth time, the words Mack had dictated, her brow furrowed in concentration.

Uncle Mack,
I need help. Please come get me. Things are so crazy now and I don't know what to do. Paul says we're going away next week and never coming back, but I don't want to go. I'm afraid of him. He calls me *la reeva royo* (?) and says someday I'll have my own shrine, but he won't explain. I tried to leave yesterday and he locked me in the bedroom. Now he watches me all the time. Today he was on the phone talking about a shipment of

guns and trampot (?) to a compomd (?). I don't understand what's happening and I'm so scared. I think he's
lost his mind.

Here the narrative ended. Sarah could almost picture the
young woman, scribbling out her frantic plea for help while
constantly glancing over her shoulder, then cramming the
page into the drawer to hide it when Paul Vernon flung open
the door. In spite of the few unreadable words, the message
was powerful and haunting. Sarah shivered. Her empathy
was working overtime, making it difficult to concentrate on
the task at hand. And if those words could affect her, a
stranger, so deeply, she wondered how much greater their
impact must be on someone who knew Kay and loved her.

Across the small table, Mack sat quietly, his hands motionless atop the torn sheet of stationery. His shoulders were
rounded in a slump, at odds with the undisguisable strength
so evident in the hard lines of his body. Sarah instinctively
knew he was a man used to being in charge, making things
happen, and she couldn't begin to imagine how helpless he
must feel now.

Tentatively, wanting to offer comfort without intruding
on his private thoughts, she brushed the back of his hand
with her own, just a feather stroke of sympathy. He smiled
crookedly, then flipped his hand to capture her fingers with
a gentle pressure. But that seemed to be all he would allow
himself. Releasing her hand, he picked up the letter again.

"Not much to go on," he said in a flat voice.

"But more than you had before," she answered. "We already know we were right about one thing. He was spooked
into moving sooner than he'd planned. See, she says Vernon was planning to leave 'next week.' Obviously she
thought there'd be time for the letter to reach you, and for
you to reach her. Now if we could decipher *these* words—"
she tapped the pad with her fingernail, indicating the words

that were followed by question marks "—they might tell us something important."

Mack shook his head. "They could be anything," he told her. "Kay has a habit of leaving out letters, sometimes whole words, when she's in a hurry. The *A*s could be *O*s, the *E*s could be *I*s without the dot. And I don't think she ever learned the difference between *N*s and *M*s. There's just no way to tell without some frame of reference."

Sarah scanned the lines yet again, gnawing at her bottom lip in concentration. There had to be something. Then, toward the bottom of the page, she latched onto a phrase. An idea began to form, tenuous at first, but growing stronger. "What about this, Mack, this 'shipment of guns'?"

"What about it? Without names or dates or places, it's just useless information."

"Maybe not," she insisted. "Remember, she used the word 'shipment,' and that implies quantity. Do you know if Vernon had a dealer's license?"

"Not in his own name," he answered readily. "He had a felony record, so he'd automatically be disqualified."

"And he's broke, too, so he wasn't doing any trading in the legitimate arms market. Without authorization from a recognized government or several million in cash, it's a closed game."

"Sarah, guns are a dime a dozen. You can buy them on any street corner."

"Mack, you're not listening!" She gestured impatiently. "We're not talking about a few Saturday night specials, we're talking about enough weapons to constitute a shipment. Think big. If you were Vernon and you wanted a cheap source for a shipment of guns, where would you go?"

"To somebody who'd stolen them and wanted to get rid of the evidence," he said without hesitation.

"And when the person they were stolen from found out they were missing, what would he do?"

"Report it to the police." He sounded as exasperated as he looked. "Sarah, where are you going with this?"

"Computers." She couldn't believe he hadn't caught on yet. "A theft of that size would automatically go into a national data bank so it could be monitored for interstate transport. And computer networks can be accessed."

He shook his head. "Look, I'm impressed with your logic, okay? But I still don't see how we can connect anything with Vernon."

"His phone records!" she nearly shouted. "Check all his long-distance calls for the past few months, then match those contacts with the theft reports. If one of the names shows up, you've got your connection."

"What?" he said in disbelief. "I don't have that kind of access."

"But I do," she countered.

"Come on, Sarah!" Mack abruptly shoved back his chair and stood. "Illegal computer access is a crime, and you know it!"

Sarah also shot to her feet. "So is breaking and entering, but you didn't let that stop you. Do you have a better idea?"

"No, damn it, I don't!" For a moment, as they glared at each other, the situation had all the earmarks of a Mexican standoff. Then he relaxed, and his eyes began to twinkle. "You're a hard woman, Sarah Kathleen," he said in a passable imitation of Patrick's brogue. "But I'm glad you're on my side."

"Yeah," she agreed. "Me, too."

For a moment, as they looked at each other, Sarah thought this was the perfect time for bells to ring, or the earth to stop spinning, or for some other appropriately romantic sensation to overwhelm her senses. Instead there was only a subtle exchange of respect and goodwill, and the gentle promise of friendship, which was certainly more practical and, ultimately, more satisfying.

Then Mack cleared his throat. "So, as one supersleuth to another, where do we start?"

"Elementary, my dear fellow," she replied, riding a crest of unadulterated happiness. "We start at the beginning."

LOS ANGELES International Airport was, as usual, teeming with people. Sarah and Mack weaved their way past gates, through lobbies, and, finally, toward the elevators that went to the parking garage. Since both of them had only carry-on luggage, they were spared the endless wait for baggage, but just the walk through the huge complex seemed to Sarah to take almost as long as the entire flight from the peninsula. And it didn't help that Mack's long legs ate up the distance at a near run, so that she had to trot to keep up with him.

He stopped only once, while they waited for an elevator, and he faced Sarah with a quizzical expression.

"Look, are you sure you want to do this?"

Sarah shook her head in exasperation. "Haven't we had this conversation before? Like, while you turned in the rental car, while we waited for our flight and *during* the flight?"

"I just want you to be sure," he said, again jabbing the Up button impatiently. "You've already had a taste of how rough this thing can get. I'm not too crazy about the idea of your getting any more involved."

"That's my decision to make," she answered, as though she hadn't said the same thing several times before. "I told you, the guy who can run the computer check lives here in L.A., and he'll only work with me." She smiled then, and her eyes lit up with mischief. "Besides, I'm having fun."

He returned her look, twinkle for twinkle. "And how much fun will it be if that muscle-bound brother of yours decides you need rescuing again?"

"Don't worry about Paddy," she said with a laugh. "He's had his shots. He'll be on the road for several days, anyway. I'll be back in Frisco before he will."

"Translated, that means he doesn't know anything about this little side trip, and you don't intend to tell him."

"You got it."

The elevator doors slid open just as another couple arrived, loaded with luggage and panting for breath, so the conversation stopped there. As the car rose, stopping briefly at the next level to disgorge the other couple, Sarah hoped that Mack wouldn't lodge any more objections to her being involved. If he objected to her presence, she'd have no choice but to go back home. And she didn't want to go home.

She'd told him the truth—she *was* having fun, and not only because of the adventure. She enjoyed being with him, talking to him, figuring out what made him tick. Aubrey Glen Macklin was a special man, intelligent, caring and loyal, but with a rough edge that proclaimed him more than capable of taking care of himself. Determined, but not ruthless; dedicated to his mission, but sensitive to the people around him. Hadn't he tried to protect her, even when he had reason to distrust her? All in all, he was a rare combination of tough and tender, and in one of those painfully honest flashes of insight, Sarah realized that if she wasn't careful, she'd find herself falling in love.

"This is it."

She hadn't noticed that the elevator had stopped and the doors had opened. Shifting her two small bags to get a better grip on them, she followed him to his car—vehicle, to be more accurate—a late-model, black-and-red Jeep Cherokee.

"My place isn't far from here," he said as he loaded their bags into the back seat. "Maybe you should get some sleep before we talk to your friend."

The offer was tempting. She'd slept only a couple of hours out of the past twenty-four, but she knew he'd mentioned it only out of courtesy. Beneath his placid expression, she could almost feel his emotions, a churning mixture of eagerness and impatience.

"Later," she answered. "We should see Dale first, explain what we need. Then we can rest while he's working on it."

He didn't try to change her mind, and she thought his eyes held a silent understanding and gratitude. Sitting beside him in the Cherokee, giving him directions, she wondered at the easy familiarity with which she read his moods, his thoughts. Not that she was unperceptive, but this instinctive awareness went much deeper than usual with her. It was almost like the rapport she shared with her father and Patrick and, occasionally, with Raylene.

Be careful, Sarah, she warned herself again. *You just met the man, so don't get carried away.* She knew the warning was justified and highly appropriate. But she also knew that if they parted company in the next five minutes, it would be a long time before she stopped thinking about him.

"What was the house number again?" Mack said, jerking her away from her disturbing thoughts.

"Oh, that's it, second from the corner."

They were on a shady, wide street, the kind that boasted two-story houses with circular driveways in front and swimming pools in back. Dale's house was no exception. Mack pulled up and stopped, eyeing the colonial columns and trimmed hedges with surprise.

"I thought you said this friend was just a computer hack."

"He is," she replied with amusement. "But he's an expensive computer hack. He troubleshoots for some of the biggest corporations in the country, and they don't mind paying for it."

Mack's surprise leaped to amazement when Dale Brown answered the door. Barefoot, wearing jeans and a torn T-shirt, he looked more like a high-school kid than a successful businessman. His eyes were large and round behind thick glasses, and his long, thin face was covered with a blond stubble.

"O'Shaughnessy!" he yelled, grabbing Sarah by the waist and swinging her around in an exuberant hug. "What brings you to the big city? Finally decide to share my ill-gotten gains?"

"Could be," she teased, feeling slightly dizzy. "In fact, I've got my suitcase in the car."

"That'll be the day." He slapped Mack on the shoulder and said, as if they were old friends, "I keep telling her she's entitled to half of everything I own, but she just won't listen to reason."

"And if I ever said yes, you'd roll over and die on the spot," she said, watching as Mack frowned in puzzlement. "Mack, this is Dale Brown. If anybody can help us, he can."

Motioning them into the house, Dale stuck out his bottom lip in a mock pout. "Just after my brain, huh? The story of my life!" He ushered them into a large room that was grossly underfurnished and waited until they were settled on the lone sofa. "You'd better tell me about it," he said. "You don't usually make house calls just to ask for a favor."

Sarah glanced at Mack, but he left the explanation up to her. "We need the name and address of every person who was called from a certain Los Angeles number for the past three months, and the same thing for a Carmel number," she said. "We also need every report on weapons thefts for the same period, not house burglaries, but anything stolen in large quantities."

"You know I can only pull up long-distance calls."

She nodded.

Dale cocked an eyebrow and looked at her down his long nose. "Gonna tell me why?"

"I can't," she answered quietly.

Dale seemed to consider her reply for a moment, then he shrugged. "If you can't, you can't. How soon do you want this stuff?"

"As soon as possible. This afternoon, if you can manage it. Will that be a problem?"

Dale frowned. "Not necessarily a problem, but it'll take time. Not the phone records—I used to work for Pacific Bell. But the other—well, it gets complicated. If we're talking about a business heist, like from a merchant, you know, it'll probably be in the regular law-enforcement network. But if it's a government rip-off, like an armory or something, it might be a different story. The feds don't always coordinate with civilians, and their system's tougher to break into."

"But you can do it?" Mack interrupted, his voice tight with tension.

Dale looked mildly affronted. "Sure I can do it. But like I said, it might take time. Give me the phone numbers, and just hang out while I work on it. Kitchen's that way—" he nodded toward the back of the room "—and the pool's out back."

Mack hastily scrawled the numbers on the back of the envelope Dale handed to him, then he settled against the sofa with a sigh after the lanky young man left the room. "Are all your friends this accommodating?" he asked Sarah, a ghost of a smile playing around his lips.

"Most of them," she answered. "And Dale's one of the best."

"Best friend or best computer hack?"

She laughed. "Both. We sort of helped each other through college. He tutored me in math. I edited his term papers. We've been trading favors ever since."

"Must have been some pretty special favors if he feels you're entitled to 'half of everything.'"

It was more a question than a statement, and she realized how odd Dale's earlier comment must have sounded. "Just his version of gratitude," she explained lightly. "When I worked on the campus newspaper, I talked him into letting me do a profile on his work in programming—he's a genius with computers. Some corporate VIP read the article and hired him to debug his company's accounting program. Dale's career sort of took off after that, and he swears that my article made him a millionaire."

Mack nodded absently, and she could tell he was only using the conversation as a way to make the time pass more quickly. She chattered on for several minutes, trying to find a topic, any topic, that would interest him, but he answered only in monosyllables, or not at all. When he stood and started pacing, she was ready to throw in the towel.

"Didn't take as long as I thought it would." Dale's voice startled them and they both jumped. "This guy doesn't seem to use the phone much. There's not much here for three months."

Sarah and Mack were too busy reaching for the papers he held to answer him. Sarah got hold of them first, nearly ripping them from his hand.

"This is great, Dale," she said enthusiastically, leafing through the pages. "We can start going over them now, while you work on the other reports."

Dale cleared his throat. "Actually, I wanted to talk to you about that. It'll be better if I wait until later to access those high-security networks, after all the offices have shut down for the night. Less risk of another hacker picking up on what I'm doing."

Mack's eyes narrowed and he opened his mouth to speak, then obviously thought better of it.

"That's fine, Dale," Sarah said quickly. "Do whatever you think is best to stay out of trouble."

After a moment Mack held out his hand. "I appreciate your help, Dale. This means a lot to me." The two men shook hands, then Mack took Sarah's elbow. "Let's go back to my place. We'll go over these numbers, and he can call when he comes up with anything else."

Dale walked them to the door, and they all said polite goodbyes. But after Mack had walked out, Dale grabbed Sarah's arm and pulled her back.

"You're not in any trouble, are you? I mean, this is some pretty serious snooping, Sarah."

"I'm okay," she answered, and kissed his cheek. "Scout's honor. But it is important."

"Life and death?"

She looked toward the Cherokee, where Mack stood, impatiently waiting for her. "That's right," she said solemnly. "Life and death."

MACK'S APARTMENT was in an older section of the city, in a renovated house that reminded Sarah of her own building, except that he was lucky enough to be on the ground floor. Inside, the rooms were large and bright, simply furnished and very clean.

He led her to a central dining room, where he spread the computer printout on an antique oak table. After offering her a glass of iced tea, which she declined, Mack immediately began going over the phone numbers.

The combined lists contained a total of twenty-three names, all but two of them called from the Carmel house. The two remaining, one in Oakland and one in Reno, had been called from both Carmel and Los Angeles. Mack eliminated six names right off the bat—two of Kay's friends, three of Vernon's employees and Mack himself.

"Here's Dolly's real estate agency," Sarah said, pointing, "and we can probably pass on all these corporate names for the time being. We'll have to check them out in person, anyway, since we don't know who to ask for."

That left only five private numbers, and with grim determination, Mack began dialing the first. After seventeen rings, he conceded defeat and hung up.

Sarah marked a big red C.B. next to the number for "call back."

The next one turned out to be the home number of Vernon's personal physician, who grudgingly agreed to meet with Mack over the weekend.

The third number put them in touch with a whiskey-voiced answering machine that delivered a peculiar message: "Cecilia is all tied up right now, but leave your number, along with any special requests, and you'll be notified of your appointment time." It would have been funny, except for the implication that Vernon might have "special requests" and that Kay might be expected to fulfill them.

Both the Oakland number, belonging to Floyd J. Carver, and the one in Reno, which was listed to A. C. Fulgham, had been disconnected.

After the last recorded announcement, Mack slammed the receiver into the cradle with disgust. "More dead ends. More wasted time."

But Sarah wasn't ready to give up. She looked over the lists again, particularly at the dates on which the calls had been placed. "When did you talk to Kay last?"

"On the third. Why?"

"And she was planning to visit you the next weekend, which would have been—what? The seventh or eighth?" She handed the list to him. "Look at these dates. Vernon called both those numbers from Carmel, one on the fourth, the other on the fifth.''

"About the time she must have written the letter."

"And about the time she would have overheard Vernon talking on the phone about a shipment of weapons."

"Then she disappeared." He rose quickly from the table, his tired eyes reanimated with hope. "This is it—it has to be! Either Carver or Fulgham, or both."

"Probably both." Sarah bit her bottom lip while she thought. "It makes sense, doesn't it? Vernon calls both of them, only a day apart, then when he disappears, so do they."

"Disconnected isn't the same as disappeared," Mack commented with a flash of humor. "But it's too convenient to be just a coincidence. The problem is, how do we prove it?"

"Right now, we'd better wait and see what else Dale turns up. If the theft reports don't pan out, we can always go to Oakland and Reno to look for them."

As things turned out, Sarah became a fervent believer in the adage "Easier said than done." She suspected that waiting didn't come easily for Mack under the best of circumstances; in his present situation, it was almost an impossibility.

He didn't want to talk; he didn't want to read; he didn't want to eat. He seemed to have turned inward, locking the world out at the same time that he shut himself in with only his dark thoughts for company. How many times since Kay had disappeared had he sat alone like this, Sarah wondered, torturing himself with what might be happening to his niece at Vernon's hands?

Sarah couldn't imagine having to go through something like this by herself. All her life she'd been surrounded by love and warmth, a family who, for all their faults, would stand by her through any crisis. Mack had no one but Kay.

Even the government was against him, because they considered Kay a criminal. The amazing thing was not that he sometimes lost himself in silent brooding, but that he managed to hang on to himself at all.

He raised his head suddenly and caught her staring at him. An expression of surprise, so fleeting she nearly missed it, touched his eyes—he'd forgotten she was in the room.

He made a soft sound that could have been laughter. "You're quite a lady, Sarah. No matter how bad my mood is, you somehow bring me out of it."

"Oh," she said, not sure how to respond. "And what have I done to 'bring you out of it'?"

"Different things. Sometimes you reason. Sometimes you shout. This time you just...cared." He paused, as if searching for the right words. "You have no idea how much that means to me."

For a moment neither of them spoke. His gratitude for what to her seemed the most ordinary kindness was almost unbearably touching.

"You said you wrote an article about Dale," he continued. "Are you a reporter?" He paused again. "Sounds funny, doesn't it, having to ask."

She nodded. "I guess we've been too busy to get around to the basics." She cleared her throat. "No, I'm not a reporter, not anymore. I worked for the *Chronicle* for a couple of years, but I decided I'd rather be my own boss. Now I'm a researcher. You know, digging up facts for other people."

"Is that how you know so much about the shady side of life—weapons, police reports, computer spying? You must have a heck of a client list if they need that kind of research."

"You mean, do I have any crime bosses wanting advice on how to pull a heist?" she teased. "Not really, just writers and reporters mostly, some graduate students and a few

overworked law clerks who want to impress the senior partners. As for the shady side of life, it's hard to research any
subject without turning over a few rocks. And what about
you? How did you get to be so good at shadowing people
and breaking into houses? Or is that routine training for all
security consultants?''

He raised an eyebrow as amusement softened his lips.
''You really know how to make a point, don't you? Okay,
I've had some training in surveillance, but it was a long time
ago, when I worked for the government. Now I'm self-
employed, trying to keep my business in the black.''

From the way he glossed over his reference to working for
the government, Sarah felt sure he wouldn't respond to any
direct probing into the subject, so she veered away from it.
''And what does a security consultant do?''

He shrugged. ''The same kind of thing your friend Dale
does, except I debug security systems instead of computer
programs. My clients want to know how to protect themselves against everything from simple robbery to embezzle-
ment. I install alarms, train night watchmen, suggest checks
and balances for the people who handle money.'' He stood
up suddenly, paced a few steps and stopped. ''What's taking him so long to call?''

''It hasn't been that long,'' she said gently. ''Tell me some
more about your work. Maybe I can get a couple of ideas to
use in my book.''

The eyebrow rose again. ''Your book?''

She nodded. ''*Kill Me with Love*,'' she explained. ''That's
why I was in Carmel. Trying to get into the mood to finish
the manuscript.''

He laughed out loud, prompting Sarah to join in. ''In the
mood, huh?'' he remarked with a grin. ''Did it work?''

''Sure did.'' Her red curls bounced as she gave him a
cheeky glance. ''I've decided to have Bothwell—he's the
hero—break into this house, looking for the bad guys, of

course. Then this lady spy gets the drop on him with a hairbrush. Sounds good, don't you think?''

"I think Bothwell had better watch his step, or he might get knocked in the head."

Sarah felt her cheeks redden. "And I haven't even asked you about it, have I? Does it hurt much?" She reached to touch the small, nearly invisible lump on his head.

He caught her hand. "It doesn't hurt at all. Stop worrying, Sarah. It was an accident."

The room suddenly seemed too warm, as warm as her skin where his fingers gently lay.

She swallowed. "Listen, why don't I fix us some soup or something? We haven't eaten all day."

He released her and took a step back, running his fingers through his hair. "Good idea. Look through the cabinets. See if you find anything you like. I'm going to try that number again, the one that didn't answer, then I'll be in to help you."

But when she had the soup heated and poured, he still hadn't come into the kitchen, so she went into the dining room, then to the living room. He was sprawled on the long, deeply cushioned sofa, his head lolled to one side. He was sound asleep.

THE FIRST RING of the telephone woke her. She blinked, trying to get her bearings. Of course, she was in Mack's living room in the old, comfortable recliner, where she, too, had dozed off.

Mack answered the phone by the second ring.

"Yeah, I've got it," she heard him say. "Thanks, Dale, you've been a big help. I owe you one." He replaced the receiver and turned to face her. "There's only one report for the past six months. Three men raided an armory in northern Nevada in September. They got enough stuff to fill a small boxcar."

"And toward the end of September, Vernon left Los Angeles and went to Carmel," she said, her pulse quickening. "It fits, Mack."

"And we got a bonus. The warrant names Floyd Carver and A. C. Fulgham, wanted on suspicion."

"And they're in hiding, like Vernon." The information was exciting, but not particularly helpful. "How do we find them?"

He stared into space, his eyes narrowed. "By finding what they stole." He grabbed her arm, pulling her through the room. "Come on, let's go."

She snatched up her purse on her way through the room. "Go where?"

"To Vernon's warehouse," he said, opening the front door. "Like you keep telling me, we have to start somewhere."

Chapter Five

The October moon was covered with clouds, which was a point in their favor, though it didn't do much for the atmosphere. Except for the dim glow from a distant streetlight, the warehouse sat in total darkness, the kind that magnified every slight noise, exaggerating the rustle of a discarded bag into the malevolent slithering of unseen monsters.

Sarah shivered, though the night was warm. "The doors are padlocked," she whispered. "And that car parked in front belongs to somebody. We're not going to get away with this."

"Come on, Sarah, where's your sense of adventure?" She couldn't see his face, but there was an odd note in his voice that told her he was actually enjoying this. "I thought you liked this cloak-and-dagger stuff."

"Not when I don't know what I'm doing," she shot back. "We need to plan it out, Mack, not go rushing in blind. What if some trigger-happy night watchman shoots us, or we trip an alarm or something?"

He took her hand and led her around the corner to the back of the building, where the darkness was even more total, if such a thing were possible. "You're on my turf now, Pollyanna," he told her. "This is my business, remember?"

She sighed. "Right. Okay. So how are we going to get in?"

"Through that window."

"What window?"

"The one I saw when I was here several weeks ago, looking for Vernon." He stepped on something that skittered across the concrete, shattering the stillness of the night. A bottle. "Damn."

Sarah froze in place, listened intently for voices or the sound of a footstep. Nothing. Mack tugged her forward again. After a few paces he stopped. "It should be right about here."

He pulled away from her, and she heard the faint whisper of his hands moving across the bricks, then the tap of fingernails on glass. "You have your purse?"

"Of course I have my purse." He'd insisted she bring it, to hold a flashlight and the small tool pouch he used to demonstrate burglary methods. "What do you want, the flashlight or the kit?"

"The flashlight first." She snapped it on, being careful to aim it at the ground. The beam seemed unnaturally bright and she glanced nervously over her shoulder. "Now hand me the kit, then point the light at the window, right up here."

The bottom edge of the window was nearly seven feet off the ground. A few inches higher, and Mack couldn't have reached it. As it was, he had to tiptoe and stretch to position the small suction device he took from his tool kit. The glass cutter made a small shriek as he twisted it, then he popped the suction cup off, leaving a five-inch hole in the pane.

"That's got it." He replaced the device in the kit, the kit in her bag. "Now I'm going to boost you up. The latch should be just below the hole. The window will open outward."

Sarah was no featherweight, but when she sat on his shoulders, he stood with no apparent effort. She stuck her arm through the hole and groped for the latch. "It's stuck. I can't budge it."

"Okay, hold on." A couple of seconds later, he passed her a screwdriver, thick but not more than four inches long. "Use this as a lever."

It worked. The latch moved with a groan of protest, and Sarah swung the window open.

"Okay, Sherlock, now what?" she said when Mack lowered her to the ground. "You're too big to fit through."

"Yeah," he agreed pleasantly, "but you're not."

"What? You're out of your mind! I don't know what to look for."

"It'll be a snap. There's a door about ten feet farther down on this wall. Right next to it, there should be a box on the wall, about chest high, with a red light. There'll also be a button. Just push the button, and the light should go out. That means the alarm is off, and I can jimmy the padlock."

"What if the light doesn't go out?"

"Then it's a coded alarm, and we're back to square one. You come back through the window and we go home."

Once again, luck was on their side. Sarah twisted her ankle when she dropped to the floor inside, but at least she didn't knock anything over or drop the flashlight. And just as Mack had said, there was an alarm box with a red light next to the door. The light went out when she pushed the button.

She tapped on the steel door with the rim of the flashlight. Then she waited, stiff with tension, while Mack made entirely too much noise on the other side of the door. Finally she heard a snap; the door opened, and she started breathing again.

"I TOLD YOU, I don't know what we're looking for." In the glow of the flashlight, Mack looked distinctly harried. "A crate full of grenades, a piece of paper with Carver's or Fulgham's name, anything that looks useful."

Sarah bit off the sharp retort that sprang to her tongue. They both knew the chances of finding anything here were slim, to say the least. Between Vernon and the IRS, who'd been through the place weeks ago, there probably wouldn't be anything left to look at. But Mack was right; they had to start somewhere.

He played the light across the floor into the corners. There were boxes, plenty of them, but most of them were already nailed and strapped. Prying the lids off would be both noisy and time-consuming. The few that were open yielded no surprises. Toys and novelties, mainly, and lots of packing material.

Mack wandered off, leaving her in the darkness. "Where are you going?" she wanted to know.

"To look for a crowbar." The light flashed across the front wall and another door. "You can stand watch. I don't want any surprises."

She picked her way across the floor carefully. It was littered with empty tools and crates, as though everything had just suddenly stopped in the middle of a busy workday.

The front door had a window through which she could see the parking lot. The car they'd noticed before was still there, still empty. She wondered who it belonged to and where they were. *Sneaking up on us, most likely,* she thought with uncharacteristic pessimism. But she couldn't help it. This place just didn't *feel* right.

She took a step backward away from the door, and bumped into something. A desk. Moving her hands across the surface, she felt the base of a lamp. It had an adjustable gooseneck and a switch on the side. Aiming the shade down as far as it would go, she switched the lamp on.

From the corner came Mack's voice. "Good idea. See what you can find."

The desk was as cluttered as the floor. Papers covered the surface, none of them stacked, just strewed about. She gathered up a pile of them, holding them under the light. Bills of lading, invoices, telephone memos. Several longer documents, some in foreign languages—letters of credit, she thought, leafing through them. Two of them were in Spanish, one in French. If any of them contained anything useful, it would be lost on her. Her Spanish had never progressed much beyond the usual tourist phrases, and her French hadn't even gotten that far. Still, she thought, she might as well look them over....

The sound of metal on wood distracted her. Obviously Mack had found a crowbar, or a reasonable facsimile, and was working on a crate. Then she heard a low curse and smiled.

"Lose a fingernail?" she asked sweetly.

"Very funny."

A bright light suddenly streamed through the window of the door. Dropping the papers, Sarah risked a quick look, then fell to her knees. It was a spotlight, and it was trained on the front door of the warehouse.

In a crouch, she ran to the corner. "There's a patrol car outside," she whispered, sharply aware of her thudding heart.

"Damn!" He dropped the crowbar and grabbed Sarah's wrist with one hand, the flashlight with the other. "Okay, let's get out of here."

He ran for the back door, dragging Sarah with him, but the sound of an idling engine brought him up short. "Now they're in back, and they're bound to see that padlock. Come on, I'll get you up to the window. As soon as they come in the back, you crawl through and run like hell!"

It almost worked. Sarah was standing on Mack's shoulders, leaning through the window, when the back door burst open. Mack shoved, Sarah hoisted, then she was through. She dangled for a moment, hanging by her hands, then dropped to the ground.

A heavy hand fell on her shoulder. She whirled around with a yelp.

"You're not goin' anywhere, lady, so relax. You have the right to remain silent. If you give up that right, anything you say may be used against you in a court of law...."

SARAH SHIFTED UNEASILY in the chair where she'd been waiting for at least forty-five minutes.

She'd never been arrested before, and it was an experience she would have gladly done without. Handcuffed, stuffed into the back seat of a patrol car, fingerprinted, photographed and grilled. Then, with no explanation, she'd been left in this small, dingy room by herself.

She supposed she'd have to call Patrick to post bond for her, and she'd almost prefer being in jail to listening to his inevitable lecture. She could just hear him now: "I warned you not to get involved, Sarah Kathleen, but did you listen? Of course not, you never listen...."

At the moment, the only bright spot was knowing that Mack probably felt worse than she did. Even if he hadn't murmured "I'm sorry" as they led him away to another room, his eyes would have said the same thing. Until now, she'd never realized how satisfying it could be to say "I told you so."

Not that she'd said it, at least not out loud. Mack had looked so utterly miserable—more for her sake than his, she knew—that she just couldn't bring herself to deal the final blow. Besides, he hadn't forced her to do anything; she'd gone along because she'd wanted to, and she could have walked away at any time. She sighed heavily, letting her head fall back until it touched the wall.

If only they'd taken more time to plan, to anticipate the problems. Both she and Mack should have known that the police made regular patrols of the business district, yet it hadn't even crossed their minds.

The door opened and she jerked her head up expectantly.

It was the police matron who'd brought her to the room earlier, a surprisingly petite woman with a nice smile. "Sarah, you can come with me now," she said, holding the door open. "We're just going down the hall to the second room on the right."

"What's going to happen? When can I see Mack?"

The matron didn't answer. Sarah walked beside her in silence, while an absurd vision from *Dragnet* raced through her mind. *"Just the facts, ma'am . . ."*

But it wasn't Jack Webb who waited for her. It was two men she'd never seen before, and judging by their grim expressions, they weren't too happy.

"Miss . . . O'Shaughnessy." The taller of the two referred to a plastic card that she recognized as her driver's license. "Please sit down." He indicated a chair, the twin of the one she'd recently vacated, straight, wooden and uncomfortable. He waited until she was seated, then continued. "I'm Norman Buckley. This is Geoffrey Potter. We'd like you to explain your reasons for being in Paul Vernon's warehouse tonight."

Sarah studied him as he spoke. Other than his height, which was several inches above six feet, there was nothing remarkable about him—he had ordinary brown hair and eyes, an ordinary face; he worn an ordinary blue suit. His companion, Potter, was blond and blue eyed, perhaps five foot ten, and nice-looking in a passive sort of way. But strangely, in spite of their opposite coloring and builds, there was a resemblance between them that Sarah found disturbing. Almost as though they were pieces cut from the same fabric, but sewn in different patterns.

"And I'd like you to explain who you are." She spoke politely, but with finality.

The men exchanged glances. "Who do you think we are?" asked Potter.

"I think you're not cops—no uniforms, no badges, no ranks. And I think that unless I see some identification, I'm not saying another word."

Buckley's mouth tightened. With an abrupt motion, he whipped a small leather wallet from his inside pocket and flipped it open.

Sarah leaned forward to read the ID card. "The CIA?" she exclaimed. "Since when is breaking and entering a federal offense?"

"Since it occurred on federal property. The IRS confiscated Paul Vernon's holdings, including the warehouse, about a month ago, so it officially belongs to the government. Now, what's your connection with Vernon?"

"There is no connection," she said, settling back in the chair. This situation was making her very nervous. "I've never met Mr. Vernon."

"But you do know who he is?"

"Yes," she answered tersely. "Look, are you going to charge me with anything? Because if you are, I want a lawyer."

Again they used eye contact to reach a decision.

"For the time being, we're merely conducting an interview," Buckley said. "And we're hoping you'll offer to cooperate in our investigation".

"I'd be glad to, if I knew anything. Like I told you, I don't know Paul Vernon. If you'd bothered to read the statement I gave the police, you'd know why I was in the warehouse."

"We read the statement." Potter had decided to take the lead. "You met Mr. Macklin in Carmel while he was conducting an investigation into the whereabouts of his niece, who is believed to be in the company of Paul Vernon, who in turn is wanted by several law enforcement agencies, both local and federal. You were sympathetic to Mr. Macklin's situation and decided to come to Los Angeles with him to help in this endeavor.

"He suggested searching a warehouse that once belonged to Vernon in hopes of turning up some piece of evidence that might lead him to his niece. You willingly aided and abetted Mr. Macklin in gaining illegal entry to the warehouse, and you maintain that it was never your intention to commit burglary or destroy property." He sat down in a chair several feet from hers. "Is that about right?"

"That's exactly right," she said.

Potter's lips turned up at the corners, but the effect was far from pleasant. "I wouldn't say *exactly*. You seem to have left out something important. Like motivation." He stood and walked to Sarah's other side. "Macklin has been to the warehouse before, as well as to Vernon's corporate offices. He's talked to Vernon's former employees. He didn't find anything then because there was nothing to find. So tell me, Miss O'Shaughnessy, why did he go to the warehouse tonight? What has he learned that made him think it was worth a second look?"

Sarah's heart sank. She'd kept her statement simple, instinctively omitting several key points, such as Kay's letter, Dale Brown and the computer printouts. She wasn't sure exactly why she'd withheld the information, except that it didn't really have any bearing on the charge of breaking and entering and she didn't want to get Dale in trouble.

Now the matter had gone past the police, straight into federal territory. And this particular fed was perceptive enough to know that she was keeping secrets.

Well, to hell with him, she thought with a burst of anger. If Mack had gotten a little consideration and cooperation from the government when he'd asked for it, he wouldn't have been forced to pick locks and pry open crates.

"Well?" Buckley prodded.

"As far as I know," she said firmly, "he hasn't learned anything new. He just felt desperate and didn't know what else to do."

"I don't believe you."

"I don't care what you believe. You have my statement. Either charge me or release me."

Potter's face was a textbook illustration of impotent fury. He strode to the door and jerked it open. "Bring him in," he barked.

Mack entered the room, closely followed by a uniformed policeman.

"You and your girlfriend have worked out quite a story, Macklin." Buckley seemed to be deliberately insulting, as though he were trying to get a reaction from Mack.

It didn't work. Mack walked to Sarah's chair, ignoring the agent, and cupped her chin in his fingers. "How're you doing, Pollyanna?"

"I'm okay," she told him with a shaky smile. Somehow the relief of seeing him had triggered that perverse mechanism that hides deep inside everyone, making her want to cry now that the worst was over. "I just want to get out of here."

"Sounds good to me," he said. "Maybe if we say pretty please, the nice boys will let us go."

"Don't get smart with me, Macklin," Buckley growled. "We could press charges and let you cool your heels in a cell."

"Then why don't you?" Mack snapped.

"I'd love to, believe me. You're lying, both of you. If I had my way, you'd stay behind bars until you decided to talk."

"Well, like the song says, 'you don't always get what you want.' So if you're through playing games, we'll be leaving."

Mack took Sarah's arm and started from the room, but Potter stepped into his path. "Make no mistake, Macklin. The only reason you're walking out of here is that we don't want any publicity on this investigation. But don't get in our way again. You gave up your status five years ago. Now you're just a private citizen, and you'd better remember that."

The vein in Mack's temple throbbed ominously. Quickly Sarah pulled him forward into the hall. "Whatever you're thinking, don't say it," she warned. "Let's just go home."

As they stood at the front desk, waiting to sign for their personal effects, Sarah could sense the tremendous tension that held his body rigid. He'd known Potter and Buckley before, maybe even worked with them during his mysterious government days. What "status" had he given up five years ago? And what had happened to cause the hostility between him and the two agents?

The mystery got deeper and deeper, extending far beyond Kay and Vernon. And she intended to probe until she got to the bottom of it.

MACK HAD LITTLE TO SAY during the drive back to his apartment, and his mood didn't improve once they were inside. For a while he puttered in the kitchen, reheating the soup they hadn't eaten earlier, then washing the few dishes.

Sarah left him alone for the most part. She knew him well enough to sense when he needed space, but not well enough to insist on invading it. After the dishes were put away, she

asked if she could take a shower, hoping he'd be more re-
sponsive by the time she was finished.

"Sure," he said, waving his hand vaguely toward the hall.
"Clean towels are on the rack."

She took her time under the hot spray, letting the water
work its magic on her aching body. It was hard to believe
that so much had happened in the past twenty-four hours,
and equally hard to believe that she was still on her feet.
She'd gotten precious little sleep before the excitement at the
beach house, and that was nearly twenty-four hours ago.

But she could sleep tonight, and so could Mack. He was
a miracle of endurance, still going strong after days of
watching the house in Carmel and only a few hours' rest at
the motel, plus a catnap early this evening. It was no wonder he was withdrawn and uncommunicative. Tomorrow
they would both feel better, and they'd be able to figure out
what to do next.

She dried off with an enormous, fluffy towel and put on
the pajamas and robe she'd packed. When she got back to
the living room, she half expected to find him sacked out on
the sofa again, but he was still awake, sitting in the recliner.

"Hi," he said when he saw her. "Feel better?"

"Lots. How about you?"

"I'm getting there." He gave her an apologetic smile.
"Sorry about the bad mood. I just had some things to think
out."

She sank into a corner of the sofa. "Anything to do with
Buckley and Potter?"

He nodded slowly. "Yeah, you could say that."

"Mack, what was going on between you and those guys?
I thought you were going to rip one another's throats out."

"Just ancient history. Call it a personality conflict."

"Conflict is right. But I think it's more than personali-
ties. You used to work for the CIA, didn't you?"

"When you get your teeth into something, you really hang on, don't you?" There was no rancor in his voice, only weariness. "No, I didn't work for the CIA, but I had to work with them on several cases. I was with the NSB."

Sarah sat up straighter. "I've never heard of it."

"Not many people have." He flexed his right shoulder and rubbed it. "The National Security Bureau. It started out as a watchdog organization in the late sixties, sort of the equivalent of an Internal Affairs Division in a police department. The original idea was to take care of problem areas within the various government branches before they became public knowledge."

"Like taking care of your own garbage before it spills out onto the street?" she teased.

He laughed. "I've never heard it put quite that way, but you're right. The FBI and the CIA were competing for power, and there were rumors of bribes, extortion, even treason. So somebody decided to set up a regulatory body."

"And a new agency was born."

"A superagency," he said with surprising sarcasm. "It worked for a while, but by the time I came along, NSB agents were actually in the field, overseeing other branches' operations. The bureau became the ultimate authority on questions of national security. But somewhere along the line, things got screwed up." He drew in a deep breath. "Their methods got dirty, Sarah, so dirty I couldn't take it anymore."

"So you blew the whistle," she said quietly.

"I tried to blow the whistle." He closed his eyes briefly, as if the mere memory still caused him pain. "My report stirred things up for a while, but in the long run, nothing really changed. The bureau protects its own, and suddenly I was the ugly stepchild. The traitor."

She bit her lip as a nasty suspicion occurred to her. "Is that why nobody listened to you when you asked for help in finding Kay?"

He didn't answer immediately, and when he did, his voice was inexpressibly sad. "I don't want to think so, but it's crossed my mind."

"Mack, if it's any comfort, I didn't tell them about Kay's letter, or about Carver and Fulgham. You're still one step ahead of them."

"I know." He smiled at her then, a smile so full of sweet tenderness that she felt her heart turn over. "Thank you for that, Sarah."

Her face glowed. "I enjoyed it," she told him. "I figured if they were worth their salt, they could figure it out for themselves. And speaking of figuring things out," she added, "what's our next move? We can go up to Oakland and—"

"No," he said, coming to his feet in a swift, fluid motion. "There isn't going to be any more 'we,' Sarah. You're too involved and it's getting more dangerous every day."

"You can't mean that," she cried. "So we got caught tonight, so what? You heard what Buckley said—they aren't going to press charges."

"Charges be damned!" He pounded the back of the recliner with his fist, startling her. "You'd be safer in jail than you are with me."

"What are you talking about?" she said, jumping from the sofa.

"I'm talking about your life. Buckley made it pretty plain tonight that it's open season on me if I don't back off on Vernon. And I'm not going to back off."

She couldn't quite believe the implication. It was too staggering. "Are you trying to tell me that they would kill you? Actually *kill* you? That's crazy."

"Sarah, there are a dozen agents who would be glad to pull the trigger. I'm the rogue, the renegade. I rocked the boat and a few people got hurt in the process." He grasped her arms, forced her to look at him. "I can take chances with my own life, but not with yours. You're going home tomorrow."

"I don't want to go home," she insisted. "This should be my decision, not yours."

His eyes grew angry, and he stepped away from her. "Look, I've accepted responsibility for getting you mixed up in this, for getting you arrested tonight. It's my fault. I shouldn't have brought you to Los Angeles. But I won't be responsible for getting you killed."

His mouth was hard and unyielding, his jaw set. It would be pointless to argue with him. And if what he said was true, if continuing the search would be so dangerous, what argument could she make? He was right. If something happened to her just because she stubbornly insisted on playing detective, Mack would have to live with the guilt.

"All right," she said, backing away. "I don't like it, but I understand. I'll go home in the morning."

"Sarah," he began, "I'm sorry..."

"Don't be. In a crazy kind of way I've had fun. Now I have to be practical." She swallowed hard, wondering why she felt so bereft. "If you've got an extra pillow and blanket, I'll make up the sofa—"

"No," he interrupted. "Take the bed. I use the sofa most nights, anyway, so I'm used to it."

She nodded and left the room.

It was a long time before she slept. She kept replaying the past twenty-four hours like a video tape. How could he have become so important to her in such a short time? *Maybe it's just the situation,* she thought. After all, they'd shared some pretty intense emotions, and it was only natural that she feel some kind of bond.

But in her heart she knew it was more than that. Leaving him tomorrow would be the easy part. The real toughie would be staying away.

THEY BOTH SLEPT LATE, so it was nearly noon before she closed her suitcase and joined him in the living room.

"I don't know what I'm going to do without you," he said softly. "You're like a magician, always pulling another rabbit out of the hat."

She tried to laugh. "It's called deductive reasoning. And you don't have to do without me—I'm always available for phone consultations."

"That's a nice thought, but a bad idea. Too much Sarah can be habit-forming." He looked away from her face, down at the suitcase. "Let me take that," he said, reaching for it.

"No, I've got it."

Their hands met, and Sarah felt the tingle all the way to her scalp. He was standing close to her, so close she could have laid her palm against his chest.

He took the suitcase, set it on the floor. One of his hands tilted up her chin; the other touched her shoulder. "Sarah, look at me."

She looked, and what she read on his face made her weak with longing. She knew he was going to kiss her, knew, too, that she'd never wanted anything so much in her life.

A gentle pressure from his fingers eased her forward, and she leaned into the kiss. At first his mouth was hesitant, undemanding. But as she responded, he gathered her into his arms, crushed her to his chest so tightly their heartbeats mingled while his lips played havoc with her senses.

When he moved his head, she uttered a small, involuntary sound of protest, but his lips were still there, trailing butterfly kisses down her cheek to her jaw.

"Sweet Sarah," he whispered. "It would be so easy to ask you to stay."

His words made her heart pound more wildly. "So ask me."

He pulled away then, and the stricken look in his eyes was like a blow. "No. Not like this. Not when it could mean your life."

He released her, and she felt cold, so cold.

WHEN SHE WALKED through the gate at LAX, she looked back one last time. He was still standing there, watching her leave.

Chapter Six

"Earth calling Sarah, come in, Sarah."

The sound of Raylene's voice jerked Sarah's attention back to the here and now, and she felt slightly ashamed of herself as she looked at the three expectant faces ranged in a circle around the table: Patrick, Raylene and Dolly, all of whom had planned the evening to be Sarah's welcome-back dinner. But so far, Sarah knew, she hadn't provided much in the way of scintillating conversation. All during the meal her mind had strayed—oh, so easily—to the night before, to her disturbingly intense reaction to what should have been a casual kiss. Even now the memory brought an uncomfortable flush to her face.

Patrick's sharp eyes caught the betraying rise of color, but mercifully he put the wrong interpretation on it.

'At least you have the grace to be embarrassed," he teased. "Dolly's been talking your ear off for the past five minutes."

"I sure have," Dolly piped up. "Where'd you drift off to?"

"I'm sorry," Sarah told her earnestly. "I guess I've just got a lot on my mind."

"Well, I don't doubt it," Dolly replied. "After what you've been through, I think it's a wonder you're not hibernating with the covers pulled over your head. When those two secret-agent types showed up and starting asking questions about you, I didn't know what to think." As she launched into a description of the men who had come to her office making "confidential inquiries" about Sarah, Dolly fairly bounced in her chair. "I was scared to death, Sarah," she said breathlessly, her brown eyes huge in her pixie face. "I mean, they weren't really threatening or anything, but they asked so many questions. Like, how well did I *really* know you, and what was my relationship to this Vernon guy, and did *you* know him, and how had he paid for the listing?" Her sleek black pageboy swung around her jaws in graceful emphasis as her had bobbed from one listener to another. "Not that I could tell them much, because Vernon's name wasn't on the listing and everything was paid in cash."

"Then when she told me about it," Raylene chimed in, "I remembered those weird calls from Ms Lambert and Greg Roberts, and I told her, 'Sarah's bein' *investigated*, Dolly. We gotta let her know.' Dolly was just gettin' ready to drive down to Carmel when Paddy called."

"And a good thing I called when I did," Patrick grumbled. "You wouldn't believe what was going on when I got there."

That remark, quite naturally, led to an in-depth recounting by Sarah of the Carmel episode, with numerous contradictions and elaborations by Paddy, while Dolly and Raylene sat enthralled.

At first Sarah was grateful for the opportunity to turn her mind to what she considered a safer topic. But as she finished the tale she realized that to her friends it was only a story. There was no way they could identify with the mouth-drying terror Sarah had experienced during that long walk down a dark hallway. No way they could feel the awful, soul-tearing fear of death and dying that had overcome her when she'd heard that single shot ring out in the night. Not even Paddy could fully understand, for he'd missed the real action.

And she couldn't tell them the rest, about what had happened in Los Angeles. She'd said only that she was doing more research for her book. The truth would just frighten them, and now that it was over, there was no point in mentioning it. But she couldn't help wondering what her friends would think of her adventures with someone like Mack. Mack, who was entangled in a dangerous web of intrigue. Poor Mack, who had been bamboozled by a hairbrush and kayoed by a sack of rocks. Irresistible Mack, who had melted her with a smile and captured her with a kiss....

"The book, Sarah?"

Startled, she looked at Dolly. "What?"

"Lord," Dolly said with justified disgust, "she's doing it again. I said, what are you going to to about the book? Can you finish it working at the apartment?"

"Sure," Sarah answered, wishing she could exercise more control over her rampant bouts of daydreaming. "I'll just have to get back into the routine, keep myself on a tight schedule. I got some great background stuff in Carmel and Monterey. And in L.A., of course," she added quickly.

"Fat lot of good it'll do if you don't start spending a little more time at home," Patrick remarked unexpectedly. Sarah was wondering if she only imagined the edge in his voice when he continued, "When my run was canceled yesterday, I couldn't even get into the apartment. Why didn't you tell me you were going to L.A.?"

Sarah stiffened. She'd expected that question sooner or later, but she wished it had been later.

"Because I didn't know. I mean, it was just a spur-of-the moment thing," she hedged, wishing the evening were over and done. She hated dishonesty, yet here she was, lying to the people who loved her most. The situation, added to all the recent excitement, had her nerves twisted into knots.

"What about your clients?" Patrick continued relentlessly. "Raylene's got a ton of messages for you. How are you going to pay your bills if you let your business fall apart while you're running the roads?"

Sarah glared at him. "Don't start with me, Paddy. It's been a long day, and I get mean when I'm tired."

For a long, uncomfortable moment no one spoke. Then Dolly laughed, somewhat nervously, and said, "Nothing like a little sibling spat to liven up a party." Everyone laughed then, and if the sound ranged from embarrassed to forced, it nevertheless had the desired effect of breaking the tension.

"So, how is Bothwell these days, Sarah?" Raylene asked in her lovely, soft drawl. "I'm just dyin' to read the whole book."

Sarah shrugged. "Not as well as I'd hoped," she said. "But I've come up with a couple of new ideas to get him back on track. Speaking of which," she continued, glancing pointedly at her wrist watch, "I'd planned to finish Chapter Eight tonight, so I'd better get home."

Luckily Dolly seconded the motion to adjourn. "Me, too, I've got an early-bird prospect tomorrow. This guy wants to see a listing at seven-thirty, if you can believe it, so I have to be up by six. C'mon, Ray, I'll give you a lift home."

"Well..." Raylene looked at Patrick from beneath long, thick lashes. "I guess you'd better, since I rode over here with you."

Sarah and Dolly exchanged amused glances while Patrick rose to his feet, then just stood, staring dumbly at the floor. Sarah marveled at his lack of initiative.

"Paddy, why don't you take Raylene home?" she said, fishing the car keys out of her bag. "I need to talk to Dolly, anyway, so she can drop me at the apartment. Just be careful with old Lucille. She's got a mushy clutch." She slipped the door key from the ring, then tossed the remaining keys to her brother, ignoring the flash of temper in his eyes.

Raylene blushed and Dolly giggled. As the small group filed out of the restaurant, Sarah prayed that Raylene would use her considerable charms to keep Patrick out until the wee hours. Something told her he hadn't really bought her explanation for being in Los Angeles and he was bound to have lots of questions. But not tonight, please. She needed some peace and quiet so she could put Mack and his problems out of her mind. She didn't want to think about Kay's desperate situation, or Mack's self-imposed isolation, or about how much she missed him. The only thing she wanted to think about tonight was *Kill Me with Love*.

AT ELEVEN-THIRTY, Sarah turned off the printer and stretched, trying to ease the kinks out of her spine. She'd been working for several hours straight; now it was time for a break, maybe a cup of herb tea and a quick read-through of the nine pages she'd just finished.

She smiled, pleased by her returning enthusiasm for *Kill Me with Love*. Initially she'd used the manuscript as a sedative. But, surprisingly enough, the automatic revisions she made seemed to become self-perpetuating, and before she knew it an entirely new Chapter Eight had emerged.

Now she puttered around in the kitchen, and in only a few minutes, she was curled in her favorite chair, a steaming cup of peppermint tea on the coffee table and a small stack of form-feed paper in her hands. Eagerly she tore the pages apart and began to read:

Bothwell pulled Traci roughly into his arms and smothered her exclamation with his hand. The darkness was almost complete, a black velvet blanket that separated safety from danger, friend from foe. And while Bothwell would much rather see his potential as-

sassin face-to-face, he realized that the inky darkness
could be a blessing in disguise—if only he could keep
Traci from giving away their position.

She struggled, and he clasped her more tightly. With
his lips against her ear, he breathed, "Trust me, babe."
She was still for a moment, then he felt her nod. What
a woman, he thought. If they got out of this alive, he
might even make a complete fool of himself and marry
her—

A sudden explosion jolted him into action. Shoving
Traci to the floor, he flung himself on top of her. The
assassin was trying to force a response, he realized, by
firing blindly. He had to get Traci to safety! Desperately he searched his mind, trying to recall the layout of
the warehouse. Somewhere, he remembered, was an
aisle of crates, large and heavy enough to afford some
protection. But which way? Right or left, forward or
back?

Sarah laid the pages aside and sipped at the tea. So far, so
good, she thought. Much better than before, and definitely
more emotional. She should have brought Traci into the
action long before now. Bothwell's character now seemed
more balanced, more sympathetic, all because he had
someone to worry about. Why hadn't she seen it sooner?

Then it dawned on her. Because until now, Sarah had seen
Bothwell as a comic-book hero, not a flesh-and-blood person. Because she had been thinking in terms of flashy cars
and derring-do, not real feelings. Because it had never occurred to her that a relationship, a commitment, could make
Bothwell stronger and more interesting.

Because, until now, she hadn't known Mack.

She groaned aloud. *Here we go again!* Every time she
turned around, Mack popped up to distract and confuse her,
even when he was hundreds of miles away. She had to stop

thinking about him. She'd done what she could to help him, even going so far as to get arrested, and the only way she could continue to help him was to stay away so he wouldn't worry about her. The adventure was over. Reality lay right here in a third-floor apartment in San Francisco. Mack wasn't Bothwell, and she wasn't Traci....

The sound of a key jiggling in the front door came as a timely diversion. Even though she wasn't particularly anxious to see her brother, she supposed it would be better than driving herself crazy with thoughts of Aubrey Glen Macklin. She was beginning to think that if it wasn't for the other people making demands on her attention, she'd probably spend every waking moment thinking about him.

When the door didn't open, Sarah sighed and rose to her feet, gathering the trailing folds of her robe in her hand to keep from tripping. She'd forgotten about throwing the dead bolt when she first got home. Patrick could play with the lock all night and not get inside.

It wasn't until she twisted the knob and began opening the door that she remembered—she hadn't heard Paddy come up the stairs, and he always made enough noise to wake the dead. But the warning flashed too late. Through the crack she caught a brief glimpse of a dark, pointy face that looked almost as startled as she felt, then the door crashed open with such force that she was knocked off balance. Before she could recover her footing, a brutal hand seized her upper arm in a painful grasp, and the next instant a cloth covered her nose and mouth.

She drew in her breath to scream, but strong, stinging fumes filled her lungs, immediately spreading to her brain. She twisted against the brutal grip, fought against the numbing chloroform. She tried again to scream, but even as she realized she made no sound, her head began to spin, faster and faster. Then the real world receded, leaving her to fall into a thick mist of fear....

MACK LAY ON HIS BED, staring at the ceiling as though the intricate design of moonlight and shadow might conceal a pattern and if he stared long enough he could find a solution to his elusive, yet troublesome, apprehension.

He couldn't understand why he was so edgy. Thanks to Sarah's help, the past couple of days had been more productive than he'd hoped, and tomorrow might be even better. True, he still had no idea where Kay was, but he intended to follow through on the leads he had, in spite of the thinly disguised threat Buckley had made. In the morning he'd start looking for Carver and Fulgham. So at this point, he should be eager, excited, possibly nervous, but not this way. Not with this skittery, jerky feeling in his gut, the kind of feeling that kept his skin drawn tight. Like he was waiting for the ax to fall. Like he'd overlooked something important. Or dangerous.

Frustrated, he flipped from his back to his side, ignoring the screech of the ancient bedsprings. Now, instead of the ceiling, he could stare at the wall.

What was it? Something in Kay's letter, perhaps, that had registered only in his subconscious? No, that didn't feel right. Whatever was bugging him, he didn't sense that it concerned his niece, at least not directly. Maybe he was just missing Sarah. But that, too, seemed wrong. Yes, he missed her, but knowing that she was safe was more important to his peace of mind. Then what?

Again he tossed, angrily tugging at the sheet, which had become tangled, leaving one leg and hip bare to the rapidly cooling night air.

When had the feeling started? he wondered. Sometime after Sarah had left, he thought, but he couldn't pin it down. If he could only relax, stop trying so hard, maybe it would come to him.

With more effort than had ever before been necessary, he finally stilled his erratic thoughts and slipped into a counting exercise that usually induced a state of total relaxation. The exercise worked. He felt calm and at peace. Soon, he knew, he would be asleep—

Nevada! That was what had triggered his internal alarm. He sat straight up in the bed, cursing himself for being a fool. The telephone number printout, the name of A. C. Fulgham who lived in *Nevada*. He closed his eyes, and as clearly as the first time he'd seen it, the number of a license plate snapped into his mind. The license plate had been on the rear of the Pontiac that had been following Sarah. When the car had unexpectedly pulled out in front of him in the parking lot at Fisherman's Wharf in Monterey, cutting him off, Mack's headlights had illuminated it: *Nevada, JQ-937.*

The sudden shrill of the telephone nearly knocked him from the bed. He groped in the darkness for the receiver and yanked it from its cradle.

"What?" he barked.

"Where is she, Macklin?"

The voice was vaguely familiar, but Mack couldn't place it. "Who is this?"

"You know damn well who it is! Where's Sarah?"

Now Mack recognized the caller, and something like pain hit him in the chest. "She's not here, Patrick. What's happened?"

"She's gone, that's what happened!" Even through the blustering, the fear in Patrick O'Shaughnessy's voice was apparent. "I found your number in her purse." He paused, and when he continued he sounded calmer, but still strained. "Look, all I want to know is if she's okay. Just let me talk to her."

"She's not here, Patrick," Mack repeated, trying not to voice his rising panic. "How long has she been missing?"

"I'm not sure. Dolly dropped her off at the apartment between eight and eight-thirty. When I got here at four, she was gone." On the other end of the line, Mack heard a swift intake of breath. "I shouldn't have called you, Macklin. She hasn't had time to get as far as Los Angeles. She didn't take her purse, and I had the car. I'm just not thinking straight. But where the hell could she be? It just doesn't make sense—"

"Give me your address," Mack interrupted. "Then wait for me. I'm on my way."

As Mack struggled into his clothes, fumbling in his haste, he hoped it was only a false alarm. But he was afraid they wouldn't be that lucky, for he had just found the last piece of the puzzle that had been teasing him for hours.

If he'd seen their license plate, they'd certainly seen hers. And as Sarah had told him, with a computer and someone who knew what they were doing, you could find out anything you wanted to know about almost anybody.

SARAH HURT. Not the kind of hurt that defines a bruise or a wound. This hurt seemed to be everywhere at once, jabbing at her muscles, twisting her joints, making each movement a separate but eloquent agony. Her first coherent thought was that this must be how it felt to be hit by the proverbial Mack truck. Her second coherent thought was that she was frightened.

After that, nothing seemed very coherent—except the fear.

"Well, looks like Sleeping Beauty's awake." The voice was high-pitched and harsh, with a strong undercurrent of anger that made it ugly to hear. "And she didn't even wait to be kissed."

Sarah raised her head to look at the speaker, or rather she tried to. But the back of her neck, torturously stretched from supporting the weight of her head, knotted in protest. She simultaneously winced and gasped, tried to move her hand to massage away the pain. That was when she realized she was tied up, her wrists firmly trussed behind the slats of a straight-backed chair, her ankles lashed to the front legs.

Through the sudden roaring in her ears, she heard the voice again, but couldn't make out the words. She wasn't really listening, anyway—she was too busy reliving her last few moments of consciousness, remembering the apartment door slamming into her, the chloroformed rag being held against her mouth and nose. And after that, nothing. Until now.

Suddenly her chin was gripped hard and forced upward. She cried out, then quickly bit her lower lip against the sound.

"Look at me, damn it!" the voice commanded.

When she opened her eyes again, she saw an expanse of dirty gray shirtfront, two buttons straining against the girth of the man who stood in front of her. She lifted her eyes marginally—even that tiny movement was painful—and let them rest somewhere between the unbuttoned shirt collar and a round, fat-dimpled chin. If the man had a neck, it wasn't, for the moment, in evidence.

The man removed his hand from her chin and her head immediately drooped again. She opened her mouth to ask something but the thought vanished before it had fully formed. *Maybe it's a dream. I'll wake up soon in my own bed and then I won't hurt anymore.* But that wish was futile, and Sarah knew it even before the beefy hand grasped her once more, her shoulder this time.

The cruel fingers dug into her collarbone and she cried out again.

"That's better," the voice said. "Nap time's over, girlie. I want you bright eyed and bushy tailed so you can tell me what I want to know."

"What..." She licked her lips. They felt dry and cracked, like her throat. "What do you...want to know?" She couldn't think, and that frightened her even more than the man did. Between the fear and the aftereffects of the chloroform, she actually thought she could feel the room moving, lifting and falling beneath the chair. Why couldn't she think?

"Ace, I told you she'd play dumb!" This was a different voice, but no less harsh and no less angry. "We don't have time for games. If you can't make her talk, I can."

Again Sarah moved her head, opened her eyes. The second man was easier to see because he stood some distance away, glowering at her with dark, glinting eyes. His black hair showed pronounced gray streaks that swept back from each temple. His rumpled clothes hung on his too-thin frame, but they couldn't disguise the restless, somehow menacing energy that seemed to vibrate through his body. His face, too, was thin, pinched looking and scored with deep frown lines across his bony forehead. It was a familiar face, and just for a moment, a hazy memory swam at the edge of Sarah's mind, then disappeared.

"Don't rush it," the other man answered, stepping back a pace. "She just now woke up, prob'ly can't remember her own name. Ain't that right, honey?"

This time when Sarah tried to look at his face she succeeded. It was broad, flushed and covered with a thin sweaty sheen. His sandy hair, what little of it there was, receded sharply from a widow's peak; beneath that, his eyebrows hovered precariously close above small, pale eyes set into fleshy sockets. All in all, it was a thoroughly unpleasant face, one she'd seen before. But where?

While she struggled to bring the situation into focus, she became aware that both men were staring at her expectantly, as though waiting for her to to say something. What had they asked? Oh, yes, did she remember her name. "Sarah," she croaked. "My name is Sarah O'Shaughnessy."

"Hey, that's good," said the heavy man, beaming at her with false goodwill. "That's just what your car registration says. I gotta hand it to you and Vernon. You're good at covering your tracks. But not good enough to fool me and Floyd." Again he seized her chin and squeezed, his powerful fingers digging deep into her tender flesh. "See, we already know who you are. Now we're just tryin' to find out how cooperative you're gonna be. Let's try again, but don't use Sarah this time. Use something else, something short and sweet. Like . . . Kay."

Kay. Kay Macklin. Awareness at last penetrated the fog in Sarah's brain. With chilling clarity, she now realized who these men were and why they had kidnapped her. The Beacon Lounge in Monterey. Two men watching her—these two men, Ferret Face and Porky. The Carmel break-in. Mack's comment about her resemblance to his niece and his theory that the beach house intruders thought Sarah could lead them to Paul Vernon.

She swallowed, hard, before nausea could overcome her. "Kay?" she said shakily. "No. I told you. My name's Sarah. I don't know Kay Macklin."

Floyd seemed to jump through the air to land beside the big one. "Nobody mentioned the name Macklin. Now stop playing games with us, lady, 'cause we're not in the mood. Your boyfriend owes us, and we're gonna collect one way or another. We know he's probably already left for that banana republic of his, but he didn't take you with him. Why not? You're the red queen. He wouldn't have left you without a reason. You getting his money out of the country, is that it? Or is it the shipment?" He slapped her hard. "Answer me! Where's that damn shipment?"

Sarah's head reeled from the blow. She squeezed her eyes shut and gulped again. *This can't be happening. . . .* But it was happening, and she had no idea how to stop it.

Lifting her chin and opening her eyes, she stared at her captors. "I can't tell you what I don't know. My name is Sarah O'Shaughnessy. I found Paul Vernon's house through a real estate agency. I moved back to San Francisco after you broke in that night. That's it. That's all I know."

Floyd cursed and lunged for her, but the other man—had Floyd called him Ace?—held him back. "Take it easy, Floyd. Kill her now, and we'll never get out of this."

Sarah wished she could believe they were merely playing their version of good cop-bad cop, but she knew it wasn't so. They would cheerfully do whatever it took to make her talk. And by the time they finally figured out that she was telling the truth, she might be dead. *Would* be dead eventually, anyway, no matter what she said. Only a moron would think they'd ever let her go, and she wasn't a moron.

Floyd backed down, but he obviously wasn't happy about it. "Maybe it's slipped your mind, lard belly, but we only got till midnight tomorrow to produce either the money or the shipment, and then *we're* dead. Now if you don't have the stomach for this, move over and let me do it."

Ace flicked his tiny eyes back and forth between Sarah and Floyd. His florid face wore an expression of uneasy resignation. "Okay, okay." He sighed. "One more time, honey. And make it easy on yourself, huh?"

For an instant Sarah was grateful for the bonds that held her in place. Otherwise she'd be nothing more than a smear of quivering jelly spread across the floor.

She drew a deep breath. "My name is Sarah O'Shaughnessy. I don't know Paul Vernon—"

A fist descended in a blur of motion, and the blow caught her on the jaw, sending a lightning bolt of pain through her head. The chair rocked and Sarah felt herself falling, then abruptly she was jerked upright again.

The man thrust his beefy face close to hers. His breath smelled of garlic. "I could tell you that this is gonna hurt me more than it'll hurt you, but I'd be lying. Now come on, Red, be reasonable. All we want is what we earned. Seven-hundred-and-fifty-thousand dollars, or give us back the weapons."

"I don't have any money, and I don't know anything about any weapons..." she began.

Searing pain shot through her head as it was yanked back with a force that threatened to rip out her hair by the roots. As the hateful voice poured into her ear, making demands she couldn't meet, threats she couldn't help but believe, she finally began to accept the reality of what was happening to her. This was no nightmare from which she would wake up. The cavalry wouldn't come to the rescue. Fear and desperation had turned these men into animals, and they wouldn't believe anything she told them. She was alone, more vulnerable than she'd ever been.

As the voice droned on, harsh and chilling, one thought gripped her mind with overwhelming clarity. She didn't want to die...

MACK RAPPED SHARPLY on the apartment door three times, then turned the knob and entered without waiting for an invitation. He found himself in a large, bright room with hardwood floors that gleamed. The furniture was old and heavy, but obviously well cared for; the sofa and arm chair were upholstered in a pale floral print that matched the flounced curtains. In every corner and on every available surface, pots of green-leaved plants waved their stems in the breeze coming through the bank of open windows. It was a cheerful room, airy and welcoming—just the kind of place he would expect Sarah to have.

From behind a long, low counter that separated the living room from the kitchen, he saw Patrick O'Shaughnessy peering at him with what could only be described as hostility. Patrick held a phone receiver against his ear. Waving at

Mack to sit down, he withdrew behind the counter and resumed his conversation.

"I don't care what your blasted policy is, my sister's been *kidnapped*! She could be dead in forty-eight hours!"

Too keyed up to sit down, and anxious to talk to Patrick, Mack strode into the kitchen and leaned against the counter.

"I *know* there's no sign of forced entry, you idiot! I'm the one who filed the report.... I've checked with all her friends.... She doesn't *have* a boyfriend, and if she did, she wouldn't go traipsing off without her shoes and her purse.... What do you people get paid for, anyway? I want my sister found, do you hear...?" He banged the receiver down so hard the glasses on the end of the counter rattled. "Damned bureaucrats, they couldn't find an elephant in a closet." He glared at Mack. "Well, it took you long enough to get here. It's almost noon."

"It's almost ten-thirty," Mack returned calmly. "I had to make some calls before I left. What's the word?"

Patrick shook his head. "Nothing. This number's switched to Raylene's answering service in case Sarah calls while I'm gone. And Dolly's been trying to get in touch with a friend of Sarah's on the police force, but he's off duty and apparently out of the city, and nobody else gives a damn."

"I take it the police don't consider her a missing person."

"Not for forty-eight hours." Patrick kicked at an unfortunate bar stool, sending it bouncing across the floor. "No sign of foul play, they said. No reason to waste manpower unless there's some indication of a crime, they said."

"Did you tell them what happened in Carmel?"

"Yeah," Patrick growled. "But since she didn't file a police report, they're not inclined to take my word for it." If looks could kill, Mack would have dropped dead on the spot. "And it's your fault."

Mack had been expecting that. "I know," he said simply. "That's why I'm here. I think I can help find her."

"Well, why didn't you say so?" Patrick exploded.

Mack knotted his fists. "Because there's this big, dumb jerk who keeps interrupting me!" he shouted back. "Now do you want to hear this or not?"

For a moment it seemed that Patrick was more in favor of fighting than listening. Then, with a visible effort, he relaxed his stance. "Go ahead."

Mack reached into his back pocket and pulled out a piece of folded paper. "Sarah and I had already dug up two names from Vernon's phone records. A. C. Fulgham from Reno, Nevada, and Floyd Carver from Oakland. They're both suspected of hijacking some weapons from an armory in Nevada, which they probably sold to Vernon. After you called this morning I did some more checking. Fulgham left Reno two weeks ago, but his sister is married to Carver. I think they're both in Oakland."

Patrick clearly didn't understand. "And you think they've got Sarah? Why?"

"Because the car that followed her in Carmel had Nevada plates. Because they think she's Kay and that she can lead them to Vernon."

Patrick rolled his eyes. "They don't even know Sarah's name, Macklin. How the hell could they have found her in a city this size?"

"They probably traced her licence plates." Mack's patience was nearly used up. "Look, we're wasting time jawing about this, and they could be getting away."

"And it could be a wild-goose chase...."

"Great!" Mack snapped. "You stay here if you want. I'm going to find Sarah." He spun on his heel and started for the front door.

"Wait a minute."

Mack stopped but didn't immediately turn around. *One more word,* he thought, *just one more word, and I'll lay him out.* But when he faced Sarah's brother at last, he saw with surprise that the big Irishman wore an expression of chagrin.

Not that Patrick O'Shaughnessy would apologize. "You oughta watch that temper of yours," he said with a slow half grin. "You fly off the handle too easy. Now, like I started to say, why don't we go find Carver and Fulgham."

Mack wavered between mashing the grin down Patrick's throat and smiling back. The smile won out. "Good idea. Especially since I don't have a car."

Patrick picked up a set of keys off the counter and jiggled them. "Then what are we waiting for? Oakland's just across the bridge."

Chapter Seven

Since neither Patrick nor Mack was overly familiar with Oakland, it took them nearly an hour to find the address Mack had scribbled on the notebook he carried in his jacket. Mack consulted the city map they'd picked up at a service station.

"Turn right at the next corner. Looks like the street's only a few blocks long, so it has to be here somewhere."

Patrick, who looked as if he'd been stuffed behind the steering wheel of the VW, peered at the neighborhood skeptically. "This place looks like a war zone. Maybe we should have brought reinforcements."

His observation was accurate. Only a minute away, the streets were clean and shady, lined with neat sidewalks in front of ranch-style homes—typical middle-class suburbia. But a couple of turns had brought them into the midst of social apathy, if not downright hostility.

Here the streets were neither clean nor middle class. The houses were ill-kempt, with the paint cracked and peeling. Windows were broken and doors hung askew, supported by only one hinge. Hulks of stripped-down, rusted-out cars littered half the yards; many of the vehicles had apparently become the equivalent of giant garbage cans, and a few had been burned. On several porches, groups of teenagers lounged indolently, surrounded by beer cans and liquor bottles. The young men wore uniforms of brightly colored headbands and sleeveless denim vests, while the girls seemed content to wear as little as possible.

About halfway down the second block, Mack noticed a short, husky youth leaning against a cherry-red '57 Chevy, modified in the low-rider style that had become popular among some Hispanic West Coast communities. The boy eyed the Volkswagen and its occupants arrogantly as he toyed with a tire iron, hefting it in his hand.

Mack tapped Patrick's shoulder and nodded toward the boy. "Do you get the feeling we're not welcome here?"

"Punk," Patrick commented. "If he's not careful, he'll wind up wearing that iron for a necktie."

Mack chuckled. "If it's all the same to you, I'd rather not put it to the test. We're outnumbered."

"Really?" Patrick raised his eyebrows. "I thought it was pretty even. A dozen for you, a dozen for me...."

"Wait. Here it is." Mack glanced down at the notebook, then at the faded number on the porch post of a small frame house on the left side of the street. The brown Bonneville with Nevada plates was nowhere in sight, but the front door was propped open with a battered suitcase.

Patrick steered the VW into the narrow driveway and killed the engine. "How're we going to do this?"

Mack shrugged. "Walk up and knock, for starters. If they're home, we keep them here until we find out where Sarah is."

As the two men got out of the car, a woman appeared on the porch. She was short and stout, with brassy blond curls and an excess of curves that didn't fit comfortably into the tight slacks she wore. She carried a suitcase and a gaudy, rhinestoned denim bag slung over one shoulder. She stared at Mack and Patrick with no trace of unease.

"If you're collectin'," she greeted them, dropping the suitcase with a thump, "you're outta luck. I'll be gone in another ten minutes, and I don't care if you repossess every stick of furniture in this sorry excuse for a house." Her voice matched her hair, loud and brassy.

Mack stopped with one foot on the bottom step. "Are you Doreen Carver?"

"Maybe," the woman challenged him. "Depends on who wants to know."

Mack had to admire her belligerence. In this neighborhood it probably stood her in good stead. "Actually, we're looking for your husband and your brother. We'd like to talk to them."

"Yeah," she returned, "you and every other hood in this whole damn state. Well, if you can find them, you're welcome to whatever you can drag outta their worthless hides. I don't know where they are."

"When's the last time you saw them?" Patrick asked.

Mrs. Carver looked him up and down carefully. "You two don't look like the type to do business with Floyd and Ace. You cops?"

Mack and Patrick exchanged a look that said, *Go easy. Don't scare her off.* "No, we're not cops," Mack answered.

"I don't care if you are," she said unexpectedly. "As far as I'm concerned, they belong back in prison. Let 'em rot." She fumbled in her shoulder bag and came up with a crushed, nearly empty pack of Marlboros. "Either one of you boys got a light?" she asked, placing a crooked cigarette between her lips.

"Sorry," Patrick answered. "Sounds like your old man has dealt you some grief," he continued, watching as the woman dug out a matchbook. "Can't blame you for wanting to see the end of him."

"You got that right." She exhaled the words along with a cloud of smoke. "And you don't know the half of it. That sorry worm never earned an honest dollar in his life, and my brother's just as bad. Thought maybe they'd straighten up when they got out of the pen last year. Floyd's parole officer had him a good job lined up, and Ace found something out in Reno. But I shoulda known. Once a thug, always a thug."

"So what happened?" Mack prodded, guessing that the woman would be only too glad to share her tale of woe.

"Floyd found him another surefire deal, that's what happened." Her mouth twisted in a bitter smile. "He was gonna make us rich, just like always. Then he got Ace rooked into helping him. I don't know what happened exactly. About a month ago Floyd split for Reno. Said he and Ace had a deal going. Two weeks later the cops are banging on my door. Said Floyd violated his parole and he was going back to jail."

"So you haven't seen your husband since he left for Reno?"

She flicked the cigarette away with an angry, abrupt gesture. "Hell, yes, I seen him. Him and Ace both. They show up here about three o'clock this morning, cool as you please, asking for money. Money!" She laughed harshly. "If I had any money, I told him, I'd have paid the damn rent!"

Mack felt a surge of adrenaline. "Where are they now?"

"How the hell should I know? When I saw they had this floozy in the car, I slammed the door and locked it. That's it, I told him. I'm through." She stared at Mack defiantly, as though daring him to disagree with her.

"They had a woman in the car?" Patrick asked, swelled with excitement. "Did you get a good look at her?"

Mrs. Carver transferred her angry gaze to Patrick. "Good enough," she spit. "Redheaded tramp, passed out in the back seat. And they wanted *me* to pay for their fun!"

She turned to go back inside, but Patrick grabbed her wrist. "Hold on," he commanded. "That 'tramp' is my sister! Now I want to know where they took her!"

The woman's eyes widened in fear and she tried to pull away. "Buster, either you let me go or I'll scream this place down."

Quickly Mack stepped in and laid a restraining hand on Patrick's arm. "Please, Mrs. Carver. Nobody wants to hurt you. But we think your husband and your brother kidnapped a young woman from her apartment. All we want to do is find her."

Mrs. Carver regarded them suspiciously, rubbing her wrist. "Kidnapping, huh? Well, that's a new one for Floyd." She seemed to ponder her options for a moment, then shrugged. "What do I care about those two? They messed me around once too often. I don't know if it'll help, but Floyd's got this friend over in Marin County, lives on a houseboat. If he's on the run, he'd probably go there. Most of his other buddies are either dead or in jail."

She gave them the name of the marina and general directions on how to get to it. Then she laughed again, but her faded blue eyes were suspiciously bright. "If you find 'em give 'em a punch for me, okay? And tell them Doreen says bye-bye."

When Patrick kicked the VW into gear and took off, Mack looked back. Doreen Carver still stood on the porch, watching them. He couldn't tell if she was laughing or crying.

WHEN SARAH CAME TO, she heard the sound of someone moaning. It took a few seconds for her to realize the moans were coming from her own mouth. She blinked rapidly, then slowly raised her head. Except for a dark young man she'd never seen before, who seemed to be completely absorbed in a magazine, she was alone.

She ran her tongue over her parched lips, winced when she felt the hard, ragged cracks in the tender skin. Her throat felt swollen, and her body ached in so many places it was impossible to separate one pain from another. In some indefinable way, she no longer felt like *her*, Sarah.

A sob formed in her chest, tried to force its way up her throat and out of her mouth. "No," she whispered aloud. "I won't cry."

The tiny sound she made alerted her guard. He jerked his eyes away from the magazine and fixed them on her. His Adam's apple bobbed nervously when he swallowed, and Sarah thought she could detect a slight tremble in his hands. "I...uh...Floyd, well, he's not here," he said irrelevantly, almost as though he were apologizing to a guest for the host's absence.

Confronted with the young man's unexpected attitude, Sarah quickly searched her mind for a memory of what had happened. She remembered the pain. She remembered pleading with Floyd to believe her. And there was something else, something important, but she couldn't quite focus on it. She must have said something they wanted to hear, because Floyd had stopped hurting her.

She concentrated fiercely, aware that the young man was watching her closely. Then it came back to her. She'd been so desperate, she'd lied to Floyd and Ace, told them Vernon had hidden the "shipment" in a warehouse in Los Angeles. She didn't recall the address she'd given them, but apparently they'd thought it was worth checking out, because they were gone.

But what good had it done her? She was still tied up, and she still hurt. And sooner or later, when they realized they'd been duped, Floyd and Ace would be back. Sarah thought she could safely assume they wouldn't be pleased with her.

"Hey, lady," the young man said, rising from his chair, "you okay? You look kinda funny."

"Yeah, I feel funny, too," Sarah tried to say, but the words came out in a garbled croak.

"What?" The young man, who couldn't have been more than eighteen, edged closer to her. He avoided looking directly at her, and Sarah realized he was frightened. In fact, she sensed that the entire situation had him ready to bolt at the first loud noise.

The uncertainty on his face gave her a faint spark of hope. "Water," she whispered, letting her head drop back. "Please, I'm so thirsty."

The boy rocked from one foot to the other. "Well...they didn't say not to let you have a drink. Okay. Just hold on."

In a few moments he was holding a glass to her lips. The water was lukewarm and slightly brackish, but to Sarah it was nectar. She gulped half the glass before she paused to draw a breath.

"Thank you," she said with sincerity. "Where...where are they?"

The boy shook his head. "Dunno. They brought the boat in about an hour ago, then took off. Said they had some phone calls to make. Just told me to stay here and make sure you didn't try nothing."

Her battered spirits sank yet again. They were checking out the address by phone, which meant they could be back here any minute. Though she didn't mean to, she groaned aloud.

Her guard looked almost panic-stricken. He offered her the rest of the water and held her head while she drank. When he turned to place the empty glass on a nearby table, she noticed the handle of a small pistol protruding above his belt.

She licked her lips. If she was going to get out of this alive, she had to think of something, and soon. The calvary wasn't on its way, because the troops had no idea where she was. No, whatever happened, she'd have to do it herself.

The young man sat down and again took up his magazine, and Sarah looked closely at her surroundings. The room was small, almost cramped, and it was furnished strangely. Like a camper, she thought, with small appliances, a bolted-down table and padded benches along the wall. There were only two windows, one on each side of the room, and they were covered with thin, café-style curtains, but through the space between the top of the curtains and the gathered valance she could see birds, sea gulls, wheeling above a number of masts. She was on a boat.

"Look," she said tentatively, "you've really been nice to me and I appreciate it. Would you do just one more thing for me? I, well, I need to go to the bathroom...." She let her voice trail away as though she were embarrassed.

Her request seemed to frighten him. "Hey, I can't do that," he protested. "Floyd'd kill me if I let you loose."

"But you don't have to let me loose," she pleaded, "just my feet. You can stand outside the door until I'm through. Please?"

His face went flat with stubbornness. "No way, lady. I'm not that stupid."

Sarah felt tears of frustration gathering in her eyes, and she let them fall. This wasn't the way it was supposed to work. She was supposed to be clever and resourceful. Or she was supposed to be rescued. She was supposed to be *alive*...

"Please, lady, don't cry," the boy exclaimed, jumping from his chair. "Cripes, how did I get into this mess?" He ran to the window and, parting the curtains, peered outside. "Okay. But hurry it up, all right? You gotta be back in that chair by the time Floyd comes back. And don't try nothing."

To Sarah, it seemed an eternity before her bonds were loosened, and when she stood up to ease her still-tied wrists over the back of the chair, her hands and feet felt as cold and heavy as leaden blocks. The numbness disappeared, however, after a few halting steps, and her circulation kicked in like a thousand tiny, flaming arrows.

She gasped and stumbled, would have fallen if her reluctant captor hadn't grabbed her around the waist.

Again he seemed apologetic. "Guess you're pretty stiff, huh?"

"A little. But I'll be okay." Even talking had become a wrenching effort.

A few more steps, each one a small and separate agony for Sarah, brought them to the door of a tiny lavatory.

"Could you turn on the water for me?" she asked.

"The water?" he repeated dumbly.

She nodded. "I don't want you to hear when I . . . you know."

"Oh," he said, dropping his eyes. "Sure."

That done, she slipped inside, gasping when she turned her shoulder the wrong way, and leaned against the door. When she heard it click shut, she sighed with relief.

The boy's voice followed her inside. "Hurry it up, lady. And no funny business."

"All right," she called back. "I promise."

Now that she was face-to-face with the toilet, she realized that she really did need to relieve her bladder, but there was no time for luxuries. She had to get rid of the rope. Turning her back to the sink, she bent her elbows until her hands and wrists were in the basin, under the running water. Every movement brought a wrenching pain, but she kept at it, twisting and pulling at the rope until it began to stretch, little by little. The rough fibers abraded her skin. By the time she finally wrenched her right hand free, it was raw and bloody.

She'd just removed the rope from the other hand, when the boy knocked on the door. "Hey, lady, hurry it up."

Her heart did a double beat. "Just another second, okay?" Nearly frantic with the prospect of escape, she looked wildly around for a weapon. Nothing, not even a bottle of Listerine. Not even a hairbrush.

A picture of Mack flashed through her mind. If she didn't make it, she thought, her biggest regret would be missing the opportunity to love him....

Snap out of it, Sarah! The game wasn't over yet. If she hurried, she still had a chance.

She stood against the wall and took a deep breath. "Okay, I'm through now," she said loudly. "But I don't think I can stand up by myself. My legs are cramping."

She heard him curse. As the doorknob turned, she tensed, breathing a prayer of relief that the door opened inward.

His head and one shoulder were inside when he saw the unoccupied toilet. Throwing her weight against the door, Sarah caught him between the door and the frame, driving the air from his lungs. She jumped backward, then dived at his stomach with outstretched, stiffened arms.

He shot backward into the galley, bounced off the stove and fell to his knees. While he was still shaking his head, Sarah jerked the gun from his belt and ran.

He yelled, and she heard him scrambling to his feet. If she could only make it to the door...

But she didn't. He caught the back of her robe and yanked her to a neck-snapping halt. Sarah whirled, bringing the gun around in a swift, hard arc. As the barrel struck him in the face, her finger involuntarily tightened on the trigger. The explosion caught her off guard and she yelped in surprise.

"Don't you move!" she shouted at him, waving the gun. "If you follow me, I swear I'll shoot you."

"Hell, I don't want to follow you!" he shouted back. "I'm getting out of here before Floyd kills me!" And brushing her aside, he rushed through the door.

Sarah took time to blink in amazement, then followed suit.

Outside the sun's brightness nearly blinded her, but she managed to jump from the deck to the pier, and for a few seconds she ran aimlessly. The narrow boardwalk seemed endless, with one intersection after another, all leading to yet more boats. Her body, pushed to the limits of endurance, began to fail her—she could no longer catch her breath, and a dagger of pain in her side nearly forced her to her knees. Though she was afraid to stop, she had no choice. Her legs simply refused to move another inch.

It was while she was holding her side, panting, that she saw them. They hadn't spotted her, but she knew she had only a few seconds at most. She staggered back the way she had come, out of their line of vision, and dropped to a crouch beside a yacht, letting the gun dangle uselessly by her side. The bay was behind her, the land ahead. And between her and the land were Floyd and Ace, who undoubtedly wanted to kill her.

Trying to calm herself with deep breaths, she ran through her options, limited though they were. She could sit there and wait to be cornered, or she could charge ahead and hope to outrun them.

Run? The idea seemed ludicrous. She could barely stand. But the alternative was death. Sarah didn't want to die.

She took a few more seconds, another small measure of blessed rest. Then she stood. "Okay," she whispered. "Here goes nothing."

She gathered the billowing folds of the robe up around her hips and held them with her left hand. In her right hand she clutched the pistol tightly. Then she sprang forward. *No matter what happens,* she vowed, *I won't look back. And if they catch me, I'll pull the trigger.*

She passed one intersection, turned right at the next. So far she heard no sounds of pursuit, no bullets whistling past her head, and a wild hope sprang up inside her. *I'm going to make it.*

From out of nowhere, two rock-hard arms fastened around her body and pulled her down onto the rough planking of the boardwalk.

She fought like a demon, kicking, punching, gouging, too intent on basic survival to worry about which one of them had caught her. Then a familiar voice penetrated her frenzy.

"Sarah, cut it out! Ouch! Damn it, stop!"

She realized she was clutching a handful of short, sandy-brown hair, and that a pair of anxious, fawn-colored eyes were now looking at her with worried bemusement.

"Oh, Mack!" She flung herself against his chest, aware of nothing except his presence and the wonderful, amazing feel of his arms as they wrapped around her.

SARAH LATER RECALLED almost nothing past reaching the car. As soon as Patrick tucked her into the back seat, she curled into a ball and withdrew from the world. Her brain, overloaded with emotion, sensation and a jumble of roller-coaster perceptions, simply refused to process the data, so she closed her eyes and retreated into a twilight of blankness.

At one point she was aware of being moved, lifted and carried in strong, comforting arms; she heard the swish of automatic doors, felt a gush of refrigerated air, smelled the medicinal odor she always associated with sickness. A soft babble of voices momentarily surrounded her, then she was placed on a cold metal surface. Gentle fingers touched her face and her shoulders, and even that light pressure reminded her of something unpleasant, something that had hurt her.

"No, please don't," she tried to say, but the words felt thick and clumsy in her mouth.

She heard her brother curse, then say, "What did they do to her?" Who was he talking about, she wondered, and why was he crying?

Then she heard another voice, sharp and angry. "What is he doing in here? Orderly, get this man out to the waiting room!"

A constriction around her arm, above the elbow, came and went quickly. She felt cool dampness here and there on her body, and stings that quickly faded to numbness. Hands, hurried and impersonal, prodded and probed, turned her to her stomach, then back again. She tried to push them away, but the effort was too great. She was very tired.

Strange voices asked strange questions: "Sarah, can you hear me? Talk to me, okay? Can you tell me what happened?"

She didn't want to answer, she only wanted to be left alone, so she took herself back to the blankness.

SHE AWOKE in easy stages, each one bringing her a step closer to real awareness. The first time she did no more than turn over and briefly open her eyes. But the room was too bright, too intrusive, and her eyelids immediately closed again.

Sometime later she felt a gentle pressure beneath her head; a woman's voice, familiar and well loved, urged her to drink; the rim of a glass touched her lips. The water soothed her dry throat and she drank for a long time. When she opened her eyes, Dolly's face wavered and took shape. Sarah tried to thank her, knew there was something she wanted to ask, but she couldn't form the words. She slept again.

The next time she woke, the room was dark except for a single dim light above the bed. Odd, she didn't remember a wall fixture in her bedroom. The bed, too, felt different. Narrower and harder, with high rails on each side.

With an effort, she sat up and looked around. The room was sparsely furnished, utilitarian in design, with only a cabinet and two plastic-cushioned chairs. In one of the chairs, a man, arms and legs sprawled, head angled back in what had to be a most uncomfortable position, was sound asleep. Mack.

She lay back on the pillow, drained by even the slight effort of sitting. Plainly she was now in a hospital, and she retained a fleeting memory of being examined, but nothing after that. She wondered how long she'd been sleeping. Not that it mattered. The way she felt, another forty-eight hours wouldn't be enough to banish the fatigue that had taken root in her body. She needed a drink of water, then she would go back to sleep.

The carafe beside the bed wasn't heavy, but she had trouble lifting it and filling the plastic cup. Then, when she raised the cup to her lips, her hand began to tremble violently. She drank every drop of the water, but when she tried to replace the cup, her nerveless fingers lost their grip and the cup fell to the floor with a dull clatter.

Mack jerked upright.

"What . . . ? Sarah?"

Even gruff with sleep and alarm his voice sounded beautiful. "It's okay. I dropped the cup."

"Why didn't you wake me?" he scolded, moving to her side. "Do you want a drink?"

She shook her head. "Just had one." Up close Mack looked terrible. His face was more haggard than ever, and he obviously hadn't had a nodding acquaintance with a razor in quite some time. She wondered if she'd ever have a chance to see him under normal circumstances, relaxed, happy and unworried. "Where am I?"

He looked blank for a moment, then grinned ruefully. "Beats me. We just stopped at the first place we came to. It's a clinic, not a hospital. For all I know, we may still be in Marin County."

"When can I go home?"

"Tomorrow," he assured her. "The doctor says you're basically okay, just banged up a little. He also said you should rest, so go on back to sleep."

"I've been sleeping." She reached out her hand and touched his arm where it rested on the bed rail. "What about you? I don't need a baby-sitter. You can stay at my apartment with Paddy." It wasn't until then that she noticed what was missing from the picture. "Where is he, anyway? Did you have him dragged away, kicking and screaming?"

Mack laughed. "Almost. Raylene and Dolly stayed until nearly midnight, and Raylene swore she'd stay all night unless Patrick left with her."

"Good for Raylene. She's just what Paddy needs, a firm hand." Sarah paused, then broached the subject she'd dreaded having to face. "Mack, where are they—those men?"

His smile faded. "I don't know, honey. We almost had them, but..."

"They got away." The news didn't surprise her, but neither did it upset her. She didn't know how she was supposed to feel. True, she hated them. They were animals and should be punished for what they'd done to her. Just thinking about it made her stomach churn. But in a way, it was a relief to know that she wouldn't have to face them again, to pick them out of a line-up or identify them to the police.

"Sarah, I'm sorry," Mack said. "We tried. Patrick chased them on foot, but they were too quick for him."

Her eyes widened. "Oh, Mack, don't apologize to me! If you hadn't been there..." Suddenly chilled, she shivered. *Don't think about it,* she commanded herself. It was over and done. And Mack was worried enough already; he shouldn't be subjected to a nasty delayed-reaction scene. "How did you get there, anyway? How did you even know where to start looking?"

"Sarah," he protested, "it's three o'clock in the morning. We can talk about this tomorrow."

"Tomorrow my foot," she said firmly. "I'm the invalid here, and invalids always get what they want. Now tell me."

"Actually," he told her, smoothing a tangled curl away from her cheek, "you did a lot of it yourself. Remember those names we pulled up, Fulgham and Carver?" He went on to tell her how he'd remembered about the license plate, about Doreen Carver and finally getting to the marina. "We'd just gotten out of the car, when we heard a shot, but we couldn't get a fix on the direction. Then we see this kid running like mad, so Patrick goes after him. I took off in the direction the kid came from and nearly fell over you. I couldn't believe it." He stopped talking and looked quickly away. "When I heard the shot, I was afraid . . ."

She sat up then and held her arms out. They fit perfectly around his neck, and for a long moment, he simply hugged her to him while she drank in his scent and the way she felt in his arms. But soon, too soon to suit her, he pressed her back against the pillow.

"Are you going to the apartment now?" she murmured.

"Not a chance," he promised, squeezing her hand. "I'm staying right here so you won't drop any more cups."

She dozed off quickly, but not before she felt his lips brush hers and heard his soft whisper. "Good night, Pollyanna."

With her hand securely tucked in his, Sarah slept again.

In the dream, she wore a long, flowing dress of scarlet silk, and she stood at the top of a turreted battlement. Below her, as far as she could see, people knelt to pay obeisance to her. "The red queen," they chanted. "The red queen, the red queen." A man stood beside her and she turned to look at him. He wore a mask and a robe, but the robe was made of bananas, hundreds of them, ripe and yellow and sweet smelling. Behind the mask she could see nothing but a pair of glittering eyes.

"What is this?" she asked.

"The Banana Republic," he answered, bowing to her. "I am the king and you are the Red Queen. Behold your kingdom."

She looked down again, and her subjects had become banana trees and the trees stretched into the distance until they disappeared from view. Far away from the battlement, a volcano rose darkly against the sky, spitting white plumes of smoke high into the air.

"What will we do if the volcano erupts?" she asked the king.

He laughed shrilly. "Why, we will eat fried bananas, of course."

"But I don't like fried bananas," she said. The King of the Banana Republic didn't say anything; he just laughed again, louder and louder, until she clapped her hands over her ears....

Sarah's eyes flew open and she sat straight up in the hospital bed, fully awake.

"Mack! Mack, I've got it! I know where Kay is...!"

At some point, Mack had moved one of the chairs next to her bed. Now he bolted from it. "What?" Blinking rapidly, he grabbed the top rung of the bed rail. "Are you okay?"

"Of course I'm okay. In fact, I feel *wonderful*." She threw back the sheet and got on her knees, absently rubbing her shoulder. "Did you hear me? I know where Vernon took Kay. Well, not exactly *where*—it's more of a *what*—but we can figure it out.... Where are my clothes?

We've got to get back to the apartment. I need my notes.... Well, don't just stand there. We've got to *hurry*."

Mack stared at her with an expression of profound disbelief. "Damn it, Sarah, you nearly gave me heart failure! What the devil's wrong with you?"

On her knees, with the hospital gown flapping open behind her, Sarah bounced impatiently. "I'm trying to *tell* you something, if you'd just listen. I heard them talking, Ace and Floyd, but I didn't think about it then, and now I've had this dream about fried bananas, and it all makes sense.... Mack, I need my *clothes*!"

He grabbed her shoulders to keep her from jumping off the bed. "You don't have any clothes. Patrick's bringing them later. And you're not going anywhere until the doctor says so." He blinked again. "Fried bananas?"

"Fried bananas?" Patrick had come in unnoticed, carrying her overnight case. "I don't think they serve those in hospital cafeterias. Why aren't you asleep?" He directed the question to his sister, then rounded on Mack. "And what are you doing here? You said you'd sleep at the apartment."

Sarah nipped Patrick's blossoming jealousy in the bud. "That's not important, Paddy. Give me my clothes and both of you wait outside while I get dressed." She made a swipe for the case and missed. The effort reminded her, quite forcefully, that she didn't feel as good as she'd supposed. The muscles in her back knotted up, and her injured shoulder felt as though it had been dislocated.

She fell on her side, hoping she didn't look as dreadful as she felt. Tiny beads of perspiration popped out on her forehead and her upper lip, and her vision blurred.

Mack cursed and Patrick dropped the case.

"Now see what you've done!" Patrick bellowed.

"Me?" Mack swung around, his hands balled into fists. "How do you figure that?"

"If you weren't in here, getting her all excited..."

"You're out of your mind. I'm trying to keep her in bed."

"I'll bet you are."

"Shut up, both of you!" Sarah had pulled herself up by the bed rail, unable to believe her eyes. "Patrick O'Shaughnessy, you say some of the stupidest things I've ever heard. Stop acting like the town bully and sit down. And as for *you*—" she pointed a shaky finger at Mack "—I thought you wanted to find Kay, but you won't listen to a damned thing I say." She plopped back on the pillow, exhausted. "Kill each other if you want to. I don't care anymore. Just get out of my room to do it."

"Sarah Kathleen, I'm just worried about you."

"And I heard every word you said, but it's a little hard to get excited about fried bananas."

"Oh, be quiet, both of you!"

When the doctor came in at seven-thirty to make his rounds, he found the nurses' station buzzing. Not only was the patient in 306 already dressed and demanding to be released, but her two male visitors had been ejected for creating a disturbance.

Strange, the doctor thought. They seemed like such nice people....

Chapter Eight

Sarah's snit lasted as long as it took her to get home, then she immediately turned her mind to more important things. Leaving Mack and Patrick standing awkwardly just inside the door, she hurried into her bedroom and dug the steno pad out of the canvas bag. She flipped through the pages until she found the transcription of Kay's letter, then started back to the other room. But as she passed her dressing table, she paused.

So far she'd avoided looking in mirrors, afraid of what she'd see. It had to be done, though, and it might as well be now, with no one around to see her reaction. Keeping her eyes down, she sat on the spindly brass stool and faced forward. Then, slowly, she raised her head and looked.

The largest bruise covered nearly the entire upper left quadrant of her face. Already it had turned an ugly, dark blue that stained her skin from the hairline, across her forehead and down her cheek. Her left eye was mottled purple, its lid slightly swollen, and the eyebrow was raised in the center by a tender lump. Gently she touched her mouth and felt the split in her bottom lip, then traced the curve of her jaw, wincing when even that slight pressure proved painful.

Unbuttoning her shirt, she pushed it back from her shoulders. Her neck bore several darkening marks, like fingerprints, and her collarbone was bruised and tender.

Sharply and with horrible clarity, the sight brought a memory of cruel fingers and hateful words whispered in her ear....

She jerked her shirt into place and fumbled with the buttons, feeling like a coward. But enough was enough. Eventually she would get used to the sight of her face and body, but not now, not today. Right now it would be all too easy to fall apart. Better to keep busy, she thought; better to think about anything except how close she had come to dying.

In the living room she found Mack and Patrick waiting in an uneasy silence. They looked at her anxiously when she entered.

"Sarah," Patrick said hesitantly, stepping forward, "shouldn't you be in bed? The doctor said—"

"Don't start, Paddy," she warned. "The doctor said I'd be sore, and he's right. But it's nothing I can't live with, and lying around in bed would only make me feel worse." She shifted her gaze between the two men and sighed. "Look, I think we'd better get a few things straight, or we're never going to get anywhere. I want you both to listen to me, and don't interrupt."

She sat on the arm of the sofa, watching as Mack crossed the room. Patrick, as if he already knew he wouldn't like what she was going to say, shuffled nervously from foot to foot.

"All right," she began, drawing a deep breath, "what happened to me was horrible, and it'll probably be a long time before I get over it, but I have to do it by myself. That's the only way I can handle it. That means no special treatment, not from the two of you, not from Dolly and Raylene. I can't put it behind me if you're constantly telling me to stay in bed or reminding me to be careful. So don't fuss over me, and don't blame yourselves or each other." She stood up and looked at them sternly. "It's over. I'm still me.

Just plain Sarah. And that's how I want to be treated. Understood?''

As she'd expected, Patrick wore his stubborn look. But underlying the bullheaded gleam in his eye, she also glimpsed a trace of hurt. And confusion. For the first time in his life, Patrick was having to face the fact that his baby sister wasn't a baby anymore and there were some things a big brother just couldn't fix.

Mack, however, surprised her. He looked neither worried nor uncertain. Instead his expression said, more plainly than words, *Atta girl. I'm proud of you.* Their eyes met and she knew, in that instant, she'd won his respect and, maybe, just maybe, something else she wasn't quite ready to put a label on.

"If that's the way you want it," he said quietly, "that's the way it'll be."

Patrick cleared his throat. "Yeah. Me, too." Then he grinned. "Does that mean you'll fix me some breakfast?"

Sarah laughed and slapped at his arm. "Fix it yourself, bozo. I've got a mystery to solve."

Grumbling, Patrick found his way into the kitchen; Sarah and Mack followed him and sat at the breakfast bar. She pointed to the transcription. "These words you couldn't read—did you ever figure them out?" she asked Mack.

"I haven't even thought about them again," he said, frowning.

"Well, I have," she announced with justifiable pride. "And I know what they mean. *La reina roja.* The red queen."

Mack gave her a keen look. "Where did you come up with that?"

"I'm not sure." She frowned. "I mean I'm not sure where I saw it in Spanish, but that's what Carver called me. He said, 'Why did Vernon leave you behind, you're his red queen,' or something like that. And in the hospital I dreamed about it.'' As she became more excited, her gestures grew expansive. ''Maybe while I was on the boat, unconscious, I picked up on their conversation and it came out in the dream. Anyway, it made sense. I think I know where Kay is.''

Patrick stopped looking for the pancake batter and leaned on the bar to listen.

''Carver said something about Vernon going to a banana republic,'' she continued. ''That's a term that usually refers to Latin American countries or islands. Then from somewhere I picked up a Spanish phrase and connected it with the red queen, which ties in with what Kay wrote, here, about having her own shrine. And farther down, the two words you couldn't recognize—they could be 'compound' and 'transport.''' She lowered the pad to her lap and looked at Mack, knowing she was right and hating it. ''Vernon's not going to resell those weapons like we thought. He's using them to buy power, either in Central or South America, and plans to set himself up as some kind of king. And Kay's his queen consort.''

The seconds stretched out. Sarah watched Mack closely, wondering what he felt behind the facade of noncommittal silence. At last, pinching the bridge of his nose, he said, ''It all fits, especially when you consider his mental problems. If you want to be a king, find yourself a revolution and strike a bargain with the rebels—arms in return for a place in the new regime.''

They all knew Vernon's cache must contain enough arms to tempt a struggling, poorly equipped army—rocket launchers and other large offensive weapons, incendiary bombs, radios and aircraft tracking devices, grenades and Uzis. Most of the equipment had been made obsolete by newer, more sophisticated models, but that didn't make it any less deadly.

"Why the rebels?" Patrick asked, wrinkling his forehead in concentration. "Why not one of the Communist governments? Seems like they've always got a rebellion on their hands."

"They don't need guys like Vernon," Mack explained. "Recognized governments, Communist or not, already have a functional army, and one of the two superpowers to call on if they need help. No, it has to be a rebel group, a small force with no sanctioned political support. They use Vernon—he uses them."

Sarah, as usual, preferred concrete facts to speculation. "We could talk about this all day and never come up with anything useful. I mean, when you get into motives, it's all guesswork. We need some facts. Such as, which Latin American countries or island republics are currently fighting civil wars. And of those, which ones show up on Vernon's shipping schedules for the past three or four months."

Patrick grunted. "It'd be easier to find out which ones *aren't* fighting. That's all you hear on the news, fighting in Central America. It's a way of life down there."

"And Vernon was basically a middleman, a contract shipper for other companies, not a manufacturer. Smuggling out rocket launchers disguised as kitchen ware and stereo equipment would be impossible, even for him. If he got that equipment out of the country, it didn't go through regular freight channels."

Sarah poked Mack's arm with her forefinger. "There you go again, setting limitations," she retorted. "With a little imagination and enough bribe money, you can smuggle anything anywhere. What we need are copies of Vernon's shipping schedules for the past three or four months. And I probably had them right in my hands when we were in the warehouse."

"You can bet they're not there anymore," Mack said with a bitter laugh. "Buckley wouldn't take a chance on leaving anything for me to find if I went back. That warehouse was probably cleaned out by the time we left the police station.''

''That's it!'' Sarah shouted. She jumped from the stool and grabbed Mack's arm, shaking it for emphasis. ''That's where I saw *la reina roja*. In the warehouse. There were several long documents in Spanish, and that was on one of them.''

''Think, Sarah,'' Mack said eagerly. ''Can you remember anything else, a city, a country?''

''No. I dropped the papers when the police showed up.''

''We'll have to think of something else then.'' He stared at the countertop for a long moment. ''Billy,'' he said. ''Billy Thomas. He worked in the shipping department.''

''Haven't you already talked to him?'' Sarah asked.

''Only about Kay, not about shipping schedules. It hasn't been that long ago, so there's a good chance he'll remember something as odd as *la reina roja*. I have to go back to L.A., talk to him—''

A sudden, loud knock echoed through the apartment, and Paddy groaned. ''That's probably the cops. I forgot to tell you, Sarah. They wanted to see you when you got out of the hospital. Mack and I both gave our statements, but they need yours, too.''

But the two men at Sarah's door weren't cops. Their badges bore the Great Seal of the United States, and their identification badges read National Security Bureau.

''Sarah Kathleen O'Shaughnessy?''

The men were both like and unlike the CIA agents she'd met in Los Angeles. They wore the same type of understated, conservative suits—one navy blue, one charcoal gray—and the same neat, conservative haircuts—short in back, no sideburns. Both were well shy of middle age, but old enough to run for Congress.

The difference was in the eyes. Buckley and Potter had been tough; these men were far worse.

Sarah felt her chest constrict, partly with anxiety, mostly with antagonism. She remembered every word of what Mack had told her about the NSB, and her instinct was to slam the door in their faces. But the rational part of her mind said that would be a very dangerous thing to do.

"May I help you?" she inquired coolly.

"We'd like to ask you some questions." The shorter man seemed to be the official spokesman. "May we come in?"

A small sound, a slight stirring of the air, made her aware that Mack and Patrick had closed ranks behind her. That knowledge made all the difference in the world.

She moved aside just enough to allow the agents passage, not enough to meet the current standards of courtesy, then closed the door behind them. Facing them, she asked baldly, "What do you want?"

The spokesman looked faintly surprised, but he, too, came straight to the point. "We want to establish the extent of your involvement with Paul Vernon and his activities."

"Yeah, there's a lot of that going around lately," Mack said. "Sara, this is John Bridges. His tall friend is Cleve Landis." Throughout the unexpected introductions, he maintained a steady—and definitely aggressive—eye contact with the men. "Two of the bureau's finest, which doesn't say much for the bureau."

Bridges's face reddened, while Landis smiled contemptuously. "Still trying to play in the major league, Macklin? After you loused up the Bakersfield operation, we thought you'd wised up, decided to leave the tough stuff to the experts."

"That's enough, Cleve." Bridges put just enough steel into the reprimand to effectively silence his partner. "Take Miss O'Shaughnessy into the kitchen there and set up the recorder. I'll question Macklin in here." He spared a glance for Patrick. "We'll want to talk to you, too, but for now you'll have to wait in another room."

Patrick, who had assumed the chest-out, head-down stance of an enraged bull, opened his mouth to speak, but Mack beat him to it. "Like hell," he said in the same tone he might have used to comment on the weather. "We stay together, and we use two recorders. Yours and ours."

"Don't push your luck, Macklin," Landis began. "You're in enough trouble...."

Sarah looked at the implacable male faces and involuntarily took a step forward. "It's all right, Mack. I don't mind talking to them."

"That's because you don't know them," he told her through tight lips. "The idea is to get you alone, rattle your cage with a bunch of empty threats and hope you'll tell them something they don't already know."

"But I don't know anything!" she said hotly. "And I haven't done anything wrong, except break into a warehouse, and those charges were dropped." She faced Bridges and pointed her finger at his chest. "Unless you want to count getting kidnapped and beaten up, but the last time I checked, that wasn't a federal offense, either. I've already been through this once with the CIA, Mr. Bridges, but I'll say it one more time. I've never laid eyes on Paul Vernon, I don't know where he is, and I'm not hiding his stupid guns. So if you want to record something, try this. Either bring formal charges against me—and make sure they'll stick—or get off my back!"

Bridges blinked. Beside him, Landis glared at her with profound dislike. A shocked silence reigned for maybe half a second, then Patrick burst into loud guffaws.

Sarah wheeled and aimed her finger at her brother, but he wasn't looking at her. His eyes were trained on the comical expressions frozen on the agents' faces.

Then she looked at Mack and saw that he, too, was enjoying the spectacle. His grin threatened to engulf the lower half of his face. "The funniest thing I've seen in years. How about it, boys," he said to Bridges and Landis. "What does the manual say about handling law-abiding citizens who aren't afraid of you?"

"Law-abiding citizens don't jeopardize government investigations, Macklin." Bridges sounded as though he had just swallowed something rotten. "You and your friends are in trouble whether you believe it or not. If you'd kept your noses out of our business, we'd have Carver and Fulgham in custody right now. And you wouldn't be facing criminal charges."

"What charges?" Sarah demanded, suppressing the urge to slap his smug face.

"The big ones are withholding information, illegal access to classified documents and questioning government witnesses without authorization, but we can probably find a few more if we look real hard." Bridges smiled without showing his teeth. "Maybe I'll drop by Leavenworth on visiting day, and you can tell me again how funny it is. Of course, if you'd like to change your mind and cooperate, we might be willing to reconsider our position."

Sarah sensed rather than saw Paddy's sudden movement forward. Grabbing his arm, which was rigid with anger and tension, she yanked on his sleeve. "Don't, Paddy." Her stomach roiled with the bile of injustice. "They're just waiting for an excuse. Tell me, Mr. Bridges, what kind of cooperation do you have in mind?"

"Nothing painful," the agent said with smug satisfaction. "Just tell us everything you know about Paul Vernon's activities, how you got the information and the names of any other parties you've discussed it with."

Sarah looked at Mack. He appeared subdued but not particularly worried, and she hesitated. How much or how little did he want her to say?

"I don't have anything to hide," she said to Bridges. "Where do you want me to start?"

IN THE END Sarah was forced to give up the transcription of Kay's letter. The original, Mack blandly explained, had been thrown away since it was too tattered and creased to be worth keeping. On the whole, however, she felt that the NSB would be leaving her apartment with considerably less than they'd hoped for.

Mack had begun by describing his reconnaissance of the Carmel house and his subsequent fight with the two men who'd broken in. Sarah filled in from her viewpoint, up to and including her discovery of the hidden letter.

Bridges countered by jumping to her abduction and fortunate rescue. How was it, he wanted to know, that Macklin and her brother had known where to find her?

Mack admitted to having seen the license plate in Monterey, but Sarah firmly maintained that he'd given the number to her and she'd done the actual tracing, eventually uncovering Carver's Oakland address.

And when had Macklin given her the license number? Bridges asked. Had it perhaps been when she'd stayed with him at his apartment in Los Angeles?

Yes, they agreed.

And what else had they talked about during that visit, for—here Bridges checked his notes—a total of six hours and twenty-seven minutes, before they had broken into the warehouse?

They hadn't talked about much of anything, Sarah stated. That part of the visit had been of a more personal nature.

Then Bridges jumped back to the letter. It was at this point that Mack had asked Sarah to show the transcription to the nice man, since the original had been thrown away.

Bridges studied the transcription briefly, passed it to Landis and continued his questioning.

Sarah, Mack and Patrick categorically denied having discussed Paul Vernon and/or the search for Kay Macklin with anyone except one another. Patrick's involvement was purely involuntary and only for the purpose of protecting his sister; he intended to forget everything at the first opportunity.

Mack swore that none of Vernon's former employees had given them any information whatsoever, and that Doreen Carver had divulged only the location of the houseboat. If she knew anything about her husband's dealings with Vernon, she hadn't shared it.

During the period of her "interrogation" by Carver and Fulgham, Sarah said they appeared to be ignorant of the whereabouts of both Vernon and the weapons, since they'd tried so hard to obtain that information from her.

Neither Bridges nor Landis mentioned the statements given to the Marin police after Sarah's rescue, a clear indication that those reports, like the ones dealing with their warehouse escapade, were now safely tucked away in some obscure filing cabinet marked "Classified." They also neglected to mention Dale Brown's name, and Sarah felt sure that she and Mack had lost their surveillance for that brief period of time.

After what seemed like hours, Landis clicked off the pocket-size tape recorder and slipped it inside his jacket. Then he and Bridges rose from the sofa and turned to leave.

Mack, who'd chosen to stand during the "debriefing," pushed away from the wall where he'd been leaning and opened the door. In spite of his apparent cooperation, he had grown steadily more withdrawn, until now open hostility poured from him.

Bridges paused on his way out. "This is your last warning, Macklin. Don't interfere again. I wasn't joking about those charges."

"You *are* a joke, Bridges." Mack appeared to be in control, but Sarah could hear the cold fury underlying his words. "Now get out of here and take your trained seal with you."

Landis cursed and made a lunge for Mack, but Bridges blocked the move and pushed his partner through the open door and into the hall. Then he faced Mack one last time, his eyes glittering like frosted-over metal.

"Grow up, Macklin. Your niece is in for the long haul, and there's not one thing you can do about it. So far we've gone easy on you because of your tender sensibilities." He sneered at Mack with undisguised contempt. "But now you've wrecked an operation and cost us two material witnesses, not to mention dragging your girlfriend into it. Next time she might not get off so lucky. Now I'm telling you, it stops here. Get in our way one more time, and I'll take you out myself."

"You'll try," Mack replied in a deceptively soft voice. "Like you've tried before."

Bridges turned abruptly and stalked down the stairs, shoving Landis in front of him. Mack watched them until they turned the first landing and disappeared.

Sarah was behind him when he closed the door, and he swung around so violently she had to skip out of his way.

"I should have killed him years ago," he said through clenched teeth. "I may kill him yet."

Alarmed, Sarah clutched at his arm. "What is it?"

"Games!" he shouted. "Always playing games. And it doesn't matter who gets caught in the middle because it's all for the 'greater good.'"

Sarah had seen him angry before, but never like this, never out of control. "Mack, please stop shouting and tell us what's wrong. You're scaring me."

Suddenly he pulled her into his arms, holding her so tightly it hurt. She could feel the pulse throbbing in his neck, the wild thud of his heart, and she heard him whisper her name. Whatever he knew, it both frightened and enraged him, and at least part of it was because of her. She clung to him and hoped he couldn't feel her trembling.

"Okay, Macklin, let's have it. What's going on?"

Mack released her slowly, reluctantly, she thought, then turned to face Patrick.

"They used us," he said, shaking his head as if he couldn't quite comprehend what he'd learned. "They've been right there, every step of the way, just waiting to see what would happen. They knew Sarah was being followed in Carmel, probably before I did. They followed us around L.A., and they knew when she was kidnapped. They knew, and they didn't even try to stop it, just to make sure she really didn't know anything."

Sarah, wide-eyed and unsteady, leaned against the back of the sofa. "I don't understand...."

Mack gave one sharp, ugly bark of laughter. "Of course you don't. People like that don't exist in your world, Sarah." He dropped heavily into the armchair and stared into space, his face nearly unrecognizable with dark fury.

"Remember what you said to Bridges, Sarah, that you didn't have Vernon's 'stupid guns'? Bridges should have jumped on that. He should have asked how you knew about the weapons, but he never mentioned it. He simply didn't notice what you said, because it was already so familiar to him."

He blinked, like a man coming out of a trance. "It was all a front. They never really thought you knew anything about Vernon, but just in case they slipped up, they figured why not let Carver and Fulgham have a crack at you. If you told them anything, the good old NSB would be right there to step in for the cleanup. And if you didn't know anything, well, that would've been all right, too. Either way, you'd have been another unsolved murder case, and they'd have one less leak to plug up."

Paddy had gone pale. "They *wanted* Sarah to die? Mack, that's crazy. Those men are government agents. They work for *us*."

"They work for a cause, Patrick. The National Security Bureau. They'd throw their own mothers to the wolves if they thought it would protect their holy national secrets."

"I don't understand," Patrick said in bewilderment. "If they already know about Vernon, why all the questions?"

"They were trying to find out who else we'd talked to, so they could plug up all the leaks. They have to keep this whole operation under wraps, because when the time is right, they're going to take Vernon out."

"'Take him out'?" Patrick repeated blankly. "You mean kill him?"

Sarah had been listening intently, putting Mack's words together with the questions Bridges and Landis had asked. Now the equation was plain.

"I believe the popular phrase is 'terminate with extreme prejudice,'" she said. The knowledge left a bitter taste in her mouth. "At least, that's what James Bond calls it." She massaged her temples with shaking fingers. "Mack's right. They want the world to think that Vernon's just another criminal who managed to skip the country before he went to trial."

Mack nodded. "And every time we mention his name or talk to people who know him or file a police report, Vernon's visibility quotient goes up another point. After a while, it will be too risky to eliminate him, because somebody might get curious and start asking embarrassing questions.''

Patrick looked from Sarah to Mack with disbelief. ''Are you saying we're in danger from our own government just because we know about Paul Vernon?''

''No,'' Mack said with a sardonic smile. ''At least not yet. I think we convinced Bridges that we're ignorant and harmless. He's too cocky to believe I could actually figure it out. But he'll be watching me—you can bet on that. Every time I turn around, he'll be standing there, waiting.''

Sarah sighed. ''So what now?'' For a moment selfishness took over and she found herself hoping Mack would say he was giving up. That they'd reached a dead end and there was nothing more they could do. But that wasn't like him—and it wasn't really like her, either. She was just so tired....

She didn't realize she'd closed her eyes until she felt Mack's lips on her forehead. ''What now?'' he echoed, smiling down at her in a way that made her tingle inside. ''For you, it's bed. You're pushing yourself too hard.''

Patrick took her arm and steered her toward the bedroom. ''Besides, you need to be rested up for tonight. Raylene and Dolly are coming over to cook spaghetti.''

''What about you?'' she said to Mack, watching him shrug into his jacket. ''I know you're planning something.''

''Just a little trip to Sacramento,'' he said innocently. ''Now that I've got some new bait, I want to do some fishing of my own.''

''Sacramento?'' She wrenched away from Paddy, thinking that there was no creature on earth as insufferable as a man. ''I thought we were going back to L.A., to talk to Billy what's-his-name.''

''*We're* not going anywhere, but we can talk about it later. I'll be back tonight.'' He kissed her again, lightly, then nudged her back toward the bedroom. "Try not to give your brother a hard time, okay?"

Before she could think of an appropriately scathing reply, he was gone. "Sarah, he's a big boy," Patrick said impatiently. "He knows what he's doing. Now get some rest."

He firmly guided her to the bedroom door, pushed her through and closed it with a last admonition.

The bed felt good, snug and familiar, and she thought she'd be asleep within seconds. But for a long time she lay awake, thinking. The spiral of danger that had brought her and Mack together was getting tighter every day, and now she lived in constant dread that something would happen to him. Where would it end? Where would *they* end? She loved him, she knew that now, and the thought of losing him was almost more than she could bear.

She sighed and snuggled into the pillow. For the time being, she wouldn't think about that. She would concentrate on helping him find Kay and bring her home, and one day, when they were free from the anxiety and fear, they could talk about their future.

Until then, she would hold the precious knowledge of her love close to her heart, safely hidden and nurtured. It wasn't enough, but it would have to do.

Chapter Nine

Greyson was late.

Mack looked at his watch, then at the large, round clock hanging on the wall of the diner. The two timepieces were still one minute out of synch, just as they'd been the first dozen times he'd checked. He hated waiting, and he especially hated waiting in public places. After a while, people would begin to look at him strangely, and if they looked long enough, they'd remember him....

With a start, he realized that he'd unconsciously fallen into an old pattern of thinking, a holdover from his days with the NSB. That mind-set was one of the reasons he'd finally gotten out, though not the most important one. The plain and simple truth was that his job began to sicken him.

There had been too much deception, too much rivalry, too much double-dealing. And too many fanatics like Bridges and Landis, to whom human lives were only statistics and who thought the end justified any and all means.

Bakersfield had been the end of the line as far as he was concerned. When a witness could be murdered under the guise of expediency to protect an agent's identity, then he could no longer be part of the system. He'd stated those sentiments in his final report, naming Bridges and Landis as the rogue agents, and two weeks later he'd been shot by an unknown assailant. Not one of his former friends in the bureau had come to visit him in the hospital.

But those years hadn't been entirely wasted. For one thing, he'd learned the techniques that had just come in so handy in shaking off the tail Bridges had put on him. And he'd made a few friends like Chuck Greyson, who was assigned to the Sacramento office of the CIA. Mack felt Greyson would help him if he could. If he balked, Mack wouldn't hesitate to use some of the leverage Bridges had unknowingly supplied him with.

A hand fell lightly on his shoulder. "Good to see you, Mack. It's been a long time."

Mack stood up and shook hands. "Too long," he responded with genuine pleasure. "You don't look any the worse for wear."

Greyson, a tall, rangy man with an open face and thinning blond hair, smiled ruefully as he took a chair. "Wear and tear is more like it. Ten years ago I hated the thought of a desk job. Last year I was practically begging for one."

The waitress took their order—iced tea for Greyson, a refill of coffee for Mack—and they exchanged more small talk until the beverages arrived and the waitress was out of earshot.

"I wish I could believe this is a friendly visit," Greyson said wryly, stirring his tea, "but I know you too well, Mack. Something's up, and it ain't the stock market."

Mack felt his mouth tighten into the grim line that seemed to be his natural expression lately. "Yeah. Do you remember my niece, Kay?"

"That pretty little girl? Sure, my kids went to one of her birthday parties. Has something happened to her?"

"Something named Paul Vernon."

Greyson was well trained, but even so, Mack saw a quick flicker of alarm come and go. "Damn, Mack, are you mixed up in that fiasco?" Like a reflex, the agent automatically lowered his voice. "I hope Kay's not implicated in it. The agency's riding it hard."

"What can you tell me?"

Greyson frowned. "Not much. My office assisted in the initial investigation, then the lid went on. Access on a need-to-know basis only, and all original files moved to Langley. I haven't seen a report in three months."

Mack knew Greyson wouldn't deliberately lie to him, but he sensed that his friend was holding something back. "Come on, Chuck. I know you've at least heard something."

Clearly uncomfortable, Greyson shifted in his chair. "There's always talk—you know that. But just among a few of us. Hell, Mack, you're not even in the business anymore."

"Listen to me," Mack said vehemently. "Kay's *life* is at stake. All I want to do is get her out, before it's too late."

Greyson sighed. "I don't even want to hear this, but you better tell me about it...."

Inside, Mack felt a minute lessening of tension. He began to talk, slowly at first, being careful to keep the facts straight, trying hard not to let his emotions get in the way. But by the time he got to Sarah's abduction and the NSB's involvement, the words were pouring out in a torrent of rage.

"Those cretins knew what was happening every step of the way, and they were willing to let her die. And they'll let Kay die, too. I just want to find her, Chuck, and bring her home. I don't care what happens to Vernon."

Greyson's face had gone slack and putty colored, like a man in extreme pain. "Bridges and Landis," he almost whispered. "Half the agents I know would love to see them disappear." He shook his head, obviously distressed. "Mack, I can't help you. This is a multibranch operation, and I'm not even on the totem pole."

"I'm not asking you to have Kay pulled out," Mack said. "It's gone past that. I want you to tell me where she is."

This time Greyson made no effort to school his features. "What makes you think we know where she is? Every agency in the country has been looking for Vernon—"

"And at least one of them has found him," Mack interrupted grimly. "I don't like playing dirty, Chuck, but I know how. And I'm prepared to do it."

The muscles along Greyson's jaw twitched. "How much do you know?"

"Enough to make life uncomfortable for a lot of people. Enough to make a million taxpayers write a million letters." He paused for dramatic effect. Greyson had to be convinced, or it wouldn't work. "I know it's a takeout operation, Chuck. Vernon has cut himself a deal with some so-called patriots who think their government needs an overhaul. He supplies all the M-16s and ammo they can use, throws in some radios, trackers and rocket launchers, and they promise him the top spot when they win."

Greyson sat like a stone, cold and immovable and silent.

"But Vernon's timing is all wrong," Mack continued relentlessly. "The latest detente treaty includes his little 'banana republic'—" he thought of Sarah and her absurd dream "—and it's strictly off limits for both the superpowers. The official line is let them have their civil war and may the best man win. Then along comes Vernon with his ugly toys. If the partisans win, using American weapons and technology, it'll be pretty hard to convince the Soviets of our sincerity at the bargaining table. At the least, we have an international incident, maybe even another Vietnam."

By now, Greyson's expression had slipped into one of bleak resignation. Mack could almost see the wheels turning in his head. *How did he find out? Does the agency have a leak?*

"Now comes the hard part—how do we retrieve Vernon before he starts another war? Regular diplomatic channels or a covert operation could pull him in, but that still leaves a whole stockpile of American weapons as evidence. So somebody, probably in the NSB, says why not infiltrate and eliminate? Blow up Vernon and the stockpile at the same time, and anybody who happens to be with him. Like my niece. No evidence, no witnesses, no problem."

Greyson's lips were white. "You're bluffing. If you knew for sure, you'd have it all, including the location, and you wouldn't even be here."

"But I am here," Mack replied quietly, hating the role he had to play. "And it's only a bluff if I don't go through with it. Now either tell me where Kay is, or I go to the press. It's already in place, Chuck. Five major newspapers break the story on the same day."

"Damn you." Greyson looked like a tightly wound spring. "I thought we were friends."

"We are. But Kay's family."

Greyson slumped in his chair. "I wasn't lying to you, Mack. I don't see the reports, and all I hear is rumor. The agency's keeping the cap on this one."

"I'll settle for rumor."

"Belen." The agent's hand shook visibly as he wiped the sweat off his forehead. "Vernon's got a compound about a hundred miles inland from San Sebastian, jungle terrain just at the base of the highlands."

"Who's your mole?"

"Mercenary named Jackson. He's reliable—we've used him before. Last I heard, Vernon got there a couple of weeks ago, and he has a young woman with him."

Mack felt his breath catch in his chest. "What's the timetable?"

"Unknown. The weapons haven't shown up yet, and we can't locate them. When they arrive, Jackson will follow them in, then the whole place goes up."

Mack stood suddenly, and his chair scraped loudly against the tiled floor. "I'd say thanks, but I don't think you want to hear it."

Greyson, too, stood. "I didn't do you any favors, Mack. Even if you get into Belen, you won't get out alive. You've got no backup, no resources and no sanction. As far as the agency's concerned, you won't even exist."

"Yeah, I know the procedure, remember? But I've got to try."

Greyson nodded. "I know." He hesitated, then thrust his hand out. "Good luck."

When Mack left the diner, he felt Greyson's eyes on his back every step of the way. And he remembered Greyson's words. *You won't get out alive.*

HE LET HIMSELF INTO the apartment with the key Patrick had given him and slipped off his shoes just inside the door. He didn't want to wake Sarah. She'd demand a full report, and he needed a full night's sleep before tackling that. Once she found out he planned to go to Belen, she'd most likely insist on coming with him, and then the fight would be on.

Her eyes would spark, her chin would jut out and she'd set her lips in that stubborn little line that meant she'd dug in her heels and didn't intend to yield an inch.

Without turning on a light, he groped through the room to the sofa. It wasn't quite long enough, but he was too exhausted to be choosy. He took off his jacket and shirt, tossed both garments onto the back of the chair. But as he started to stretch out on the sofa, he paused.

Maybe if he just looked in on her, she wouldn't hear him.

The doorknob turned silently, but one of the hinges squeaked. He stopped and listened. There was no movement from the bed. After a moment he sidled through the door and tiptoed across the room.

She lay on her side, one hand tucked under her cheek and one knee drawn up. The moonlight illuminated her hair, turning it into a shining halo of curls, and her skin looked like white satin. He didn't know how one little spitfire had managed to get such a hold on his heart, but she'd done it. She was the most amazing blend of softness and steel, honor and ruthlessness, innocence and sexuality. And when he got back from Belen—*if* he got back—he intended to make their relationship more permanent.

She stirred then, and he heard her breathing change.

"Mack?" Her voice was throaty with sleep.

"Shh. Go back to sleep. I just wanted to check on you."

She sat up and rubbed her eyes. Standing so close, he could feel the warmth radiating from her body, smell her sweet scent.

She reached for his hand and pulled him to the bed. "Stay with me."

Oh, how he wanted to! He ached for her the way he'd never ached for another woman. But once he made love to her, he wasn't sure he'd be able to leave her. And he had to leave....

As though she'd read his mind, she whispered, "Just to sleep, that's all. Just sleep with me."

He lay down beside her and wrapped her in his arms. With a contented sigh, she snuggled against his chest, and almost immediately her breathing changed again, becoming slow and regular.

Oh, Sarah girl, I do love you so.

He closed his eyes. With the smell of her hair in his nostrils and the gentle rise and fall of her breasts against his skin, Mack slept.

SARAH HAD BEEN HAVING a delicious dream. She couldn't remember the specifics, only a sense of warmth and security, and more happiness than she'd ever known. Mack, of course, had been part of it. . . .

Mack. She opened her eyes and found that her lashes were tangled in the fine, golden hairs covering his chest. Beneath her cheek, she could feel the easy rhythm of his breathing and the faint thumping of his heart. She lay on his arm, and its imprint tingled through her skin where it curved around her, his hand resting comfortably on her hip.

In repose his face was relaxed and peaceful, and his lips seemed fuller and softer. She could still see faint smudges under his eyes, but they were much less pronounced than the last time she's seen him. With her fingertips, she lightly stroked the hollow of his throat, fascinated with the tiny pulse that beat there. She smiled complacently. A girl could get used to waking up this way.

He shifted slightly, turning his head on the pillow, so she eased away from him and propped herself on one elbow. *Let him sleep,* she thought. *He's certainly earned it.* Of course she was eager to know why he'd gone flying off to Sacramento the day before, but that could wait. Some things were more important than curiosity.

Outside her closed door, she heard the sound of Patrick's bare feet slapping on the hardwood floor, followed a few seconds later by the whir of the electric can opener.

Slowly and quietly, to keep from disturbing Mack, she slipped out of bed and into her favorite fuzzy robe. There was a half bath adjoining her bedroom, but she knew the pipes would rattle when she turned on the water, so she decided to use the big bathroom on the other side of Patrick's room.

She paused to look at Mack again. Already he had stretched his long legs across the space where she had lain, and one arm was flung carelessly across her pillow. Smiling a secret smile, she closed the door noiselessly behind her.

She hurried through the morning routine, humming to herself. When she emerged from the bathroom, the smell of freshly perked coffee drew her into the kitchen.

"Top o' the mornin'," she said, using her father's favorite wake-up call. "Something sure smells good."

"Coffee's ready," Patrick said unnecessarily, without turning around.

A box of pancake mix sat on the counter, along with milk and eggs. His preoccupation with measuring the ingredients into a mixing bowl might have accounted for his terse greeting, Sarah thought, but not for the rigid set of his shoulders.

"Did you sleep well?" he asked after another interval of silence.

She suddenly realized what was wrong with him. Mack's clothes were in the living room, but Mack wasn't. She poured a cup of coffee before she answered.

"I slept beautifully," she said, cradling the hot mug between her palms. "Patrick, if there's something you want to say, do it now, before Mack wakes up."

He pushed the bowl away with an angry gesture. "That's typical. He sneaks into your room in the dead of night, takin' advantage, and you want to protect him."

"He didn't sneak, Patrick. I invited him."

His face was a study in conflicting emotions. Embarrassment battled with indignation, and the result was a comical color somewhere between red and purple. "Invited him, is it? Sarah Kathleen, this is not what your mother raised you for. If she could see you now, she'd be turnin' over in her grave."

"If she could see me now," Sarah commented, trying not to laugh, "she wouldn't *be* in her grave, Patrick."

"You know what I mean! Haven't you been hurt enough, Sarah? He walks a tightrope every day of his life, and if you don't stay away from him, you'll wind up dead."

Mack's voice, quiet and unexpected, startled both of them. "You're absolutely right, Patrick." Still shirtless and barefoot, his hair rumpled from sleep, he walked into the kitchen. "I've gotten Sarah and you mixed up in a dangerous game, and I wouldn't blame you if you punched my face in."

"It's occurred to me," Patrick growled.

"But you're wrong about last night," Mack continued, ignoring Sarah's attempt to interrupt. "It's been a while since I had to justify myself to somebody's big brother, but for what it's worth, I was on her bed, not in it. As for the rest, I'm leaving today. Carver and Fulgham are probably in Mexico by now, and the NSB won't be back if I'm not here. Sarah can get back to normal and you can stop worrying about her."

Patrick, the wind taken out of his sails, dropped his eyes and said nothing. Sarah, on the other hand, had quite a bit to say.

"Don't you dare talk about me like I'm not even in the room," she stormed, banging her coffee cup down. "Nobody got me into anything. I got myself in, because that's the way I wanted it. I make my own decisions, Mack, so get off your guilt trip. And as for *you*," she blazed, turning to face her brother.

He held up one hand, forestalling her. "I know what you're gonna say, and you're right. Your bed is none of my business."

"Exactly." She reached for a paper towel and began mopping up the coffee that had sloshed out of her cup. "Now then, what did you find out in Sacramento?" she asked Mack. "And what's all this about you leaving today?"

"Sarah," Mack began, "let's have breakfast first...."

His tone confirmed the suspicion that had started growing a few minutes earlier. "You're trying to put me off because you don't want to tell me about Sacramento."

"I'll tell you, but not right now. I want Dolly and Raylene to hear it, too, and there's no point in going through it twice."

Sarah's heart sank. Whatever he had to say, she wasn't going to like it.

"Well, getting them here won't be a problem," Patrick said with a puzzled frown. "Since it's Sunday, we decided to go bowling. They'll be here about eleven."

"What's wrong, Mack?" Sarah asked. "Why do you want to see Raylene and Dolly?"

He turned away and reached for a cup. "Nothing's wrong. Just let me do this my way, Sarah. You'll know all about it in a couple of hours."

She started to argue, but seeing the set of his jaw, she abandoned the idea. As he'd said, she'd know all about it soon. But she thought she'd already figured it out—Mack had found Kay, and he was going after her. And he intended to leave Sarah behind.

SARAH HAD TO ADMIT that Patrick made better coffee than she did, but he didn't know beans about pancakes. She prodded the soggy mess in her plate and looked balefully at Mack.

"This stuff is terrible."

"Not really. *My* pancakes are terrible. This is just bad."

"Well, I'm not going to eat it."

"Fine."

"I'm going to throw it out and make some oatmeal."

"Fine."

"And I'm going to make toast. Whoever heard of oatmeal without toast?"

"Toast is good. I'll have mine with light butter."

"Fine." She got up, whisking his plate out of his hand.

As she marched to the sink, he captured her wrist in a gentle grasp and pulled her to a halt. "Sarah, stop pouting. I'll tell you about Sacramento when—"

"When Dolly and Raylene get here." She pulled her arm away and went to the sink, where she began scraping the pancakes into the garbage disposal. "That's what you've been saying for the past hour. And I'm not pouting, I'm worried."

Mack moved up behind her and put his arms around her waist. "I know. But I've got my reasons. Trust me, okay?"

Dropping the bowl into the sink, she turned in his arms and leaned her forehead against his chest. "It's serious, isn't it?"

He kissed her, and for a moment she forgot about Sacramento, forgot about everything except how much she loved him. But when he released her, she quickly regained her memory. "Just tell me why you sent Paddy out to buy more tapes and I won't ask any more questions."

"Sarah, you'll always ask questions." He kissed her again, just a peck, then tilted her chin to look at the bruises on her face. He touched her cheek gently. "Have I ever told you how pretty you look in green?"

She pinched his arm, only half-playfully. "Keep it up, buster, and pretty soon we'll be color coordinated." Pushing him away, she returned to the breakfast bar and sat down. "Mack, I'm really worried." She couldn't say what she really thought—that she was afraid she'd never see him again.

But he seemed to read her mind. "Don't think that way. I'll be all right."

Of course he would, she told herself. He could take care of himself. She was working herself into a state over nothing. Except that it wasn't nothing. He would be gone soon, into what could only be described as a life-and-death situation, and all she could do was smile and wave goodbye.

Sarah had never dreamed that being in love would be so hard.

THE GROUP GATHERED in Sarah's living room was a solemn one. They had all listened in stunned disbelief while Mack explained the reason for his trip to Sacramento and the outcome of it. But it was even more difficult for them to accept the need for the promise he extracted from them.

"I'm going to Belen to find Kay," he said, turning off the tape recorder, "and you four are the only insurance I have. You have the story on tape, and if anything goes wrong, it's your responsibility to see that it's made public."

Sarah barely heard him. In a voice that bore no resemblance to her own, she asked, "When are you leaving?"

"I don't know," Mack replied. "There's still a lot of legwork to do. Greyson said that so far the weapons haven't arrived in Belen, so there's a good chance they haven't been shipped yet. If I can find them, I can follow them right to Vernon's camp."

"That's a mighty big *if*," Dolly remarked, still looking somewhat dazed. "Where would you start?"

"Back in L.A., with Billy Thomas. If he doesn't remember the shipping schedules, I'll just go on to Belen and scout around until I find the compound."

He spoke with conviction, but Sarah knew it was hard won and tenuous. A million obstacles still lay ahead, and he was as aware of them as she was.

After Dolly and Raylene left, Sarah tried to reason with him. "You know this is crazy, don't you? If you try to leave on your passport, Bridges or Landis will pick you up. And even if you get to Belen, what good will it do? You can't expect any support from Greyson's man. He said so himself."

"I'll work it out," he said, drawing her to him and holding on tightly. "It might take a little time, but I'm too close to give up. Try to believe in me, Sarah. Tell me you trust me and that you won't worry."

In that moment she knew what she had to do. This man—this stubborn, foolhardy, lovable, honorable man—was the most important person in her life. If she lost him, she lost everything.

"I'm not worried," she told him, pulling away, "because I'm going back to Los Angeles with you."

"The hell you are!"

"Sarah, be reasonable," Patrick added. "You're in no shape to go anywhere."

"There's nothing wrong with me except a few bruises," she insisted, "and they won't keep me from helping to plan the trip and tie up the loose ends." She touched Mack's arm, willing him to look at her. "This is something I'm good at—planning and looking ahead. You need me."

"I need to know you're safe."

She had one trump card left to play, but she hated having to do it. "I'm no safer away from you than when I'm with you, and I've got the bruises to prove it. I've paid my dues, Mack. I've got a right to see this thing through. You owe it to me."

"That's blackmail," he said flatly.

"It's the truth," she countered.

He didn't give in immediately, and the argument continued throughout the afternoon. Sarah wasn't worried, though. She'd made her point and won the match, even if she had used underhanded methods. When Mack left for Los Angeles, she knew she'd be going with him. And although he didn't know it yet, she was also going to Belen.

THEY LEFT the next morning, but not in the way of ordinary travelers. First they drove to the zoo, wandered aimlessly for an hour along the winding paths, and eventually walked to a nearby restaurant and ordered a meal. Minutes later, they left through the kitchen exit and crossed an alley, eventually winding up at another restaurant, where Mack phoned for a cab to take them to the airport.

They got on a commuter flight, and by five that afternoon, they'd picked up the Cherokee from the airport and were on their way to talk to Billy Thomas. Neither of them felt much like talking. Mack was still angry with her, and she was edgy, expecting to see NSB agents lurking behind every bush.

So they rode in silence. Mack concentrated on surviving the Los Angeles freeways, and she looked for the exit sign he'd mentioned.

"This is it," she said, pointing when the sign came up.

Mack took the ramp and turned right at the first traffic light. The boulevard, wide and congested with traffic, led to a pleasant community of small, well-tended stucco homes. The sidewalks and lawns teemed with children on bicycles and in swings, and most of the adults Sarah saw were under middle age. A young community, made up of couples who'd already started living their futures.

Mack parked in the driveway of a one-story, cream-colored stucco house. As he and Sarah approached the front door, it opened and a young woman, plumply pregnant, stepped out.

Mack introduced himself. "Billy's not here?"

"No, he's on a fishing trip with his brother. They've been gone several days."

Sarah sensed Mack's frustration. "It's very important, Mrs. Thomas," she said. "Is there any way we can reach him?"

The young woman shook her head. "They're just camping. But if he doesn't come in tonight, he'll probably call— he usually does. Can I give him a message?"

"Have him call me," Mack told her urgently. He recited his number and she repeated it back to him. "Remember to tell him that it's important."

They left Mrs. Thomas with a bewildered expression, and she was still watching them as they drove away.

Mack held the steering wheel in a death grip and cursed. "*Maybe* he'll be back tonight. *Maybe* he'll call. I don't have time for maybes!"

"You'll just have to hope for the best . . ." she began.

"Hope isn't going to get me to Belen, Sarah. Even if Billy does call, there's a chance he won't know anything about a Belen shipment. I've got to have something to fall back on."

"Like what? I know what you're thinking, Mack, but you can't just go charging down to Central America and hope you stumble over Vernon. It could take weeks to find him in the jungle, if you can find him at all."

He took his eyes off the road long enough to glare at her. "What do you suggest? That I give up, let Kay die?"

"Stop it! You know I didn't mean that. But there has to be something we haven't thought of."

He glanced in the rearview mirror. "We'll debate it later. Right now, I think Bridges has picked us up again." He reached over and checked her seat belt. "Hold on. I'm going to take the next exit. Watch for a dark blue Chevy."

Before she had time to react, he cut the wheel sharply to the right, crossing two lanes of traffic to reach the exit ramp. The maneuver left a wake of screeching tires and honking horns, but no one followed them off the freeway. At the next intersection, he pulled into a McDonald's and stopped. After five minutes, he seemed to breathe more easily.

"False alarm," he said. "I must be getting paranoid."

"Okay by me," she said, "as long as it keeps us alive."

He made a visible effort to relax, but Sarah could tell he wasn't completely convinced he'd made a mistake, especially when he decided to park two streets over from his apartment and sneak through alleys and yards to his own back door.

As soon as they were safely inside, he called Mrs. Thomas again and cursed when she told him Billy still wasn't home.

"Mack," Sarah protested, "it's been less than an hour."

He didn't answer. Instead he flipped through the *Yellow Pages*, found what he was looking for and dialed. She listened in stunned silence as he made an airline reservation under a phony name, destination Nicaragua.

She understood the deception. The NSB might be monitoring the airlines, waiting for Mack to try to leave the country, so he couldn't use his own name or his true destination. He'd fly into Nicaragua and make the final connection from there. She even understood his reasons for doing it. But understanding didn't make it any easier to bear. If he went into Belen blind, asking questions, snooping around, his chances of failure would quadruple. And in this case, failure could mean death.

"It's just in case, Sarah," he said when he hung up and saw her face. "If Billy hasn't called by tomorrow, I have to leave. Those weapons could be on their way to Belen right now. Once they arrive, Vernon's dead and so is Kay."

She merely nodded, because she couldn't trust herself to speak. He gathered her close and held her for a long time while she pondered a bitter irony—the very qualities that made her love him were the same qualities that could take him away from her forever.

"Do you know we've never been on a date?" His breath was warm against her ear.

"A what?"

"A date," he repeated. "A real date." He tilted her face up. "Miss O'Shaughnessy, would you like to have dinner with me tonight?"

She laughed in surprise. "I would've thought restaurants would be the last thing on your mind. What about Bridges?"

"We'll just go out the way we came in." He kissed her nose. "Don't think this is just for your sake, to get your mind off things. I need a healthy dose of normalcy, and I need to spend time with you. This may be our last chance to be just an ordinary couple...until I come back from Belen."

She clung to him, knowing that what he was really asking for was a memory, something joyous to take with him. *This won't be our last night together,* she wanted to say. *I'll be with you in Belen, and we'll all come back together.* But she didn't dare say the words aloud. If he knew what she planned, he would tie her up and send her back to San Francisco in a crate.

So she kissed him and smiled. "I'd love to have dinner with you tonight, Mr. Macklin."

THE RESTAURANT was all she could have asked for. She felt a bit underdressed in slacks and sandals, while most of the other women were dressed to match the elegant decor, but she didn't mind. With wine and candlelight and Mack sitting just across the table, she had no need for jewels and silk dresses.

Later she couldn't really remember what they had talked about. There was so much they didn't know about each other that they found it easy to move from one topic to another, discovering the little everyday details that mean both nothing and everything.

More important was what they *didn't* talk about. Neither of them mentioned Belen, or the NSB...or the future. It was as though they'd made an unspoken agreement to live only from moment to moment, at least for the evening. The real world, with its attendant problems, would intrude soon enough.

They finished a bottle of wine and watched the candle burn down to a nub, and eventually Sarah noticed they were the only customers left. "Do you get the feeling we've overstayed our welcome?" she said, nodding toward a waiter who hovered a short distance away.

Mack grinned. "Maybe if I tipped him a buck, he'd let us stall all night."

"Not likely." The waiter, scenting their imminent departure, was already heading their way, wearing an expression of utmost relief.

Mack paid the bill, then asked Sarah to wait while he tried to call Billy Thomas one more time, and the lingering romance of the evening was blown away like mist in the wind. Already the world was intruding, and they weren't even out the door yet.

But she couldn't blame Mack for being anxious, and she fervently hoped he'd get through this time. She glanced at her watch. Eleven o'clock. If Billy was coming home tonight, surely he would be there by now.

She watched while Mack dialed, prepared to see him hang up in disgust. But this time he hit pay dirt. As he spoke into the receiver, she hurried to stand beside him.

"Anything going to Belen?" she heard him say. "Yeah, that's it...! What kind of equipment...? Where did it go from there...? Yes, I understand. Do you remember the ship date...? Thanks, Billy, I appreciate it."

"Well?" she asked breathlessly, grabbing his arm.

"Vernon moved out a huge shipment of farm equipment a day ahead of the IRS. It was going to a mission in Belen. La Iglesia de la Reina Roja."

"The Church of the Red Queen!" If they needed any final proof, this was it. "We've found it, Mack."

"Not quite. Billy doesn't know exactly where it is now, just somewhere in the port, but he remembers that it wasn't scheduled to ship until late in the month."

"Then we've got it made. Today is only the twenty-fourth."

"Yeah, but I still need to find the actual shipment. Following those weapons straight to Vernon's front door is the only way I can be sure of getting to Kay before that compound is blown sky-high. How the hell do you find one shipment in a place as big as the Port of Los Angeles?"

"By asking. Mack, the port has a public information office that keeps a current list of all cargo and destination. All we have to do is call them tomorrow and ask which ship it's going on and when."

His mouth dropped open the tiniest bit. "Ask for it? It's that simple?"

"Yep," she replied, trying to laugh at him. "It's that simple."

He hugged her so hard she couldn't breathe. "Sarah, you're a miracle. I don't know what I'd do without you."

"I don't intend to let you find out." She tugged at his sleeve. "Come on, let's go home and plan strategy."

They walked outside into the night, still laughing. Sarah was elated. At last all the pieces had come together and they could form a clear, workable plan. Soon, maybe in as little as a week, they could have Kay home and start living a normal life.

Mack had left the Cherokee in the parking lot at the side of the restaurant rather than on the street, and the lighting was dim. He fumbled with the keys, trying to find the door lock; they slipped from his fingers.

As he stooped to pick them up, Sarah heard a faint spit of sound and the window of the vehicle exploded. She stumbled backward, too stunned to cry out; then suddenly Mack yanked her to the ground, rolled her under the Cherokee.

Another spit. This time the bullet ricocheted off the pavement not two feet from Mack's head.

Sarah still hadn't found her voice, but she finally understood the message. Someone was trying to kill them.

Chapter Ten

Mack pushed her farther under the vehicle.

"He's on the roof," he said in a near whisper. She felt him press something into her hand. They key ring. "Give me three minutes, then get in the car and drive out of here."

"Not without you . . . !"

"Three minutes, Sarah. If I'm not back by then, you leave."

He crawled away, leaving her alone. For a few seconds, she could hear the slight rasp of his soles on the pavement as he sprinted away; then even that bit of comfort faded as the sound dwindled and died.

She had no way to judge the time; it was too dark to see her watch, so she tried counting.

One, two, three, four . . .

She was afraid to move, afraid to breathe, because even a whisper of sound might give her away.

Forty-three, forty-four, forty-five . . .

She could see nothing, hear nothing, not even a gust of wind. The universe seemed to have frozen in place.

Sixty-seven, sixty-eight, sixty-nine . . .

A prisoner of time, deprived of sight and sound, she became aware of other sensations. The rough, gritty feel of the pavement beneath her palms; the sharp burn of pain in her knees where the skin had been abraded through the thin material of her slacks.

One fifty-five, one fifty-six, one fifty-seven...

A trickle of sweat crawled down her forehead, across her right eyelid. She blinked the sting away.

One seventy-eight—Mack, where are you?—one seventy-nine, one eighty...

She scooted from beneath the Cherokee and crouched beside the door, listening. The night was quiet, too quiet. No footsteps, no Mack. She aimed the key at the lock and missed, tried again and made it. The interior light came on when she opened the door, and she dropped to the ground again, her heart thudding.

She slid across the seat, closing the door with faint click. Again the key was contrary; or maybe it was her hand that was so traitorous. At last the key slipped into the ignition.

She started the engine and the roar was deafening. But she couldn't leave, not yet, not even to get help. She would wait a few more minutes. If he wasn't back by then, she would have to look for him.

A sudden clatter from behind the restaurant wrenched a gasp from her. *Mack.* She had pulled the door handle, was opening it, when a man burst around the corner, running hard and fast across the parking lot. Mack was right behind him.

Sarah threw the car into gear and it leaped forward, directly into the man's path. He hit the front fender with a thud and rebounded, landing on his back, while Sarah stomped on the brake. She watched as Mack bent over him and took something from his hand. A gun. The man stirred, then groaned and fell back.

Then Mack was in the car, telling her to drive like hell.

The Cherokee felt big and ungainly as she urged it into a tight circle, and she missed the driveway, bouncing over the curb and into the street.

"Where are we going?" she asked when her teeth stopped rattling.

"Not to the apartment." He flexed his right hand as they passed under a streetlight, and she saw that the knuckles were scraped and raw, his thumb swollen. "And we need to ditch the car. They'll be looking for it."

She shivered, and it had nothing to do with the weather. "Why don't we go to the police?"

"I know Bridges, Sarah. If he hasn't already got out a warrant on me, he will as soon as he finds out what a lousy shot he hired. The next best thing to killing me is locking me up for a few weeks so he won't have to worry about keeping me out of Belen."

"Okay, no apartment, no cops. And we don't dare try to check into a hotel looking like this." She thought for a moment. "We can stay with Dale."

"Bad idea, getting somebody else mixed up in this."

"Well, we can't drive around all night. I'm going to find a phone."

A few minutes later, she spotted a service station that was obviously closed for the night. She pulled behind it and parked, then ran to the pay phone in front, praying that Dale would be home.

He was. Yes, he told her, they could stay with him; yes, he would pick them up; no, he wouldn't ask any questions.

She ran back to the Cherokee, where Mack leaned against the fender, waiting. "He's on his way, but it'll be about twenty minutes." She shivered again, hugged her arms against her body.

"Come here." He took her into his arms, and she realized that was what she'd been waiting for. For a while, she listened to his heartbeat, reassured by its steady, strong rhythm.

"Why?" she asked finally. "All you did was come back home. Why should they try to kill you for that?"

She felt his shoulders tighten. "They must have a tap on my phone. Bridges found out I called the airlines."

Burrowing her face against his chest, she breathed in his scent. "I thought you weren't coming back," she said in a muffled voice.

He ran his hands up her back, to her head, and threaded his fingers in her hair. "I'll always come back to you, Sarah. Always."

DALE, BLESS HIS HEART, was as good as his word. He was there in eighteen minutes and he didn't ask a single question, except "How ya doin'?"

At the house, he gave them keys to the back door and to a year-old Porsche, which he said he didn't drive. "My knees hit the steering wheel," he explained. Then he showed them the bedrooms and the bath, gave Sarah a handmade silk shirt to sleep in and went to bed.

A shower helped restore Sarah's equilibrium, and the prospect of hot tea helped even more. She padded barefoot into the kitchen, where she found that Mack had already started to heat the water.

He looked her up and down, grinning, "Love the outfit," he teased. "New designer?"

"The latest from L.A. Nightshirts by Dale." She rolled up the sleeves some more so they wouldn't cover her hands, and got two cups from the cabinet.

"I guess the first thing we ought to do is get you some new clothes," he said. "You'll stop traffic if you go out dressed like that."

She turned to face him. "And what's the second thing we ought to do?"

He knew what she meant. "Nothing's changed, Sarah. Tomorrow we call the port and get the name of that ship. After that we play it by ear."

"Okay. I've got a couple of ideas, depending on what we find out tomorrow. But I think I know how you can get out of the country, and Bridges will never know."

"Why don't we talk about it now?"

She swallowed. "No, not now. In the morning. Right now I want to sit down and drink a cup of hot tea. I want things to be the way they were in the restaurant, just for a little while longer."

One of the things she loved most about Mack was that you didn't have to talk something to death to make him understand.

He kissed her, just once, and it was sweet and loving and undemanding. Then he pulled out a chair, bowed her into it and served her a cup of hot tea.

WHEN SARAH WENT into the kitchen at eight-thirty the next morning, she found a note from Dale propped on the coffee maker:

Gone to save major corporation from financial ruin. Call Sheraton in Houston if you need me. Take what you want and leave the rest—remember half of it's yours, anyway.

Yours (and I mean that sincerely),
Dale

She was still smiling when Mack walked in. He read the note and laid it on the table.

"He's a nice guy, Sarah. And he's crazy about you."

"Is that your subtle way of asking why I haven't settled down with good old Dale and raised a family?"

He chuckled, a nice, mellow sound that made her feel good. "Yeah, I guess so."

She brushed a tangle of curls away from her eyes. "It just never happened. There's no spark. I mean, I love Dale, but I don't *love* him, you know?"

"Yes," he said quietly. "I know."

When the silence drew out to the edge of awkwardness, she looked away. "I guess I should think about fixing us some breakfast. We've got a big day ahead. Do you like French toast?"

"Sarah, wait a minute. I just talked to the public information office at the port." He touched her cheek, drew his finger down to her chin. "You were right. All I had to do was ask."

"And?"

"And there are eight large crates of farm equipment going to San Sebastian, Belen, aboard the Liberian flagship *Helena*."

"When?"

"On the twenty-seventh. Day after tomorrow."

Day after tomorrow. The words rang hollowly in Sarah's head, and the enormity of what he'd undertaken hit her all over again, almost as though she were hearing it for the first time. All along, while she thought she'd been anticipating the goal, she'd only been looking forward to the thrill of each new discovery.

The goal was in sight now, but it wasn't thrilling. It was sobering. The *Helena* would sail day after tomorrow. They had only two days to prepare, and a double threat to prepare for: Vernon and Bridges.

"Well," she said on a deep breath, "I think we'd better talk. We've got some serious planning to do."

They both decided to settle for toast, juice and coffee, and Sarah performed the small domestic chores automatically, her mind already racing to pull her thoughts together into a cohesive whole.

"The first thing is getting you into Belen, and since Bridges will be watching all the airlines, your best bet is to sail with the *Helena*."

"You mean book passage? Bridges is sure to have it covered, too."

"I mean stow away." The toast popped up, and she placed it on a platter. "It wouldn't be very comfortable, but it's the simplest solution. Here, put some butter on these."

"Simple? Sarah, I can think of a few things to call that idea, but 'simple' isn't one of them."

"Okay," she conceded after a moment, "maybe *simple*'s the wrong word. Let's say it's the most workable plan, because it gives us several options. You could buy a longshoreman's card, or try to hire on the tug that will service the ship, but the time factor's against you. I think you should bribe one of the tug's crew to let you ride out on the barge when the ship is refueled."

"You've really put a lot of thought into this, haven't you?" he said, studying her face. "You must have been awake all night."

The coffee maker gave a final hiss as she poured the orange juice. "I didn't have to stay awake, thank goodness. I've had this worked out for a long time."

"Just in case you ever needed to stow away, huh?"

"Don't be cute," she said, tossing him a jar of marmalade. "It's something I used in my book. I did a lot of research, Mack, and talked to a lot of people, so I know I'm on solid ground."

He brushed the back of her hand with his own. "I trust you, Sarah. That amazing mind of yours has gotten us this far, so you don't have to convince me of anything." He twisted the lid off the marmalade and spooned some onto a piece of toast. "Okay, I think I can handle the bribery—my savings account is fairly healthy. But how do I know who to bribe?"

"The public information office again. I'll call and get the names of the owner's representative and the ship's agent. Then you call the agent, tell him *you're* the rep and ask who's handling the refueling."

He had raised the toast to his mouth, but he stopped in mid-bite. "Sarah, this is beginning to sound mighty complicated."

"That's just because I'm throwing everything at you at once. We'll take it one step at a time, and it'll work out fine. Just remember the main objective. You want to get on the fuel barge. The barge is pushed out to the lightering position by a tugboat. When the bunkering is completed, the *Helena* will lower a Jacob's ladder, and the captain of the tug will go on board to get a receipt for the fuel. That's what you'll be waiting for, the ladder."

"And I just climb on board while nobody's looking?"

Sarah ignored the trace of sarcasm in his voice. "Basically, yes. Then you find the cargo hold and stay there until the ship docks in San Sebastian." She saw the beginning of mutiny in his expression and sighed. "I'm sorry, Mack. I don't mean to sound smug. I'm just trying to give you the overall picture. We'll go over the details again, as many times as you like. This is just the groundwork."

"I know. But it's like learning a new language. Agents, owner's representatives, bunkering." Though his features were perfectly composed, there was a note of worry in his voice. "I know I said I trusted you, and I do. But are you absolutely sure this will work? If something goes wrong..."

Anyone else might have thought he was worried about his own safety, but Sarah knew better. He was thinking about the time that would be wasted if he got caught. "I can't give you a guarantee," she said gently, "but I truly believe this is your best shot. Otherwise I wouldn't even consider it."

For several minutes they ate in silence. Sarah watched Mack with something akin to awe. She had just outlined a proposal that any other man would have laughed at, yet he not only listened to it, he assumed that she knew what she was talking about. In essence, he trusted her to come up with a plan that would protect not only him, but Kay, as well.

He spun his coffee cup on the table, then raised his eyes to meet hers. "Okay. From now on, you're the tactical commander and I'm the troops." He smiled, and for Sarah it was sunshine after a rainy day. "You're my good-luck charm, Pollyanna. Lead on."

Every day she thought she couldn't possibly love him more, and every day she did.

ODDLY, once he had committed himself to a course of action, he seemed to relax instead of growing tenser, as she would have expected. She supposed it had something to do with his training, his years with the NSB—it was almost as though he used the stress, digested it and turned it into a different kind of fuel.

Whatever the reason, his mood was remarkably light. He laughed often and made silly little jokes. A stranger meeting him for the first time would never have suspected he was in training to become a one-man assault force. And if that mind-set was what he needed to function most effectively, Sarah was more than happy to foster it.

Humming off-key, he started a list of the equipment and supplies he would need, while Sarah called the port. She scribbled the names of the owner's representative and the agent of the *Helena* on a paper towel, looked up the agent's telephone number and gave the information to Mack.

She listened to the call he made with only half her attention. The other half was busy making her own plans. She intended to try to convince him that she should be on board the *Helena*, too, but she already knew how he would react. As he would say, she needed a contingency plan.

Running over the possibilities in her mind, she focused on one man who not only had the clout to help her, but who owed her a favor. Oscar Witherspoon.

Mack hung up the phone with a triumphant flourish. "The tug belongs to Garibaldi Brothers, and it's captained by Willie Rose. They refuel the *Helena* tomorrow morning at ten, and it sails at four." His arms circled her waist and he whirled her around in a funny little dance step. "It's all falling into place. We're close, honey, really close." He kissed her with a loud smack. "I don't know how I'll get along without you in Belen."

"You don't have to get along without me—"

He clamped his hand over her mouth. "No. Absolutely not. Don't say it—don't even think about it. You're not going to Belen." He spun her around again. "You're going shopping."

"Shopping? Right now?"

"Unless you intend to go bar hopping in Dale's shirt."

"Mack, you don't even drink. And in case it's slipped your mind, you're leaving tomorrow morning."

"Not unless I do some heavy-duty bribing tonight," he reminded her. "And everybody knows the only place to conduct bribery is in a dark, smoke-filled room. Come on, cover up those gorgeous legs of yours and let's go. We've got a lot of ground to cover."

HE INSISTED that his own clothes didn't need any attention. With only one button off his shirt and a small smear of grease on his jeans, he wouldn't look any worse than anybody else. But Sarah's problem was a bit more drastic. Her blouse had also gotten grease on it, but somehow the effect was more startling on beige linen than on blue denim. She wiped her slacks with a damp cloth and looked at them critically. Dale's shirt would hide the worst of the damage, and with the shirt belted she would look passable, if not exactly fashionable.

Their first stop was a huge sporting goods store. Sarah could have spent hours browsing through the unbelievable array of camping equipment—tents, stoves, lanterns, clothes for all seasons, including an outfit that made her mouth water. She looked at the khaki walking shorts and matching military-style shirt each time she passed the display, but the price tags told her they were definitely out of her league.

Mack didn't seem to be inhibited by either the variety or the prices. He knew exactly what he wanted. A sturdy waterproof knapsack, a compass, two canteens, a utility knife and a mess kit. Sarah threw in a first-aid kit for good measure, a cigarette lighter and a lightweight, long-sleeved men's shirt.

Mack had already stuffed the purchases in the Porsche and closed Sarah's door, when he headed back into the store. "Forgot something," he called over his shoulder.

Five minutes later he slid behind the steering wheel and tossed a bag into Sarah's lap. Inside the bag she found a pair of khaki walking shorts and a matching shirt. They were even the right size.

"Mack, they're too expensive."

"Well, the clerk said I couldn't return them, and they won't fit me."

He wouldn't let her say thank-you, but he did accept a hug.

Buying a dozen assorted foil-wrapped pouches of dehydrated foods at a supermarket was an in-and-out operation, but they spent considerably more time at a boutique, where Mack insisted that a proper bar-hopping outfit was a matter for serious deliberation.

Sarah fell in love with a turquoise dress, sleeveless and simply cut, while Mack held out for a black sequined jumpsuit. Sarah won the argument, but he insisted on throwing in a pair of sandals and a long silk scarf swirled with aqua and lavender.

The boutique ended their shopping spree, and the next stop was short and essential: an automatic teller. Then they went to the port.

Mack drove around the sprawling complex until he found Garibaldi Brothers, a metal building with a faded sign over the door. He parked some distance away, and for perhaps half an hour they sat in the Porsche, watching the foot traffic in and out of the building. Mack seemed particularly interested in a thin young man with dark hair and rounded shoulders who was working on a disassembled engine of some kind.

"That's our mark," he said after a while.

"Do you know him?"

"No, but I know the look. He's hungry."

Eventually Mack left the car and spent several minutes talking to the boy, and when he came back, he said, "Well, you've got a reason to wear that new dress. Nine o'clock tonight at a place on the waterfront called Jackie's."

She returned his smile, but her heart wasn't in it. Ever since they'd gotten to the port, she had felt the buoyancy slipping away from her bit by bit. She'd let herself be carried along on the crest of Mack's high spirits, willing to put the reason for their outing aside and simply enjoy the experience. But this reminder was too strong to be ignored. The magic was gone, and she didn't think she would be able to recapture it.

She sensed that Mack was feeling much the same. He still laughed and teased, he'd lost none of the tenderness he'd been bestowing on her, but the change was there. She could see it in his eyes, they had a distant look now, and she knew that no matter what he looked at, he was seeing Belen.

As soon as they entered the house, Mack shooed her away. "I'm making dinner," he told her, heading for the kitchen. "Find something to do for an hour and don't look over my shoulder. We chefs are a temperamental breed."

"Can't I slice or dice or something?"

"Absolutely not."

"I guess I could call Paddy. It'll probably take an hour to explain what's going on."

She turned to leave the room, but his voice stopped her.

"Sarah, be careful what you say. There's a good chance your phone is tapped."

Of course. Bridges was probably frantic since she and Mack had dropped out of sight, and he wouldn't overlook the possibility that she might get in touch with her brother. She'd have to find some way of getting her message across without really saying anything.

Patrick answered on the first ring, and she knew he'd probably been haunting the apartment, waiting for her to call.

"Hi, Paddy. It's me, Frances." Frances had been their mother's name, the only one she could think of that might put him on guard.

He didn't respond at once, but when he did, his voice was blessedly normal. "Hi, Frances. I was just thinking about you."

"Hey, I'm sorry I didn't call sooner, but you know how it is, there's always so much going on."

"Tell me about it," he said dryly. "It's the same way around here. You never know what's going to happen next. What's on your mind?"

"Well, I was just thinking that we haven't been bowling in a while, and I wondered if you were free tonight."

She could practically hear the wheels turning in his head. "Yeah, tonight's good. What time?"

"About eight. I sure hope you can make it. We've got a lot to catch up on."

"I wouldn't miss it for the world. See you at eight."

She heard the click when he hung up and, a split second later, another click, different in tone but clearly audible. Mack had been right. The NSB was still making its presence felt. Bridges wanted Mack in the worst way, and she found herself wondering how much of his obsession could be attributed to his warped interpretation of patriotism, and how much to a desire for revenge that had been festering for five years....

SHE DECIDED to dress for dinner, since Mack was going to so much trouble to give them another memory to hold on to. The new dress was perfect for her coloring, and when she draped the scarf around her shoulders, the mirror told her she couldn't have made a better choice.

Mack's bon voyage dinner was a masterpiece of understated elegance. They ate in the formal dining room instead of the kitchen, to the accompaniment of soft music from Dale's stereo. The steaks were perfectly pink, the salad fresh and crisp, the wine slightly fruity and not too dry. He'd even found a candle for the center of the table.

"The temperamental chef has my compliments," she said when they were finished.

"Since this is the only meal I know how to make, I try to do it up right. And Dale gets credit for the wine. He picked it out. I just poured it."

"Ah, a temperamental, *modest* chef. A rare combination."

"The best things are always rare," he said, bowing over her hand.

She laughed, enjoying the absurdities, enjoying a side of Mack she hadn't suspected. Since this morning, when he'd made up his mind which course to follow, he'd been a different person. No, not different, she amended. Today he'd been the *real* person, the man who had been buried under an unbearable weight of tension and anxiety.

"So," he said, breaking her train of thought, "what did Patrick have to say?"

"Nothing yet." She told him how she'd used the coded conversation to arrange to call Paddy at the bowling alley. "And my line is tapped. I heard a double click when Paddy hung up."

He simply nodded,. "I know Bridges, Sarah. I know how his mind works. That's the only way I manage to stay ahead of him."

"You're ahead of him now, but what about later, when you get back from Belen? He's not going to just give up. He hates you, Mack."

He took her hand and held it against his chest. "Remember what you told me this morning? We take one step at a time. The first step is getting to Belen, and you're helping me do that. What happens after that is my responsibility, and you're not to worry about it."

But she did worry about it, along with everything else on her worry list. She worried about it while she loaded the dishwasher. She worried about it while she called Patrick at the bowling alley, assuring him that she was safe and trying to answer his hundred and one questions over the crash of balls and pins.

She continued to worry about it when she and Mack sat at a dirty booth in Jackie's Bar and struck a deal with a nervous young man named Trini who needed money to pay off his gambling debts.

As they drove home from the bar, she thought about the serenity prayer: *Lord, give me the strength to accept the things I cannot change, the courage to change the things I can and the wisdom to know the difference.* Until now, those words had always made sense to her, but no longer.

She couldn't change the situation, but neither could she accept it. The only thing she could do was worry about it.

AT ONE O'CLOCK in the morning, Sarah rolled up the sleeves of Dale's silk shirt one more time and shifted position on the sofa. Mack sat next to her, looking impossibly sexy in a pair of pajama bottoms he'd found in Dale's room.

"Remember," she said to him, "stay in the cargo hold at least forty-eight hours. By then the ship will be in international waters, and the captain probably won't go to the trouble of putting you ashore."

"Sarah, that's the fourth time you've told me."

Actually, she'd gone over everything at least four times, drilling him on the ship's construction, compartments and personnel. She'd explained the duties of each member of the crew so he would be able to approximate their whereabouts at any given time and repeatedly reminded him to conserve his water.

She'd even double-checked the knapsack against the list he'd made, just to be sure he hadn't left something out.

"I don't want you to forget it."

He laid a finger on her lips. "Sarah, enough is enough. We've covered it all, and I'm as ready as I'll ever be. Now it's your turn to listen. As soon as you drop me off at the port, I want you to come straight back here. Call Paddy to let him know you're okay, but whatever you do, don't go back to San Francisco. You'll be safe with Dale until this is over."

"I don't want to be with Dale. I want to be with you."

He sighed. "This is something else we've been over too many times. You're not going to Belen, Sarah."

"Mack, listen to me. We're a good team, and you're going to need help. I know it's going to be dangerous, but I can take care of myself. Whatever happens, I can handle it."

"Sarah, stop it. I don't want to fight with you."

"I don't want to fight, either!" she said, bouncing off the sofa. "And we wouldn't be fighting if you'd listen to me!"

His eyes went suddenly flat, like two pieces of stone. "Now *you* listen, and pay attention, because this is absolutely the last discussion we're going to have about this. You're one of the most resourceful people I know, Sarah, but that damned optimism of yours is going to get you killed someday. Come here, I want to show you something."

He took her wrist in a firm grip and pulled her into the bedroom, where the knapsack lay propped against the wall. Jerking it open, he pulled out the pistol he'd taken from the man in the parking lot. "This is what nearly killed us last night. It's ugly, isn't it? Ugly and deadly. Look at your face! You don't even want to see it. Can you load it? Can you point it at another human being and pull the trigger? Last night it was only one man, but in Belen it could be two or three or twenty, and you don't know how to meet them on their terms, Sarah."

He dropped the weapon back into the knapsack. "Then there's the heat and the terrain. Have you ever walked twenty miles in hundred-degree heat, fighting snakes and mosquitoes every step of the way? And what if we're captured, Sarah—have you given any thought to what a band of guerrilla fighters would do to a woman?"

She hadn't thought about it; for all her farsightedness, the logic she prided herself on, that possibility had never once occurred to her. Stunned, she wondered what else she had overlooked in her complacent determination to get her own way.

He suddenly grasped her shoulders and shook her gently. "You're the most precious thing in the world to me, Sarah O'Shaughnessy, and I've come close to losing you twice. Don't ask me to live through it again."

With a small cry, she threw herself into his arms and clung to him fiercely. "Don't you understand yet? I've lived with the same thing, and now you're asking me to go through weeks of it, with no way to know what's happening, if you're safe, if you're hurt, if you're dead! We've taken care of each other so far, and it would be the same way in Belen. We'll both be safe as long as we're together.''

She heard a soft rumble in his throat. It was laughter, but there was nothing happy about it. ''You almost make sense, Pollyanna. You don't know how easy it would be to give in and take you on that ship with me tomorrow.'' He took her face between his hands and looked at her with hunger in his eyes. ''That's part of the problem, Sarah girl. You make life too easy for me. You bring out everything in me that's good and noble, you ease my way, you make me believe in myself. Yes, I want you with me, every day and night, even in Belen.''

''Then let me come with you,'' she whispered.

''No. Your best chance is here. I have to know that you'll be here, alive and well, when I get back.''

His torment echoed within her, and she longed to ease his pain—*their* pain—even if only for a short time. ''Then I want tonight,'' she said, running her palms over the smooth strength of his shoulders. ''Belen can have you tomorrow, but I want tonight.''

The longing in his face made her tremble with need, and she traced his lips with her fingers. With a groan, he swept her against him, kissed her with an outpouring of passion that left her shaken. His hands touched her with gentle reverence, then with greedy desire; he whispered magic words that touched her soul; he offered her every secret he possessed. And when at last she lay on the bed and he covered her body with his, she cried out at the keen sweetness of it.

Then, wrapped in a feeling of fulfillment and unity that she'd never before dreamed of, she cradled his head between her breasts and held him while he slept.

THE PERSISTENT CHIMING of the doorbell finally penetrated her sleep. Mack, one arm thrown across her, began to stir, and when she slipped out of bed, he sat up.

"Where are you going?" he murmured sleepily, reaching for her.

"To answer the door." She fumbled on the floor for the silk shirt.

The chimes sounded again, and Mack came fully awake. "Sarah, stay here. Whoever it is, they're looking for Dale, not us."

"It might *be* Dale," she answered, trying with only modest success to get the shirt buttoned.

"Dale has a key."

"Maybe he lost it."

Grumbling, he pulled on the pajamas and followed her to the front door. She peeked through the security lens, then looked at him with astonishment.

"Who is it?" he demanded, alarmed. "Bridges?"

"Almost as bad." She threw the lock and opened the door for her brother.

"It's still dark, Patrick," Sarah said, fixing her brother with a killing look. "The top of the morning doesn't happen until the sun comes up."

"Sarah Kathleen," he said mournfully, "is that any way to greet a man who's come nearly four hundred miles to visit his baby sister?"

"Cut the blarney, Patrick," Mack told him. "What are you doing here?"

Patrick beamed at them both and hoisted a knapsack in his hand. "Why, I'm going to Belen with you. I hope I got everything I need. Sarah was talking pretty fast when she told me about it, so I might've missed something."

Sarah couldn't believe this was her practical, conservative brother. "What about your job, Paddy? You make good money with that rig. You can't just walk away and leave it.''

He shrugged. ''I'm tired of being on the road all the time, so I sold the rig yesterday. Got top dollar for it, too. When we get back, I'll look around for something else.'' He fixed her with a knowing look. ''And don't try to tell me it's too dangerous. If you had half a chance, you'd be going, too.''

Sarah certainly couldn't argue with that, since he was exactly right.

But Mack could argue with it, and did. ''Are you crazy?'' he demanded. ''You can't go to Belen.''

''Why not?'' Paddy asked reasonably. ''I'm strong, fairly intelligent, good with my fists, and I know how to stand my ground. Besides, you need all the help you can get, and as far as I can see, I'm the only game in town.''

''But you're not trained for this,'' Mack protested.

''I learn fast.''

''You'd just be one more thing I'd have to worry about. You'd slow me down.''

''Wrong. You could move faster than ever because you'd have somebody watching your back. It's called the buddy system.''

''This isn't your fight. It's different for me. This is something I have to do.''

Patrick looked at Mack consideringly. ''Maybe it's something I have to do, too. I owe you one, Mack.''

That was Patrick's last word on the subject. He'd made his decision, and he intended to stick by it. ''Now if we're through jawing, why don't you catch me up on what's happened so far?''

Mack threw up his hands in disgust, and Sarah left him to cope with the situation as best he could. She wasn't going to try to change her brother's mind. He obviously felt very strongly about this. If, as she suspected, this was Patrick's way of repaying Mack for rescuing her, she could only applaud his motivation.

The men talked for nearly an hour, and as Sarah moved about in the kitchen, making coffee, fixing breakfast, she somehow found the drone of their voices comforting. She still had a drastic decision to make and she was feeling edgy. Self-doubt was alien to her nature, but Mack had made a pretty convincing case for why she shouldn't go to Belen. Knowing she was exposed to that kind of danger would be an agony for him, and the last thing she wanted to do was cause him any more anguish.

But she couldn't rid herself of the conviction that she was meant to be with him, that there would come a time when his life would depend on her presence. She smiled at the thought. Put in those terms, it sounded as though she'd had some sort of mystical revelation, yet she knew herself to be the most pragmatic person on earth. Still, the conviction stood, unshakable and immovable, even with the knowledge that Mack would now have Patrick to lend support.

Elbows propped on the table, she leaned her head into her hands. No matter what she did, one of them would suffer. And she *knew* she was right. Mysticism or not, she simply couldn't silence the voice that told her to go.

She stood up and brushed the hair away from her eyes. She would see Oscar Witherspoon later today. Right now, she would call her lover and her brother in to eat breakfast.

AT EIGHT-THIRTY, Sarah watched the taxi pull into the circular driveway. She'd wanted to drive them to the port, but Mack had said it would be easier to say goodbye here.

Patrick hugged her, then swung both knapsacks over his shoulder and walked outside.

Mack held her shoulders and kissed her once, hard.

"I'll be back, Sarah."

She watched the taxi until it was out of sight, then she went inside and called Oscar Witherspoon.

Chapter Eleven

Sara rode the elevator up to the fifth floor of the large newspaper building where Oscar had been conducting business for most his seventy-five years. Though most people had never heard his name, he ruled an extensive publishing empire and had amassed several fortunes during his colorful lifetime.

His ultraefficient secretary smiled and waved Sarah through to the inner sanctum.

"Sarah," he bellowed in his softest voice when he saw her. "Why the hell haven't you been to see me sooner? How's the book coming?"

Oscar was one of the few people she'd trusted with the secret of Bothwell, since he'd been the first to encourage her to take the plunge. "The book is great, Oscar, but that's not why I'm here. I need a favor."

He scowled, pulling his thick, white eyebrows together. "Hell, why didn't you say so? Been waiting to do something for you ever since you spotted the glitch in that Ackerman story. Saved us one helluva lawsuit, you know."

Sarah grinned. "Don't commit yourself yet, Oscar. You haven't heard what I want, and it's a biggie."

"Anything," he roared, gesturing her to a chair. "Already said so."

"Good. Because now you can't say no even if you want to. Oscar, I want to go to Central America, but I need you to arrange a charter flight for me. And I'll need press credentials."

For a second or two he gazed at her intently, silent except for his loud breathing—he suffered from chronic bronchitis, but refused to give up his cigars. "Where in Central America? No place legal, or you wouldn't need me."

"Belen," she answered. "I have to get into the country without anybody knowing. It's important to me, Oscar."

"Belen?" he exploded. "That piece of swamp is a powder keg, girl. Hasn't been a journalist allowed in since last summer. Out of the question."

She'd expected him to say that. "Come on, Oscar. You owe me, remember? Not five minutes ago you said I could have anything I wanted. Well, this is it. Fix it for me and we're square."

"I never said I'd help you get yourself killed! Tell me why, Sarah. Maybe I'll think about it."

"At the risk of sounding melodramatic, it's a life-and-death secret mission. Honest to God. And it's personal."

Oscar seemed to be chewing on her request, but she couldn't read his eyes behind his thick glasses. At last he said, "I don't like it, but if you tell me it's that urgent, I believe you. When do you want to leave?"

She let out her breath in relief. "As soon as possible, tomorrow at the latest. Can you do it that quickly?"

He pointed his cigar at her. "I can do any damn thing I want, girl. Give me two hours."

As Sarah stood up to go, he winked at her, then picked up the telephone and barked an order into it. The ultraefficient secretary didn't even glance up when Sarah passed the desk; she was too busy scribbling down Oscar's commands.

Oscar would come through for her, she thought as she waited for the elevator. He had more contacts than Colonel Sanders had franchises, and he'd been around long enough to garner IOUs from all of them. She was as good as on her way.

When she called him two hours later, he gave her the details of her flight and said she could pick up her credentials and documentation from the downstairs desk on her way to the airstrip. She was now officially on an exclusive assignment for a magazine under his directorship.

"Oscar, you're wonderful," she told him. "You have no idea how much this means to me."

"I don't know what you're up to, girl," he answered, "but you take care of yourself. I've outlived most of my other friends. It'd be a hell of a note if I outlived you, too."

FORTY-EIGHT HOURS LATER, Sarah was looking at the Red Queen.

La Iglesia de la Reina Roja sat nestled in the most beautiful valley Sarah had ever seen, completely circled by low, rolling hills that sparkled like emeralds under the hot Belen sun. The walls were constructed of massive blocks of rose-red native stone, with that special sense of antiquity that doesn't exist in the United States, simply because the country isn't that old.

She walked into the central courtyard of the church, admiring the rose garden and pretending to be a feature writer for a prestigious magazine, while beside her Sister Teresa nattered on about the glory of La Reina. "And our school is worthy of a separate story, on its own merits. Last year we graduated sixty-two young people, and several of them have gone on to university. Father Bonifacio himself teaches a course in animal husbandry, which is part of the new Regeneration Program."

"I've heard of it," Sarah said. "The church started it several years ago to help the farmers become self-sufficient."

"Yes, and it has been a miracle for our people. We have a . . . cooperation?"

"Cooperative," Sarah supplied.

"Yes, a cooperative that covers more than seventy acres. We now sell our produce everywhere in Belen."

"Then the church isn't dependent on patrons for funds?"

"Not like before. Five years ago La Reina was falling to pieces. If one of your American organizations had not sent aid . . . Well, that is past, is it not? God has truly been good to us, and we give thanks every day that our prayers were answered."

Sarah stopped walking and sat on a marble bench beneath a tree heavy with oranges. "Sister Teresa, this American organization, do you happen to know the name of it?"

The nun frowned. "The name? No, I am sorry. I only know that their generosity helped La Reina become as she was in the past, and that each year a representative visits us during the festival."

"What about this representative, then? Do you know his name?"

"Oh, it is a different person each year, and I do not have a good ear for American names."

Sarah made one final stab at getting something concrete out of this lovely, but maddeningly vague woman. "Paul Vernon. I understand he's one of the patrons of the church. Have you ever met him?"

"Oh, no," Sister Teresa said quickly. "I had never even heard the name before yesterday."

For a moment, Sarah thought she must have misunderstood. "Yesterday?"

"Why, yes. I do not know who Señor Vernon is, but he must be a very famous man in your country. Another

American was here yesterday, and he also mentioned Señor Vernon. He even showed me a picture.''

Sarah lingered long enough to praise the rose garden again, then she hurried through the arched gate to the dilapidated automobile waiting just outside the mission. *Another American,* she thought. It certainly couldn't have been Mack. The *Helena* wasn't due in port for three more days.

She started the engine, such as it was, and shifted into first. With a rattle of bolts, the old DeSoto lurched onto the road and began its labored chugging.

So far she hadn't managed to accomplish a single thing in the two days she'd been here, except uncover another mystery. And she wasn't looking for mysteries; she was looking for solutions. She'd hoped to smooth Mack's way by being able to lead him directly to Vernon's compound. Admittedly it was an ambitious project. After all, if the CIA couldn't find Vernon, who could? But it had been worth a try, because if she'd succeeded, they could have had Kay out of harm's way by a safe margin, and Mack wouldn't have had time to be angry.

Mack. It seemed she spent most of her time thinking about him. When she wasn't missing him, she was dreading his reaction when he found out she was in Belen. Then she would start missing him again. Like now.

He was probably going crazy, shut up in a dark cargo hold, with only hungry rats and a crazy Irishman for company and nothing to do except think about rescuing Kay. Maybe, like Sarah, he used the memory of their last night together for comfort.

She missed him more than she would have believed possible. *I wonder what he's doing right now....*

''BLASTED RATS,'' Mack said with a curse. He aimed a flashlight behind the crate that made up the walls of their temporary home, looking for the rodent that had made off with a pouch of trail mix. "I wouldn't be surprised if he came back with his friends and took the whole damned knapsack."

"Don't be selfish," Patrick teased, shaking with laughter. "All God's children gotta eat."

"Let 'em find their own food," Mack snapped, clicking off the flashlight and letting it drop beside him. "We don't have any to spare."

"Sure we do," Patrick said. "Sarah packed enough stuff for a Boy Scout troop."

Mack grunted. "Not the way you eat."

"But I'm a growing boy," Paddy protested. "I gotta keep up my strength to fight off the bad guys. Speaking of which, once we get to San Sebastian, how do we get off this tub?"

"Just stroll down the gangplank, I guess. It won't make any difference who sees us then."

In the dark, Mack could only imagine the way Patrick would be tilting his head to one side as he considered the logic behind that statement. "Yeah, I guess you're right," Paddy conceded. "After all, what are they gonna do, throw us off the ship?"

Mack grinned. He had to admit that having some company in this stinking hole made life a little more palatable. "Exactly."

"And what then?"

"We follow those crates over there, since that's the only way we can find Vernon. After that we play it by ear."

Paddy didn't say anything for a long time, but Mack could hear him shifting position on the hard floor. Then, Paddy asked, "Do you ever think about what you'll do if . . . well, if Kay's not there?"

Mack closed his eyes wearily. "If she's dead, you mean." He could feel the bile rise in his stomach. "Not often. Once that kind of doubt takes hold, you can't shake it. But sometimes it creeps up before I can stop it. That's when it hits the hardest, when I'm not expecting it."

"Must be rough." Paddy hesitated. "Look, I want you to know you can count on me out there. This isn't just a grandstand play for me. I really want to help."

The sincerity in the big Irishman's voice was unmistakable. Again Mack was aware of how much better he felt knowing that he wasn't in this completely alone. "I know, and I appreciate it."

But Patrick wasn't quite finished; the words kept coming, as though they had been damned up, and now, in the darkness, they could finally spill over. "There's something else, too. I know I come on pretty strong where Sarah's concerned. Sometimes I act like a real jerk...." Mack felt a rush of sympathy for him, knowing the effort he was making. "Anyway, I just wanted to tell you that it wasn't personal, against you, I mean. When we were kids, Pa always told me to take care of her, so I did, and I guess it got to be a habit. The trouble was, she grew up and I didn't see it."

For a while neither of them spoke, but the silence was a comfortable one. Mack felt almost relaxed, and for the first time since they'd climbed up that Jacob's ladder, some of the tension left his neck and shoulders.

Paddy's voice, when he spoke again, was softer. "How long were you with the NSB?"

"Twelve years. Which was about eleven years too long."

"Do you ever miss it?"

"No," Mack replied without hesitation. "I'm glad I had the experience, especially now. But it was dirty. Toward the end I began to feel dirty."

"But you don't regret doing it," Patrick persisted.

Mack knew Paddy had something in his mind, had known since the day he showed up in Los Angeles with his knapsack slung over his shoulder. "No, I don't regret it. Like I said, as rotten as it was, something good came out of it. My training, a few good friends."

Again Patrick fell silent, and Mack could almost hear the wheels turning in his head.

"I wanted to be a cop," he said finally. "When I was a kid, it was all I thought about. I was gonna be *Dragnet*, *Adam-12* and Broderick Crawford, all rolled into one." The wistfulness in his voice made him sound absurdly young.

"So what happened?"

"I'm not sure. Ma died, for one thing, and it really scared me. I was sixteen, and I'd never thought about dying before. By the time I got out of school, I was finding all kinds of reasons for not filling out that application for the police academy."

"That happens. We grow up and we don't look at things the same way anymore."

"But that's not what happened to me. I just plain got scared, so I gave up. I settled for driving a truck because I was scared to be a cop."

Mack thought he understood. "And this is your emancipation proclamation."

"My what?"

"Oh, I was just thinking that's what Sarah would call it. An emancipation proclamation."

Patrick sighed. "Sarah. She's what got me started on all this. We were a lot alike when we were kids—always dreaming, always taking chances. But I changed, and Sarah didn't. If there's something she wants to do, she does it, and to hell with what anybody thinks. She always—I don't know how to explain it. It's like she's constantly testing herself, just to make sure she's got what it takes. If it doesn't come out right the first time, she does it again. And she won't ever have to look back and wonder if she could've done it, because she already has." He paused. "Me, all I can do is wonder."

Mack chuckled. "Not anymore. You picked one hell of a way to kick over the traces."

"It's all Sarah's fault," Paddy replied, and Mack could almost see the grin on his face. "She set a bad example. You know she wanted to come with us."

"So bad she couldn't stand it," Mack agreed. "But I couldn't take that kind of chance. She's too important to me."

"Yeah, I sorta figured that out." Patrick chuckled. "You know you're gonna have to marry her, don't you?"

Mack tried to imagine life without her and couldn't. "Yeah, I know," he said softly. He let himself picture her the way she had looked that last night, soft and lovely and vulnerable, incredibly desirable in that silk shirt that hung almost to her knees. Sometimes he missed her so much it was almost a physical pain. "I wonder what she's doing right now?"

Patrick chuckled. "If I know my sister, she's planning a full-scale invasion of Belen, just so she can beat us to the punch."

IN HER ROOM at the only hotel in San Sebastian, Sarah was dressing for dinner, remembering the last time she'd worn the aqua dress with the silk scarf. Mack had cooked the bon voyage dinner, and they'd gone bar hopping. Later they'd fought, and then...

"Oh, stop it," she said to her reflection. Thinking about him all the time only made things worse. She should be concentrating on the here and now, doing what she could to make things better.

She leaned closer to the mirror and examined her face to make sure the bruises were completely covered by makeup.

They were fading quickly, but not quickly enough to suit her. Every time she saw them, she remembered....

She shivered. Sometimes she had to remind herself that the past week hadn't been a dream. So much had happened, and it had happened with frightening speed. A week ago she'd been writing a book. Since then, she'd been followed and threatened, kidnapped and beaten, arrested and shot at. She'd committed assault, breaking and entering and bribery. And forgery, if one wanted to count the press credentials Oscar had gotten for her.

She'd also met Aubrey Glen Macklin, and that compensated for everything else. *Yes, indeed, Sarah Kathleen. You've had a very busy week.*

She ran a comb through her hair and took one final inventory in the mirror; then she went downstairs to the hotel dining room.

It was still early by Latin American standards, only seven o'clock, and the dining room was nearly empty. Two men in business suits were seated at one table, and a family of four at another. All foreigners, probably, either tourists or investors who were interested in Belen's recent oil development.

She took a table near the window, where she could look out at the dusty street. The marketplace was deserted, the stalls empty and the vendors gone home for the night. Seen like this, in repose, San Sebastian wasn't a bad little town. She wondered what Mack would think about it—

"'Scuse, *señorita*."

Sarah jumped. "Oh. Good evening," she said to the waitress. "I'd like to have dinner. Could I see a menu?"

"'Scuse," the woman said once more. "Capitán Ávila ask you to dinner, *por favor*."

"Captain who?"

The woman gestured. Standing beside a table in the corner, a man in uniform smiled and bowed from the waist. "El

Capitán would be mos' pleas'. You eat alone, not good. ¿*Por favor?*"

"Oh, I don't think so. Thank the *capitán* for me, but no thanks."

The waitress pursed her lips in what Sarah interpreted as disapproval and brought her a menu that was, thank goodness, printed in both Spanish and English.

"Excuse me."

Sarah looked up to find the capitán standing beside her.

"Please don' misunderstand, *señorita*. But since we two are separately alone, I wonder if perhaps we could share a table. A meal is so much better with pleasant company, don' you think?"

Her first instinct was to refuse again, more forcefully this time, but she remembered how miserable last night's meal had been and reconsidered. She really didn't want to spend the evening brooding over what Mack might or might not do when he discovered she was here, and besides, the *capitán* looked harmless. Short and slight, perhaps forty, with an honest face.

"Thank you," she said, reaching her decision. "My name is Sarah."

He bowed again. "I am Ernesto Ávila, *a sus ordenes*. May I sit?"

Sarah nodded her permission and he pulled out a chair and sat down. Maybe he would let her practice her Spanish on him, she thought. He looked like a nice little man. . . .

Ernesto Ávila was a nice little bore. He began by ordering Sarah's meal, overriding her original choice. She wouldn't have minded, except that the food, when it came, was inedible. And he probably wouldn't have objected if she'd practiced her Spanish, but he wouldn't stop talking long enough for her to ask.

By the end of the meal, Sarah had learned that he was from the capital city and that he had a very important job.

Unfortunately the job was top secret and he wasn't permitted to talk about it, but he was sure she'd understand, being a woman of the world. He himself preferred American women, although there was a lot to be said for the Germans, and the Dutch weren't bad, either. Of course, he was married, although his job kept him from home a great deal. His wife understood these things, though, because she, too, was a woman of the world.

He drained his second bottle of wine into his glass, and Sarah began looking for a break in the flow of words so that she could tell him she was leaving. But as she opened her mouth, he said his first interesting thing of the evening.

"I don' do this work all the time, you understand, only when there is no one else. I work in the capital city, where the criminals are more important than . . . stowups?"

Sarah began to listen more closely. "Stowups?"

"No, that is not the right word. You help me, okay? A person who rides a ship without paying, what is that?"

Sarah licked her lips, because they'd suddenly gone dry. "Stowaway?"

"Yes, stowaway! This is a small criminal, you understand, not what I am used to. But also I am not a stupid man. So I think, why send an important man like me to catch a little criminal. An' you know what I say to me? I say, Ernesto, this little criminal is not little, after all. He is a big American criminal that is top secret."

She picked up her napkin and dabbed at the corners of her mouth. "I think you must be right, Ernesto. They wouldn't waste you on an ordinary stowaway."

"Of course I am right. Sometimes I am wrong, but this time, no. Because I ask another question of myself. I say, Ernesto, if this man is a little criminal, why is he being picked up by an official American?"

Sarah's chest was tightening by the second, constricting her lungs. "I agree completely."

"Of course you do! Because I am right. I have had time to think about this. Ernesto Ávila is not a stupid man...."

Outside the window, a military jeep jerked to a halt, sending a thick cloud of dust billowing against the pane. But the dust wasn't so thick that Sarah couldn't see the official American sitting in the passenger seat.

John Bridges, agent for the National Security Bureau.

THE DARKNESS in the hold was absolute. After three days, Mack still hadn't gotten used to it. He supposed there were some things human beings were genetically incapable of adapting to—things like breathing water, drinking through their ears and living in a pitch-black, cavernous hole in the belly of a ship.

Or maybe it was just him. Patrick didn't seem to have any adjustment problems. In their cubbyhole behind the crates, he was snoring contentedly, and the sound was driving Mack crazy.

He stood and stretched, trying to loosen the knots that were beginning to form after too many days without exercise. The large muscles on each side of his neck felt as though they'd been cast in concrete, and his knees were getting stiff. He picked up the flashlight and turned it on, following the beam of light until it played out into nothingness. Neither of them had done any exploring since they had boarded. It was possible that somewhere in this megadungeon there was an open space large enough to be used as a track, or at least as a very small gymnasium.

Stepping from behind their "wall," he made his way through the access corridor that had been left between sections of cargo during the loading process. He'd been to the end of this particular stretch a couple of times, but no farther. He hadn't wanted to risk even the slightest noise. But now he was restless, and caution didn't seem half as important as the illusion of freedom.

The thin beam of light guided him from one turning to another, each one taking him farther from the irritating buzz of Patrick O'Shaughnessy's snores. Unfortunately each access aisle was exactly like the one before it. They led nowhere, except to another corner and another.

High above him a door opened, and he snapped off the flashlight. Voices floated down to him from the heights of the catwalk, muffled by distance, but he thought there were at least two men. He stood frozen in place, straining to hear.

Apparently the men weren't acting in any official capacity. No lights had come on, and they were still talking quietly, occasionally laughing. Mack relaxed his stance. Probably a couple of goldbrickers, he thought, playing hooky for a few minutes.

From somewhere within the maze of aisles, he caught the sound of a faint, familiar rustling. Foil. Patrick was awake and hungry, digging through the knapsack for something to eat. The cubbyhole would keep him from hearing the men on the catwalk, but Mack had no faith in the flip side of the coin. He had to assume that if he could hear Patrick, so could the others.

Damn! To think that everything hinged on a foil pouch....

He'd have to find his way back, try to silence Patrick before the entire crew came shinnying down the ladder. He turned around and began feeling his way back, moving in slow motion. At the first corner he turned right. At the second corner, right again.

The third corner... He couldn't remember. Right or left? His hand brushed against the metal rim of a barrel, and something flicked against his wrist, something alive. He jerked away, but not quickly enough to avoid the rat that leapt on his chest and tried to climb up his head.

He stumbled against a crate, and the corner struck him between the shoulder blades, sending his arm flying in a wild arc, and sending the flashlight crashing to the floor.

He heard an exclamation from the catwalk, the sound of running feet, and the hold was suddenly flooded with a million watts of blinding light.

CAPTAIN GIORGIO ASIMOKOPOULOS was a big man, barrel chested and muscular, saved from roughness by kind eyes and a courtly manner. Considering the circumstances, he'd been remarkably considerate, going so far as to visit the stowaways in their confinement and offer them a chance to explain.

The simple truth was, Mack liked and trusted him, enough to tell him the truth. The Greek had listened quietly until Mack was finished.

"The usual action in cases such as this is to put the offenders ashore at the first opportunity," he'd said with an odd little smile. "I hope you will not be too distressed to learn that our closest port of call will be San Sebastian."

Now the ship had docked, but instead of being put ashore immediately, they'd been escorted to the bridge by two burly seamen.

The captain paced in silence for a few moments; then he stopped in front of them and pressed the heel of his hand against his forehead.

"I must tell you that I have thought a great deal about your situation," he said in his courtly English. "I sympathize with you most deeply. I feel that if I were in your position, I would act as you have."

He coughed—somewhat self-consciously, Mack thought—before he continued. "If you look down at the wharf," he said, pointing, "you will see a railroad track running beside that platform. Our cargo will be offloaded, which will carry it into the warehouse at the end of the dock. From there it could be moved by rail or by truck, or it could remain in the warehouse until the consignee picks it up. I do not know what arrangements have been made for the crates you are following." He offered them an apologetic smile. "I have tried to help in some small way by arranging for your crates to be the last out of the hold. Perhaps that will enable you to watch them more closely."

Mack didn't know which muse of fate had lead him to this man's ship, but he was damned grateful for it. "It'll help more than you know," he said. "Thank you."

The captain nodded at the first officer, who stepped forward and handed Mack a bundle of clothing; then he cleared his throat again. "I make the suggestion that perhaps you should not be observed leaving the vessel, and I think these will help. The townspeople are accustomed to our seamen, so perhaps you would not be conspicuous if you dressed accordingly."

The captain solemnly shook Mack's hand, then Paddy's. "I wish I could do more. You are honorable men."

"No more than you," Mack responded fervently.

Asimokopoulos beckoned to a crewman, who stepped forward smartly. "Akima will see that you get safely ashore when you have changed clothes. Beyond that, I can do no more."

He nodded to each of them. "Go with God."

SARAH HAD BEEN HAUNTING the docks ever since she'd caught sight of the *Helena* offshore, nearly bouncing in her impatience. So far she hadn't seen the obsequious little Ernesto, but she hadn't yet seen Mack and Paddy, either. According to Ernesto she shouldn't have to worry about bumping into John Bridges, but just in case, she'd covered her blaze of curls with a fringed shawl.

When she'd seen the agent last night, she'd said the shortest goodbye in recorded history and made a wild dash for the stairs. Surprisingly, considering the two bottles of wine he'd drunk, Ernesto had been right behind her, insisting on seeing her to the room. Since he was close at hand and seemed in no danger of being struck dumb, she'd asked a few more questions.

Apparently Bridges wasn't anxious to be seen, so Ernesto was to have the ship searched and, when the stowaway was found, Ernesto would deliver him to Bridges in secrecy. And since Ernesto was obviously in no hurry to do his duty, Sarah still had time to find Mack and Paddy and warn them.

The dock bustled with people, and Sarah sometimes had to push and shove to stand her ground, but she wasn't budging until Mack and Paddy walked down the gangplank.

She caught sight of a group of seamen on the deck dressed in regulation blue. When they reached the gangplank, Sarah started forward, hoping that Mack would figure the safest plan was to hide in a crowd, but she'd taken only a few steps, when she was roughly shoved from behind.

She stumbled forward and felt the shawl slipping from her hair.

"Damn!" she said under her breath. She straightened the shawl, pulling it tightly around her shoulders, and looked through the crowds, trying to spot the seamen.

They were already past, moving in a tight cluster. The cluster shifted for a moment in deference to an old man with a wicker cane, and Sarah suddenly caught sight of a familiar blue knapsack.

Patrick. And Mack, walking next to him.

She started after them in a trot, and again she was jostled to one side. By the time she'd shoved past a man with a donkey cart, her quarry was going out the gate.

And coming in the gate was Ernesto Ávila.

She whirled, putting her back to him, and prayed that he hadn't seen her. In sneaked glances, she watched until he was safely past and on the gangplank, then she dashed for the gate.

But it was too late. When she got to the street, Mack and Paddy were nowhere in sight.

THE STREETS of San Sebastian were clogged with pedestrians, carts and animals, and the noise level was nearly deafening. After days in a hellish black pit, relieved only by the excitement of being confined to quarters, Mack felt assaulted by the mélange of sensations. Women in brightly colored dresses haggled with storekeepers on dusty sidewalks, while their boisterous children played tag around their skirts. Recalcitrant donkeys, dwarfed by their enormous loads, trotted by, led by nut-brown peasants armed with switches. On the nearest corner, a group of young men loitered, hands in pockets, occasionally relieving their tedium by tossing insults at one another.

The scene was straight out of *National Geographic*, a layout of still shots accompanied by text entitled "San Sebastian: The City that Time Forgot." Even knowing what he did about the political situation, it was difficult for Mack to reconcile this bustling domesticity with the notion of civil war. There was no sign of soldiers, no burned-out houses or shell-cratered streets.

Unknowingly Patrick echoed his thoughts. "Looks peaceful enough. Think anybody'll give us a hard time?"

"Not unless we give them a reason," Mack replied grimly. "They're used to seamen and foreigners. We'll browse, visit the local cantina. After a while they won't notice us anymore."

"What about the warehouse?"

Mack looked over his shoulder at the port. The warehouse sat at the northernmost end, in plain view from the streets. "We'll just watch the loading area. If nobody's picked up the crates by dark, we'll have to move in closer so we don't lose sight of them."

"Since the shipment's going to the mission," Paddy asked, "why not wait there for it? We could probably find a vehicle of some kind, and when Vernon shows up, we follow him."

"We can't afford to second-guess him," Mack said. "The crates might go to the mission, but then again, Vernon might move them directly to the compound. My only link to Kay is sitting in that warehouse, and I don't intend to let it out of my sight."

Patrick accepted his verdict with a shrug. Hefting his knapsack, he nodded toward the cantina across the street. "Let's get into character then, before we get arrested for loitering."

It was more a café than a cantina, with an adjoining patio that caught the last of the fading light. Mack chose to sit at an outside table, taking the chair that faced the warehouse.

A rotund little man wearing a white apron hurried toward them, beaming.

"Dos cervezas, por favor," Mack told him. The little man's smile faltered when he realized the rich sailors intended to contribute only a pittance to his establishment, but he was unfailingly courteous in his service.

Before they were served, Patrick suggested they stow the knapsacks behind the low decorative border that edged the patio.

"We look like a couple of overgrown Boy Scouts," he said, "and people tend to remember things like that. They'll be safe back there, and we can pick them up anytime."

They nursed their beers for a while, watching the loading zone. So far, there hadn't been much to see. A few vehicles had pulled up, but they'd carried away small parcels, nothing near the size of the crates addressed to the mission.

"Hey, Mack," Paddy said, nudging him with his elbow. "Look at that. And they say American women dress funny."

Mack glanced toward the market square. Near one of the stalls stood an odd little figure, a woman with a shawl over her head and shoulders, and bare legs. She seemed to be looking for someone, from the way she turned and fidgeted.

A sudden gust of wind whipped through the town, and the woman threw up her arm to shield her eyes. The abrupt movement raised the edges of the shawl to reveal a pair of khaki walking shorts.

Patrick gaped and Mack swore.

"Blast, damn and hell. It's Sarah."

Chapter Twelve

Sarah didn't see Mack until he grabbed her arm and spun her around.

"What the hell are you doing here?" His face was ashen, and he trembled with rage. Patrick, who had followed him across the street, looked distinctly uncomfortable.

She stepped back, breaking from his grip. She'd known he would react this way, and she'd been trying to prepare herself for days. But she still felt as though she'd been hit in the stomach.

"I'm looking for you," she told him, moving closer to Paddy. "John Bridges is here. I saw him last night."

There was no way Sarah could have described his expression if she'd been asked to. The emotion on his face was raw, naked; it was the look of a man who'd lost faith in the concept of justice, and seeing him that way made Sarah feel like a voyeur.

Almost instantly his mask was in place, revealing nothing. "Where is he now?"

"I don't know. They're searching the ship now. He's waiting somewhere to take custody of you when you're found."

The line of his jaw was so tight that Sarah was surprised when he managed to speak. "We've got to get off the street."

"I have a room in the hotel. We can all go there."

She didn't wait to see if he agreed; she just walked away, leaving him to follow or not, as he pleased.

Patrick walked beside her, his arm around her waist. "Pretty dirty trick to play on a guy, Sarah. I hope you've got a good reason."

She sighed and let herself lean on him, just for a moment. "I have, but I don't think he'll ever let me explain it to him."

"Faith and begorra!" he said, widening his eyes in mock dismay. "That's what I call throwing in the towel before the bell ever rings."

She slapped his arm, but she was smiling. Something had happened to her relationship with her brother since the night he'd come charging to the rescue at Carmel, something good. At least she wouldn't feel completely alone; he might even buffer some of the hostility that was sure to be flying back and forth between her and Mack.

The desk clerk looked up from his magazine when she walked through the lobby with two sailors, then quickly looked away again. "By tomorrow morning, you'll either have an eviction notice or a stack of dinner invitations," Patrick said on the way upstairs.

Behind them Mack said, "She won't be here in the morning."

Sarah stopped on the landing. "Then where *will* I be in the morning?"

"You should stop jumping to all those conclusions, Sarah," he said coldly. "You'll be right next to Paddy and me, trying your damnedest to stay alive."

IT DIDN'T TAKE HER LONG to repeat what little she'd found out from Ernesto, and even less time than that for her to have another argument with Mack.

"We're leaving later tonight, before Bridges shows up," he told her, eyeing the shorts she wore. "Change clothes before we go, put on some jeans."

"I don't have any jeans. I brought only what I had with me at Dale's house, plus a couple of sundresses and a linen suit."

"Then it doesn't make any difference what you wear," he said, "because they're all useless." He stationed himself at the window and leaned against the sill, staring outside.

"What he means," Patrick said, intervening tactfully, "is that jungles are full of things that sting, bite and cut. Your legs are going to be a mess."

She sighed. She'd planned to buy some more things here, after she'd had a chance to see what would be most practical. But she'd kept putting it off and now it was too late, so she'd just have to take her lumps. "Can I ask where we're going when we leave here?"

Just when it began to seem as though he wouldn't answer, Mack pointed out the window. "Right across the street."

"What's across the street?" Sarah wanted to know.

"The warehouse," Patrick explained. "That's where the weapons were unloaded. Mack wants to stay on top of them until somebody comes to pick them up."

Mack called Patrick to the window. "Look down there. The fence runs all the way around, but we can climb over pretty easily. Those trees will be good cover after dark."

"But what kind of cover do we have once we're over the fence?" Paddy asked. "We can't just squat beside the building."

"We go *inside* the building," Mack told him, sounding faintly amused. "There's a rear door—I spotted it a little while ago. It'll be locked, but we'll cross that bridge when we get to it.''

"Speaking of bridges, what about the one who's after you? He's gone to a lot of trouble on your account. I don't think he's going to just give up and go home.''

Mack laughed shortly. "No, he's way past that. When I don't turn up on that ship, he'll try something else. But not openly. I think he's gone beyond his sanction in coming after me, or he'd be searching the ship himself. That's why we're safe here, for the time being.''

"You still haven't answered Paddy's question,'' Sarah said, forcing him to acknowledge her presence.

"I don't have an answer, not right now,'' he said flatly. "We stay out of his way until I do what I came here for. If he finds us before we get out of the country, I'll deal with it then.''

Sarah didn't press him further, but the specter of John Bridges stayed in her mind. She was as afraid of him as she was of Vernon, maybe more so. Vernon was an obvious villain, and that somehow made him easier to deal with. But Bridges hid his duplicity behind the guise of patriotism, and he had all the resources of his position behind him. If he could find out about the *Helena*, when Mack had been so careful to cover his tracks, he could find them in San Sebastian, no matter where they were hiding.

Throughout the rest of the afternoon, she sat cross-legged on the bed, listening to the man talk. Mack seemed to have no clear plan for getting out of the country; they would cross the northern border out of Belen, he said, and contact the American embassy. But as for how they would get to the border, that was another bridge to be crossed when the time arrived.

Sarah made no comments, offered no suggestions, because she knew Mack wouldn't listen, no matter how valid her point. His anger was too deep, his sense of betrayal too strong.

Finally, when it was fully dark but still early, she ventured an opinion. "I think we should eat a real meal while we have the chance. Besides, I'm starving."

Paddy readily agreed. "Sounds good to me. My stomach's beginning to think my throat's been cut."

In the hotel dining room they ate in silence. Sarah tried several times to talk to Mack, ask questions, but more often than not he ignored her, leaving Paddy to fill in the gaps. By the time Mack decided it was safe to climb the fence, Sarah was ready to climb the walls.

Patrick paid for the meal, and he and Mack left the hotel to pick up the knapsacks they'd left at the café. After a moment, during which she took a deep, calming breath, Sarah followed them, lifting her bag with hands that weren't quite steady.

As MACK HAD PREDICTED, the fence presented no real problems. He went over first, using the chain links to pull himself up, and caught the knapsacks and Sarah's bag as Patrick threw them over. Patrick boosted Sarah up. She heard her shirt rip as she topped the fence, and was abnormally aware of Mack's hands when he caught her waist and eased her to the ground. He let her go quickly, and if he was reminded of another night when they'd broken into another warehouse, he kept it to himself.

A moment later, Patrick landed in the dirt beside them with a grunt.

They crouched behind the warehouse, hugging the wall. The moonlight, filtered through thin clouds, afforded plenty of visibility. Mack told Sarah and Paddy to stay put; then he disappeared around the corner.

Several minutes later he was back. "I don't know what they use for security around here," he said in a near whisper, "but for now we're okay. And we're in. Stay low and be quiet."

He led them around the corner to a door. In the faint light Sarah could see where the hasp had been pried loose from the outer wall. Patrick entered first, pulling Sarah behind him. Mack brought up the rear, cursing softly when the door made a faint squeak. Then he turned on his flashlight, darting the beam here and there until he found a narrow passage that took them into the very back of the building behind a high stack of boxes.

"If we move out, everything stays here except the gun, one flashlight and the utility knife," he said. "Sarah, do you have a scarf?"

She pulled a blue kerchief from her bag and handed it to him. With a sharp motion, he ripped a thin strip off the scarf and looped it through the metal ring on the end of Patrick's flashlight. "Fasten it through one of your belt loops," he said, tossing the flashlight to her. "Paddy, here's the utility knife. Hook it to your belt and make sure it's secure." He stuck the pistol into his own waistband, then emptied a small box of cartridges into the remains of Sarah's scarf and tied the scarf tightly to eliminate any rattling. This, too, he kept with him, unbuttoning his shirt to slip it inside.

"I'll take first watch. You two stretch out and get as much rest as you can. Paddy, you can take over in three hours. If nothing's happened by dawn, we leave the same way we came in and start all over again."

Sarah wanted so badly to touch him she found herself reaching out without thinking. He must have seen the motion, for he stiffened abruptly and moved away, clicking off the flashlight as he walked up the narrow aisle.

She felt Patrick's hand on her shoulder and allowed him to pull her close. "Don't worry," he whispered. "He'll get over it." Sarah wanted to believe him, but she'd been running a little short of faith lately.

A LIGHT TOUCH on her thigh brought her awake.

"Something's happening," Mack whispered. "Come on."

Moving as quickly as she could in the darkness, guided only by her grip on the back of Mack's shirt, she became aware first of the rumble of motors from outside, then of her erratic heartbeat.

Mack pushed her through the door and Patrick grabbed her arm, pulling her with him as he ran for the back of the warehouse, where they stopped and leaned against the building.

"Two trucks," Paddy panted, "military types, with the canvas covers."

"Deuce-and-a-halfs," Mack supplied. "How many men?"

"Four that I saw. I'm pretty sure that's all."

"Okay, we move on around to the opposite side, but stay close to the rear. The moon's down, so if we stay against the wall we'll be all right."

Again Mack took the lead, and the tiny procession crept over the ground at an excruciatingly slow pace. Once, Sarah put her foot down on something soft and yielding, something that quickly slithered away, leaving her momentarily frozen into immobility. Then Patrick prodded her back, and her legs began to respond to the messages from her brain.

After an eternity, they rounded the corner and, silent as ghosts, went another twenty paces. At Mack's whispered command they stopped.

Huddled in a crouch next to Patrick, Sarah listened to the noises made by men and machines. Suddenly, assailed by grim reality, she didn't want to know what was going on. She didn't want to know who the other men were, even though one of the voices obviously belonged to an American. She simply wanted to get on with whatever they were going to do; she wanted to find Kay and go home, back to a friendlier world.

Patrick touched her arm. "You okay?" he whispered.

She managed to nod, trying to shed the strange feeling of apathy.

Then Mack was kneeling beside them. "These are our boys," he told them. "From what I can make out, one of them is Jackson, the mercenary Greyson told me about. They're using a forklift to move the stuff, but it's still taking all four of them to get it packed in. I figure when the first truck's loaded, they'll move it out of the way. If we work it right, we can climb in and ride it straight to the end of the line. No muss, no fuss."

Sarah listened in amazement. Since the action had started, Mack's tension seemed to have vanished. Now he was totally calm, almost relaxed, just as he had been in L.A., the day before he'd left. She thought she was beginning to understand. Even though he'd left the NSB, he was still an adventurer at heart. The part of him that had been drawn to the bureau in the first place was enjoying this.

But she didn't have time to think about it, for he was giving the orders and she was determined to do her part. "Don't move," he said. "Don't even breathe, unless I give the signal. Paddy, when I tell you to go, get to the truck as fast as you can and don't waste time looking back. I'll be covering you and if something goes wrong, you'll know soon enough."

One of the truck motors roared to life. Sarah saw headlight beams cut a swath through the darkness as the truck rolled slowly past the warehouse. The vehicle braked no more than thirty feet away, and the driver went back toward the loading dock.

Mack waited until he was sure the man was inside, then continued. "Sarah, even when Paddy's in place, stay put until I say otherwise. Move fast but don't run—it's too noisy. Once you're inside, get as far forward as you can. Then don't move again. Understood?"

Then it began. Mack led them along the wall until they were mere feet from the front corner. Light poured from inside the warehouse, illuminating the loading bay and the second truck, but falling short of the target vehicle by several yards. They stood motionless for so long that Sarah felt her knees lock. When Patrick darted away at an angle, she realized she'd missed Mack's signal. She had to pay attention. She was next.

She watched her brother skim soundlessly over the ground until he was all but invisible in the darkness. She steeled herself. There was a tap on her shoulder, and Mack's whispered command: "Go!"

Her feet moved, dragging her reluctant body along, but only for two steps. She stumbled, flailed, fell, heard her own grunt as she hit the ground. Before she could take another breath, she was jerked up by her collar and thrown backward.

Mack pressed her against the wall of the warehouse. A voice shouted a question in Spanish; another answered in English. "I'll check it out."

Mack's body was rigid. He pushed her deeper into the shadows, seemed to spread himself into no more than a thin protrusion on the wall.

Footsteps, light and quick, coming nearer. A leg, then a body, appearing from around the corner.

The man was barely into the shadows, when Mack sprang, so swiftly Sarah barely had time to register the fact. One arm snaked around the man's neck; the other jammed a gun into his temple. The man's arm jerked and something hit the ground with a nearly inaudible thud. With his knee, Mack nudged the man toward Sarah.

"His gun," he whispered.

Sarah forced her body forward, forced it to bend, forced her nerveless hand to pick up the weapon from where it had fallen. The only thought she could focus on was that she had nearly gotten Mack killed. She had risked her relationship with him, given in to her mystical conviction that she could save him, yet she was the one who had just put him in grave danger.

"*¿Qué es?*" The voice, from inside the warehouse, startled her and she jumped.

Mack tightened the pressure on the man's throat, then eased it slightly.

"Nothing," the man called back in an amazingly normal tone. He hesitated, and again Mack squeezed and released. "I don't see anything," the man continued, "but I'll check the back."

Mack force-marched his prisoner to the rear of the warehouse, while Sarah followed so closely she might have been his shadow. When Mack halted, he spoke quickly, urgently.

"You're Jackson?"

The man nodded.

"I know about Vernon," Mack continued. "I'm not here to interfere. I want the woman who's with him, that's all. Then we're gone."

"You must be Mack."

Sarah sensed Mack's reaction, his shock. "You know Kay?"

"She talks about you." Jackson raised his hands higher. "Ease up. I'm listening."

"Nothing else to say." Mack held his stance a moment longer, then abruptly released his choke hold. "I came after Kay. You can have Vernon."

Jackson seemed to find that amusing. "I've already got him."

"Don't play games. Yes or no?"

Jackson shrugged. "Why not? She's a good kid. You're after the truck?"

"Not the truck, just a free ride."

Jackson considered the proposition. "Not through the gate—they search every vehicle. Not even very close. Vernon has regular patrols that sweep a five-mile radius. I'll let you off about ten miles out. Wait until dawn and walk due east until you hit a stream, the follow it north three miles. There's a hut you can use until you hear from me."

Sarah heard heavy footsteps. Jackson jerked his gun from her hand and walked quickly around the corner. "Just a dog," she heard him say. *"Un perro."*

Mack waited until Jackson's footsteps had faded. "Come on," he urged, "on the count of three."

This time when she ran for the truck, it was much easier. Mack was with her.

THEY BOUNCED for hours. Every time the deuce-and-a-half bucked, which was approximately three times a second, she felt the jolt clear to her teeth. The vehicle swayed and rattled with every revolution of the tires, and she didn't know how it managed to stay in one piece. Apparently Patrick shared her discomfort, for he cursed so often it had turned into a monotonous drone. When the motion stopped abruptly, she felt disoriented.

The driver's door opened, then slammed. The passenger raised his voice in an angry burst of Spanish, and Jackson said, "Relax. It'll take only a minute. When a man's gotta go, he's gotta go."

Then he was at the rear of the truck, just a shadow in the predawn light, motioning them out. "East, then north," he reminded Mack in a whisper, waving them toward the cover of dense vegetation that crowded the road.

They slipped into the dew-wet growth and didn't stir until the truck was out of sight.

Patrick squeezed her shoulder. "How're you holding up?"

She managed a shaky smile. "I keep counting my teeth to make sure they're all there."

"Let's go," Mack commanded from across the road. "There's enough light to see, and we're too exposed here." He set the pace, and they started the march eastward.

They walked steadily, without talking. As far as Sarah was concerned, she didn't have any breath to spare on conversation. Every square inch of the ground was thick with jungle growth, and the trekkers had to fight for every foot they gained. Short, lush bushes, lacy ferns, wrist-thick vines twisting around tall, slender-boled trees—they all crowded together in competition for the earth.

And after the sun came up in earnest, so did the humidity and the insects. At times Sarah felt that she was trapped in a gigantic steam room, that if she took another breath of the liquid air, she'd surely drown. At others, the clouds of tiny, hungry gnats that swarmed after her like bad luck made her want to scream. They covered every available inch of her body, and soon she began to feel like a walking itch. Then she'd see Mack's sweat-soaked back weaving just ahead of her, arrogant in its tirelessness, and she would plunge forward again.

Sometimes she stumbled, sometimes she became tangled in the dense foliage, and Patrick would turn back to help her. At those times Mack would stop and wait, his features set in a permanent mask of impatience.

Eventually he allowed them one rest period, but as far as Sarah was concerned, it was almost worse than being on the move. The gnats were worse than ever, covering her arms and legs like a living net. By the time Mack signaled them to march again, she was almost eager to go.

When at last they reached the stream, Sarah all but threw herself in it, not to get wet, but to get cool. She fought her way to the bank and waded in. The shallow water flowed around her ankles and calves like cool silk, and she gratefully splashed it on her arms, her chest, her face. She didn't think there was a square inch on her body that hadn't been bruised, scratched or bitten.

Patrick joined her, and for a few moments Sarah actually found herself laughing as he cavorted like a big red seal. His antics distracted her, allowed her to let go of the tension and anger that kept her knotted up inside.

Then she noticed Mack standing on the bank, glaring at them.

"If you're through," he said acidly, "I'd like to get out of here."

Sarah had had enough. Enough of his arrogance, enough of his temper, enough of his superiority. Enough of *him*.

Hands on hips, chest heaving, she stood in the stream. "As a matter of fact," she enunciated, "I'm *not* through. I like it here, and I'm going to stay awhile. Please feel free to leave without me. I certainly don't want to hold you up."

"Uh-oh," Patrick muttered, wading to the bank.

"Damn it, Sarah, we don't have time for this!"

"No, *you* don't have time for this. *I've* got all the time in the world."

"Look, you're the one who just had to be here, so if you don't like the rules, that's tough! But I'm leaving, with or without you."

"So go!" she shouted. "I don't need you to take care of me. Just get out of here, leave!"

He started to say something else, but thought better of it and walked swiftly away.

Patrick motioned to her from the bank. "Come on, Sarah, this isn't getting us anywhere." When she didn't move, he came after her and took her hand. "He's crazy about you, you know that. He just doesn't remember it right now."

"I don't care if he never remembers it!"

But she did care. Of course she cared. As she stiffly followed Mack down the path he had chosen, she cared with every step and every hard-won breath, and she knew she would never stop caring as long as she lived.

THE HUT could hardly be called a "structure." It leaned heavily, and the warped boards couldn't keep out anything, certainly not rain or bugs. But at least it was a place to get out of the damned jungle. And it was a place to try one more time to talk to Mack.

Patrick had suggested it. "You've got to get it straight between you," he told his sister. "I'll get out of your hair for a little while, give you some space."

She had agreed, although reluctantly. She knew he was right. This thing between her and Mack was taking a toll on all of them. But still she hesitated. Right now her love for Mack was in danger of being overshadowed by her anger, and if she said the wrong thing, it would be worse than saying nothing at all.

She framed a sentence, rehearsed it, discarded it and framed another, which sounded no better than the first. Finally, sighing with weariness and frustration, she decided to take a chance and say whatever came to mind.

She found Mack scraping at the bark of a tree with the knife, testing it with his tongue. He glanced at her when he heard her approach and went on with what he was doing.

"Mack, how long are you going to keep this up?"

He didn't answer.

"You can ignore me, but I'm not going to disappear. I'm here, and you'd better start dealing with it."

He turned. "Are you absolutely determined to have this conversation?"

She nodded. "Absolutely determined." The pain she'd been trying to hold at bay for nearly two days came to the surface, as smothering and oppressive as the heat. If the breach were to be healed, it would have to be soon, because this limbo of uncertainty was unbearable.

She stepped closer and touched his arm. "Mack, I love you. I love you so much it hurts. Why do you think I'm here?"

His eyes flashed dangerously. "That's what I keep asking myself. Why is she here? Why would she deliberately do the one thing she knew would rip my guts apart? And you know what answer I come up with?" He flung the knife to the ground. It stabbed into the earth the way his pain and fury stabbed at her heart. "That she's so selfish and irresponsible she doesn't care what happens to anybody else as long as she gets her own way!"

"Then you came up with the wrong answer!" she cried, clutching at his arm. "I'm here because I love you, because I thought I could help, the way I've helped before. Because I thought if I was here, maybe I could keep you from dying." Her throat closed up, choking her. "Because if you die, I don't want to live without you...."

His face was stricken and drawn. "You still don't understand, do you?" he said, sounding desolate and sad. "You've put me in the position of having to choose between you and Kay. I can't be in two places at once, Sarah. If I go in after her, it would leave you unprotected, and if I don't, she dies. And I can't make that choice."

"I'm sorry," she whispered. "I'm so very, very sorry. But I had to do what I thought was right, and I can't change things now. I'm here, you're here, Kay's here. Just do what you have to do for her, and trust me to take care of myself."

He shook his head. "How do we work through this?"

She touched his face. "I don't think we can. Some things can't be worked through, they just have to be accepted, and I guess this is one of them. We either put it behind us and go ahead, or we don't go anywhere at all. But I have to know which it's going to be, because I'm hurting inside and it's killing me."

Almost reluctantly, it seemed, he reached for her, as though touching her were somehow dangerous or forbidden. "I know. It's killing both of us, and I don't know what to do. I only know I don't want to lose you."

"You can't lose me." She smiled then and touched his face. "I'm in for the duration."

He sighed and pulled her closer. They simply stood like that, not moving, not talking, for a long, long time. For Sarah, the heat, the bugs, even the danger receded into the background; it was going to be all right, her heart sang. Everything was going to be all right.

PATRICK CAME BACK to the hut accompanied by Jackson. The mercenary was red faced and sweating, obviously exhausted.

"I don't have much time," he panted. "Vernon trusts me for now, but if he gets suspicious, it could blow everything." He unsnapped a canvas pouch from his belt and tossed it to Mack. "Here's a map and a few tinned rations. Be outside the compound a little before dawn tomorrow, and I'll try to get Kay out to you. Then get the hell out, because that place is gonna go up like a volcano."

"What about the patrols?"

"I told Vernon I'd heard reports of troop movement to the north, so he's sending them in the opposite direction tomorrow."

Mack unfolded the map. "I make it about four miles from here."

"Right." Jackson pointed to a spot on the map. "Wait on this ridge and stay out of sight. You get in trouble, I won't back you up."

"I wouldn't ask you to," Mack replied. "You've already done more than I expected. Any particular reason why?"

Jackson grinned. "I knew you'd ask that sooner or later. The truth is, I'm not sure. Maybe I'm getting tired, or just old. This is my last job, and maybe I want to retire feeling that I've earned the right, you know? Besides, like I said, Kay's a good kid. She didn't ask for any of this."

"You seem to know her pretty well," Sarah remarked.

Jackson spit. "Vernon keeps her under guard. Since he trusts me, I draw the duty most of the time. He's gone a lot, recruiting, I guess, so Kay talks to me."

"Then I'm glad you were there for her," Mack said, extending his hand. "Thanks."

Jackson considered the hand before accepting it. Sarah had the impression he was slightly embarrassed, but he covered it well.

"Remember," he called over his shoulder as he walked away, "before dawn."

"Before dawn," Mack repeated, almost as if he were talking to himself.

Sarah knew what he was thinking. In twelve hours it would be over, one way or another. She moved to stand beside him and took his hand, felt his love flow into her, binding them. Together, she knew, they could make it through whatever came with the dawn.

THE RIDGE WAS CLOSE to the compound, so close that Sarah could almost count the buttons on the guard's shirt. He stood in front of the main house, holding his weapon at the ready. Behind him, the building's windows blazed with light.

Smaller structures on either side of the house, which she assumed were barracks, completed a semicircle. Behind all these buildings, separate both in style and size, was a massive, barnlike structure; Mack had said it was probably the armory, and would be the main objective in the attack.

The deuce-and-a-halfs were parked behind the armory; in front of the main house, near the guards, sat a jeep. The compound itself was ringed by coils of barbed-wire fencing.

"Where *are* they?" Mack demanded, watching the first faint blush of pink in the eastern sky. "He said he'd get her out before the attack." His voice was tight with apprehension.

Sarah put her hand on his shoulder, offering what comfort she could. But in the final analysis, she knew, each of them would have to find his own comfort. Facing death was a personal thing. She, like Mack and Patrick, was coming face-to-face with destiny, and she would be taking with her the sum total of her hopes and dreams.

She felt Mack's hand brush her cheek, then fall away. Her comfort was in knowing that she had made the right decision. Whatever happened, she was where she was meant to be, next to the man she loved....

Patrick nudged Mack and pointed. Outside the compound, approaching the gate, Sarah saw several dark figures emerging from the jungled forest like wraiths. Two, four, then seven and more, they advanced in stages, crouched low. Inside the fence, another figure moved toward the gate. As Sarah watched, this figure opened the gate, allowing the invaders to enter.

Mack swore. "I'm not waiting any longer." He pulled the gun from his waistband with a deft movement and began half running, half sliding down the steep slope toward the compound, Paddy on his heels. Sarah was right behind them, midway in her descent when the first rattle of gunfire shattered the stillness of the dawn. The world suddenly erupted into a maelstrom of confused shouts, pounding feet and the sharp coughing of automatic weapons.

She reached the open gate just as the first shell hit, rocking the ground under her feet. She kept running, past the barracks on her right as it exploded into an orange fireball, lighting up the entire compound. Men poured out of the other barracks, some only half dressed, all carrying weapons. The constant rat-a-tat of gunfire drowned out everything but the loudest screams and the explosions of bursting shells.

A man darted in front of her and she threw herself to the ground, expecting at any moment to feel a bullet rip into her. But he passed her at a dead run, heading for the burning barracks. Scrambling to her feet, Sarah saw Mack and Paddy gain the porch of the main house, saw a uniformed man raise his weapon. She screamed, but Mack didn't hear. Then the soldier jerked and fell backward. Jackson jumped over the body and grabbed Mack's arm.

Sarah stumbled onto the porch in time to hear "Locked in with Vernon, couldn't get to her." The door to the house gaped and Jackson dashed inside, the others close behind. A soldier appeared from a hallway, but Jackson shot him before he could aim his weapon. "Back there!" he shouted, gesturing down the hall. "I'll cover you!"

He whirled and started firing toward the front door, buying them as much time as he could, and Sarah flew down the hall behind Mack and Patrick. Along the corridor, all the doors except one stood open, and from behind it came a woman's terrified screams. Holding the pistol high in one hand, Mack kicked the door once, then twice, and it flew inward.

"Let her go!"

Sarah skidded to a halt in the open doorway. Her mind froze the scene before her into a surrealistic tableau. Mack stood in a wide-legged stance, aiming the pistol at a man who held a struggling, kicking woman by her waist. Paul Vernon. Using Kay Macklin as a shield, Vernon held his own weapon to her head. Sarah could see the weapon jerk as Vernon's hand trembled with the palsy of fear. "I'll kill her," he screamed. "I swear I'll kill her."

Patrick spun to the side, trying to circle, but he wasn't fast enough. Vernon's arm moved like lightning. He fired twice and in spite of his erratic aim, one of the bullets found its mark.

Sarah saw her brother go down, felt the icy grip of terror squeeze her heart. "Paddy!" she screamed, and ran toward him.

He raised his head. "Get out of here!"

She hesitated, and a movement at the door caught her eye. Jackson, hidden from Vernon's view, pointed toward her, mimed a throwing motion and pointed again. She looked down at herself, at the flashlight that still dangled from her belt loop, and she understood. If she could distract Vernon just for an instant, Jackson could take him down.

She ripped the flashlight free, gripping it tightly. Vernon's attention was on Mack, who was slowly but inexorably moving forward, pressing Vernon into a corner. On a deep breath, she stepped forward and lobbed the flashlight across the room. Vernon saw the movement from the corner of his eye and in shocked confusion turned his head to follow the missile's flight.

In the split second that Veron's head was turned, Jackson darted into the room, knocking Mack aside with the same swift motion that brought his weapon up. He fired, and Sarah saw Vernon jerk like a puppet. In his death throes his arm tightened around Kay's waist, and she fought wildly to twist free of his grasp.

Sara dived across the room and grabbed Kay's wrist, tugging her toward the door. Patrick still lay where he had fallen, his shirt drenched with blood from armpit to waist.

She dropped to her knees beside him, but Mack pulled her away, urged her forward. "I'll take care of him. Get Kay out of here."

Sarah called on an inner reserve of strength and turned away from her brother. Dragging Kay behind, she streaked down the hall and through the front door.

Outside, hell still reigned. A shell exploded near the gate, and the concussion knocked the women to the ground. Jackson appeared from nowhere, pulled Sarah to her feet and shoved her forward. "The jeep!" he yelled.

Kay moved like an automaton, stiff and unyielding, but Sarah forced her to the jeep, pushed her into the back seat. Looking over her shoulder, she saw Mack, bent double with the weight of Patrick's body, and behind them, rounding the corner of the house, two of Vernon's soldiers. "Mack!" she screamed, but the din of exploding shells drowned the cry.

Jackson darted toward the struggling men, firing short bursts to cover their progress. When he reached them, he grabbed Patrick's other arm, helping to support him until they reached the jeep. Then he grinned and saluted, turned and ran toward the back of the compound, toward the armory.

Together, Sarah and Mack got Paddy into the back seat beside Kay. Mack rounded the back of the vehicle as Sarah jumped into the passenger seat. Halfway across the compound she could see Jackson, still running, and she thought that the self-respect he'd craved had been earned a thousandfold.

Suddenly Jackson went down, his back arched, his mouth open in a wordless scream. Sarah clutched her throat in shock and horror.

Mack had seen Jackson fall. "Start the jeep!" he shouted. "I'm going back for Jackson."

"It's too late!" she cried, but he was gone.

She slid behind the wheel, turned the key and pushed the ignition button, and the engine sprang to life.

Mack was only a few yards away from Jackson's body, firing his pistol toward the barracks. As she watched, tiny puffs of dirt spouted in the ground in front of him; then his leg folded and he collapsed like a rag doll.

"No!" she screamed. She wouldn't let this happen.

Chanting his name like a mantra, she rammed the jeep into gear and let out on the clutch. The jeep bucked but didn't die, and she wheeled it in a tight circle and drove straight for Mack. She braked to a jolting stop beside him and leaped out. He was propped on one elbow, trying to lever himself into a sitting position. Sarah grabbed him under the arms and yanked. Suddenly Kay was beside her, helping her. He scooped his gun from the ground and struggled upright. He hopped once and managed to gain the jeep. Using only his arms, he boosted himself in, falling heavily into the front seat.

Sarah, turning back to look at Jackson, could tell that the final spray of bullets had ended his life.

When Kay was safely in the vehicle, Sarah jumped behind the wheel again. The jeep slewed wildly as she straightened it out, but then they were racing toward the gate, through the gate, past the gate....

Behind them a mighty roar exploded as the armory went up, and the fireball rose high in the air, bright as the sun at noontime. Sarah heard someone shriek—maybe herself—and the jeep rocked with the concussion of the explosion. She pressed harder on the accelerator and drove until the stench of destruction no longer threatened to choke her.

She braked the jeep in the middle of the road and leaned her forehead against the steering wheel, breathing in deep, jerky gulps. "It's okay, honey," she heard Mack say. "It's over now. You got us out."

His face when she looked at him was ghastly white, and his lips seemed twisted in a grimace. His blood-soaked leg was stretched at an odd angle, perhaps broken, surely agonizing. Then he gave her a thumbs-up, and she realized the grimace was a smile.

Kay leaned forward from the back seat and, crying unrestrainedly, threw her arms around Sarah's neck, while Paddy demanded in a weak voice, "Can I open my eyes now?" He kept his hand pressed against his side, but his color was good.

Sarah, letting her eyes travel from face to face around the vehicle, thought it would be hard to find a more motley, raggedy group than they were—or a happier one. She leaned over and touched Mack's lips with her fingertips. "How bad's the leg? Can you last a little longer?"

"Do I have a choice?" He felt the wound, pushing at it, and sweat popped out across his forehead. "It's stopped bleeding. I'll last a while yet." He searched her face, and Sarah felt her pulse leap. "Remind me to tell you how much I love you—"

The crack of a rifle cut off his words. Sarah heard the whine of the bullet as it narrowly missed Mack's head.

On a hillock, partially hidden by the trees, stood a lone gunman. *Bridges.*

"Get down!" Mack shouted, drawing his pistol.

In the back seat, Paddy and Kay slid from the seat to the floor.

Sarah jabbed the ignition button. The engine ground but wouldn't catch. She cursed and tried again. Nothing.

A bullet crashed against the windshield. Mack returned fire, and Bridges darted for cover, but he clearly had the advantage.

Mack pushed her out of the jeep and to the ground, falling on top of her as another bullet slammed into the hood. "You get Kay and Paddy to cover," he told her. "I'll be right behind you."

He fired four shots, carefully spaced to keep Bridges down while Kay and Patrick crawled out of the jeep. "Go on," he urged when Sarah hesitated to leave. "Kay can't move that big guy herself."

Reluctantly Sarah turned away. She and Kay supported Patrick across a small clearing and into the dense undergrowth. They had gone perhaps twenty yards, when Paddy collapsed. She knew they hadn't gone far enough, and she whirled with relief when Mack limped through the brush behind them.

"He can't go any farther," Kay said, holding Paddy's head in her lap.

"I'll draw Bridges away, in the opposite direction," Mack said to Sarah. "When you think it's safe, get the jeep started and get back to town."

"Draw him away? Mack, you can barely walk."

"I can walk far enough to get Bridges," he said grimly. Then his mouth relaxed as he looked at her frightened face. "I'll be back, Sarah."

Then he was gone.

Sarah looked at Kay. "I've got to go after him," she said half-apologetically. "If we're not back soon, try to get the jeep started, like Mack said."

Kay's eyes were wide with fright, but she nodded. When Sarah left, she was still huddled on the ground, cradling Patrick's head and crying.

SARAH KEPT MACK in sight until he came to a shallow ravine. She saw him descend into it, but when she reached the spot, he had disappeared.

Frantic, she slid down the shallow slope and examined the ground. A thick, spongy layer of vegetation covered the earth, and she could see where his limping steps had left a trail. She followed it, down the ravine, lost it, found it again. He had left the ravine, and after a few yards she lost the trail for good.

She tried to escape the panic that welled up, clouding her thought processes. *Just stay calm,* she told herself over and over. But it was impossible. Mack was gone, and she had no idea in which direction.

Suddenly a faint sound brought her to rigid attention. A man's voice. She followed the sound, trying to move noiselessly, and as it got louder, she identified the speaker. It was Bridges.

"You can't hide forever, Macklin," he said. "It's just a matter of time before I find you."

Sarah crept closer, dropped to her knees, then lay on her stomach and crawled through the dense brush.

"I've got you now, Macklin," Bridges said. His voice was ugly with hatred. "This time it'll be finished, the way it should have been five years ago."

Now she could see him. He stood just yards away from a clump of trees thick and heavy with vines. Somewhere behind that green curtain, she knew, Mack was hiding.

Bridges fired into the trees and Sarah flinched. She had to distract him, but how? There was no way she could disable him, nothing to use as a weapon.

She heard a movement and froze. Mack had circled behind Bridges, would have had him if he hadn't stumbled.

Bridges had heard him, too, and he spun and fired. Mack ducked into the cover of the trees, and Bridges followed him.

Sarah leaped to her feet and sprinted across the ground, taking advantage of the noise Bridges himself made. She was close now, but no better off than before. Bridges was armed; she wasn't.

Suddenly Mack stepped into the open. His pistol was leveled at Bridges's chest. "Looks like a Mexican standoff, John," he said. "Now drop the rifle."

Instead Bridges whipped the rifle up and fired. The bullet struck Mack's shoulder, spinning him around and knocking the gun from his hand.

Sarah found herself flying through the air. She landed on Bridges's back, her arms locked around his neck in a death grip. He staggered, but didn't fall, and he began clawing at Sarah's arms, trying to dislodge her.

She was aware of a growing noise in her head, a thunderous roar, but she paid no attention to it. Perhaps, she thought vaguely, this was the sound death made when it approached. But her mind had no room for fear; it was filled only with the need to keep Bridges away from Mack.

Then Mack was pulling her away. He had the rifle, and it was pointed at the agent's head. Mack's mouth was moving, but she couldn't hear what he said. The roar had grown louder, nearly deafening. When the forest began to shake with wind, she looked up.

It wasn't death at all. It was a helicopter.

SARAH SAT PROPPED AGAINST a tree, wondering if she would ever have the strength to move again. A short distance away, Mack stood talking to a man she'd never seen before, a man who had put a pair of handcuffs on Bridges before pushing him toward two other men, who led him away.

Mack slapped the man on the back and grinned. "Chuck, if you're a hallucination, I don't want to know about it."

"No hallucination," Chuck replied. "Damn, I'm glad to see you. I was afraid we'd be too late."

"You nearly were. Next time don't cut it so close, okay?"

Sarah closed her eyes. Chuck. Mack's friend. It was really over. She let her head drop back to rest against the trunk of the tree. Relief flowed through her like a heady drug, leaving her too weak to move and too elated to want to.

"When Bridges went off the deep end, Landis came down here to stop him," she heard Greyson say, "but he couldn't find the compound and he couldn't find Bridges. He wasted a lot of time asking questions, trying to handle it alone. By the time he called us for help it was nearly too late."

"Yeah, I figured Bridges had gone too far this time. And for a while, I was afraid he'd get away with it."

Sarah listened for a few moments longer, then she tuned the voices out. She didn't care how it had happened. Let somebody else figure it out. All she wanted to do was rest, and know that Mack was alive....

"Sarah?" Mack was shaking her shoulder gently. "Sarah, it's time to go." He pulled her to her feet and into his arms.

She melted against him. His arms were warm and strong and real, and she wanted them to stay around her forever. "It's over, isn't it? I'm not dreaming?"

"No, Sarah girl," he whispered. "You're not dreaming. You're going home."

"We're both going home."

Epilogue

The huge mall teemed with shoppers, some of them juggling packages and small children in and out of stores, others strolling more sedately, content to window-shop and talk to their companions. A good many of them, however, were clustered around a table in front of a bookstore on the second level.

The store's entrance was garlanded with colorful balloons and banners, the largest of which read AUTOGRAPHING TODAY—SARAH O'SHAUGHNESSY. Judging from the number of people who vied with their neighbors for more favorable positions closer to the table, the bookstore was in no danger of losing money on the promotion.

Sitting at the table, Sarah Kathleen O'Shaughnessy Macklin smiled brightly, if somewhat wearily, at a large, smooth-coiffed woman and accepted the paperback book the woman thrust in her face.

"Your book is *wonderful*! I stayed up all night reading it." The woman had raised her voice to compete with the babble around her, and Sarah winced. "Just write 'To Nancy, Your Good Friend, Sarah.'"

"'To Nancy,'" Sarah repeated, trying to hold her smile in place. It had been a long two hours, and her fingers were cramped from holding the pen. She autographed the title

page, letting her fingers trail across the bold, black print:
KILL ME WITH LOVE. She'd autographed hundreds of copies
during the past two weeks, but the words still induced a thrill
of pure elation. "I'm so glad you enjoyed it," she told
Nancy. "The sequel will be out in September."

"A sequel!" Nancy squealed. "Oh, I can't wait! What's
it called?"

"*Mission to Belen*." Sarah gave the book back and waited
politely for her to move on.

Nancy, however, wanted to talk. "Belen? You mean that
little country in Central America? There's been something
on TV about that lately, Senate hearings or what-have-you.
Is that what the new book is about?"

"Not exactly, but I have done some research in that area."
Sarah couldn't bear to watch the televised committee hearings; the memory of how close they'd all come to dying was,
even after nearly a year, too vivid, too chilling. Mack, on the
other hand, watched them every chance he got. He wanted
to see the dissolution of the NSB as it happened.

She looked past the crowd, found the benches in the center of the mall where her husband waited with Patrick,
Raylene and Kay. Mack was holding Kay's hand, and they
were deep in conversation. Probably another pep talk, she
thought. Though the nightmares were less frequent and
she'd recently found a job, Kay still required a good deal of
emotional support.

Funny, Sarah mused, how Belen had changed all of them
in different ways. Kay had become withdrawn, while Patrick had become more relaxed and less critical. Two months
after their return to the States, he and Raylene had been
married, and he now looked forward to impending father-
hood with nary a whimper about the burden of responsibility.

For Sarah the change had been less dramatic, more evident in her writing than in her personality. Bothwell's char-

acter had changed from reckless to reasonable, from macho to mature, from careless to committed. The insouciant ladies' man was gone, and so was Sarah's adolescent dream of reckless adventure.

Only Mack seemed to be the same—sometimes unpredictable, but always dependable. Sometimes intense, but always tender. Sometimes restless, but always *there*.

"Excuse me." The voice was tentative and not very loud. It belonged to the tiny, older woman who had taken the ebullient Nancy's place in line, and Sarah wondered, with some chagrin, how long she'd been waiting. "I wonder if you'd autograph my copy of *Kill Me with Love*?"

"I'll be happy to," Sarah said warmly, taking the book. "What's your name?"

"Emily. Emily Franklin." Her soft, pearly skin was lined, her head crowned by snow-white hair, but her blue eyes were bright and undimmed by age. Not so many years before, Emily Franklin had been a stunningly beautiful woman. "I have to tell you, dear, that Bothwell is very special to me. He's so... well, you know." Surprisingly, she dropped her gaze and blushed. "He's the perfect hero. I guess that sounds silly coming from a woman my age."

Impulsively Sarah squeezed her hand. "It's not silly at all. Everybody needs a hero."

"The truth is, I knew someone like Bothwell, a long time ago. He's...gone now, but I've never forgotten him. We had wonderful adventures, and we were so happy together." Emily cocked her head and regarded Sarah thoughtfully. "I have a feeling it's that way for you, too. You have that special glow."

Sarah caught sight of Mack threading his way through the crowd. She'd long since memorized every detail of his face and body, but each time she saw him this way, from a distance, her pulse leaped anew. "You're absolutely right, Emily. It's that way for me, too."

She opened the book and wrote two lines, closed it and handed it to Emily. "I'm so glad we met," she said.

Then Mack was there, his eyes filled with love and pride, his tender smile for Sarah alone. He reached for her hand and bent to kiss her.

At the edge of the crowd, Emily Franklin paused to look back. A tall man with rough features and kind eyes was standing behind the lovely young writer, one hand resting on her shoulder.

Emily opened the book and read the inscription: *For Emily, who was lucky enough to have had the real thing.*

No luckier than you, Sarah, the old lady thought with a secret smile. *No luckier than you.*

Harlequin Intrigue

COMING NEXT MONTH

#107 A DEATH IN THE HOUSE by Stella Cameron
What happened long ago at Airstone Hall that was
coming back to haunt the present? Sue-Ellen Hill
was not only determined to turn the Elizabethan
house into a bed-and-breakfast but also driven to
find out the mystery of the past. And Edward
Ormsby-Jones, Lord of Airstone, was the one man
to whom she could turn for help. But was there
enough time to stop the menacing evil before it
destroyed their love?

#108 SKY PILOT by Laura Pender
Rachel Morgan, crack pilot and newspaper
publisher, grew suspicious when her best reporter
turned up dead on the Puget Sound wharves. The
only one who'd listen was police detective Jake
Connors. With him she not only explored a sinister
paper trail but also her own heart, on the brink
of blossoming.

Harlequin Temptation dares to be different!

Once in a while, we Temptation editors spot a romance that's truly innovative. To make sure *you* don't miss any one of these outstanding selections, we'll mark them for you.

EDITOR'S CHOICE

When the "Editors' Choice" fold-back appears on a Temptation cover, you'll know we've found that extra-special page-turner!

THE

Temptation

EDITORS

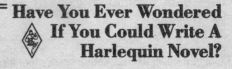

Have You Ever Wondered If You Could Write A Harlequin Novel?

Here's great news—Harlequin is offering a series of cassette tapes to help you do just that. Written by Harlequin editors, these tapes give practical advice on how to make your characters—and your story—come alive. There's a tape for each contemporary romance series Harlequin publishes.

Mail order only

All sales final

TO: **Harlequin Reader Service**
Audiocassette Tape Offer
P.O. Box 1396
Buffalo, NY   14269-1396

I enclose a check/money order payable to HARLEQUIN READER SERVICE® for $9.70 ($8.95 plus 75¢ postage and handling) for EACH tape ordered for the total sum of $_____*
Please send:

☐ Romance and Presents   ☐ Intrigue
☐ American Romance   ☐ Temptation
☐ Superromance   ☐ All five tapes ($38.80 total)

Signature_____
                                          (please print clearly)
Name:_____
Address:_____
State:_____ Zip:_____
*Iowa and New York residents add appropriate sales tax.

AUDIO-H